Praise for *Land Marks*

"Maryann Lesert has witnessed an av̶ Michigan. *Land Marks*, her savvy, mindful, and dramatic novel of intergenerational education and place defense, is writing as nonviolent direct action, principled and powerful."

—Stephanie Mills, author of *Tough Little Beauties* and
In Service of the Wild

"Through complicated characters and a compelling fictional narrative, Lesert gives readers a taste of the dedication and commitment of real people and groups working to protect the Great Lakes . . ."

—Gail Collins-Ranadive, author of
Dinosaur Dreaming, Our Climate Moment

"Readers will be both entertained and inspired. This outstanding novel is about our common fight for the natural places and systems we hold dear, but it is also about our society's soul."

—Liz Kirkwood, Executive Director of
FLOW (For Love of Water)

LAND
MARKS

LAND MARKS

A Novel

Maryann Lesert

SHE WRITES PRESS

Published 2024
Printed in the United States of America
Print ISBN: 978-1-64742-646-0
E-ISBN: 978-1-64742-647-7
Library of Congress Control Number: 2023914325

For information, address:
She Writes Press
1569 Solano Ave #546
Berkeley, CA 94707

She Writes Press is a division of SparkPoint Studio, LLC.

For Corinne

Contents

Showing Up

Showdown

Showing Up

Chapter 1

TV Ticker

I don't know why I turned on the television in the first place, except to provide a little white noise. It was that time of the semester when the essays were piling up, and I had heard more about my students' lives and their problems than I could possibly carry. (Couldn't they see the stack of essays I was hauling away from class?) After teaching all day and into the night, I didn't want to remember the excuses or the hardships. I wanted noise, simple white noise.

I climbed the dark carpeted steps to my second-story apartment, thinking about the one man who had ever shared the space with me. It was Sam who suggested the golden yellow color we painted the entryway and dinette. Recalling our better days, I strolled through my tiny dinette, loving those golden yellow walls and the drop-sided table with two wooden chairs. I knew what I was doing, indulging in the escapism of romance. This was the time in every semester when I started thinking about getting a dog, maybe even dating again.

Sam had been so attuned to color. The landlord loved the pinky salmon he'd picked out to trim the exterior window casings. She said they made the windows pop, and she credited me two months' rent for our labor. Sam was fit and active and he loved to be outdoors, but I soon discovered that he didn't love the trees or the darkness of wet soil or the ways different leaves let go of water. He loved moving *through* the outdoors, preferably on wheels and as fast as possible. Why I needed to stand under a white pine, touching its trunk with one hand and my heart with the other, was something he would never understand.

I opened one of those tart red wine-beers and passed back through that golden yellow dinette before I paid the television any attention, but as soon as I saw the face on the screen, the smooth beige of her skin and the short haircut that brought her sandy brown hair up in curls, I knew. It was Sonya. One of them had finally done it—gotten themselves arrested.

There was nothing more than a ticker below her photo. "Woman arrested, possibly child, sabotage at northern Michigan frack well site. Details at eleven."

My first thought was, Hank? Why on earth would they have Hank out there with them? And then I was annoyed with yet another demonstration of right-now journalism's grammatical failures: *possibly* child? Did that mean there was one person arrested whose age was in doubt? Were there actually two people in custody, one adult and one child? And how could you have someone *possibly* in custody?

The weight of the bag of essays still hanging from my arm came to me, and viewing those essays in a whole new light, I lifted them gently over the back of the couch. If I hadn't been overwhelmed by the thought of adding another twenty to the pile of sixty already stacked and waiting, I never would have turned on the TV. I would have missed this.

Eventually, Brett or Kate or Mark would have called or texted; at least I hoped so. The last time we talked we agreed to stay in touch but not too closely. They hadn't taken that to heart, had they? My suggestion for distance? I didn't mean for them to go silent on me.

I sat in front of the old television that I only occasionally used for weather reports, trying to find some patience with the converter box. Part of me used to enjoy watching Sam fight with the rabbit ears, him begging me to get cable and a flat panel. By the time that first winter had set in, his love for color wasn't enough, and I asked him to leave.

The *Live at Eleven* teaser began with a quick zoom to a headshot of Sonya. It was oddly small, as if the station had gotten hold of a school or license photo and quickly scanned it in, but her classically proportioned face, the smile that could have come from an archaic Greek sculpture, was unmistakable. The text ran again. "Woman arrested, possibly child, northern Michigan frack well site," before a live shot of what looked to be a tree-lined clearing.

I sat forward, scanning the graying bands of darkness that faded back from the light stack on the news truck, searching for the telltale pink and orange flags, the lights, the noise of a well pad, but there was nothing. Justin Thompson, the same spiky-haired reporter who had covered their Winter Campout, swept his arm over a dark, empty field as he entered the shot, backed by a tree line like any in northern Michigan, mixed hardwoods and pines.

"Justin Thompson reporting from a northern county frack well site where at least one person has been arrested in what appears to be attempted sabotage. Stay tuned for the full report at eleven."

Had they somehow managed to get Thompson into their fold? He had to have known to end up hitting the story from what appeared to be an empty, half-excavated field.

They were good. I had been exceptionally proud of the protests and events they had planned. But I also knew, as they stepped closer and closer to direct action, how things could go wrong. Were they trusting a news guy to wait for the right time? What a coup that would be.

Had someone tipped Thompson off?

Thompson had seemed sympathetic when he'd covered their Winter Campout. He'd gotten quite a bit of screen time, too, thanks to the bizarre thunderstorms that came out of January's snow clouds. He called the report "Environmentalists Occupy Frack Well Site," and for a new reporter, he had gotten some unforgettable shots. In one day's time, temperatures had plummeted, falling from nearly sixty degrees to near zero, ending a heat streak that was way too warm for a January

thaw. Snow clouds rolled in off the lake, filled with pinkish red lightning, and a rather new meteorological term came into vogue: thundersnow. The icy snow, blowing across the field as a constant presence,
held on to light and sound for long periods of time, elongating the
rumble of thunder and the lightning's eerie pink glow.

There was a flash as Thompson wrapped up his winter report,
and both he and Brett had ducked as pink light flickered overhead
and remained. The camera panned the campers' tents, orange and
green glow worms in the windblown field, and when asked what the
group wanted, Brett had taken the opportunity to connect fracking
and all sorts of unconventional extraction methods—boiling bitumen
in open pits, steaming it up from the ground, blowing the tops off
mountains—to our third January of thundersnows. "This," he had
said, pointing to a night sky swelling with morning-like light, "is the
very real face of climate change."

Brett had turned to the camera, looking a bit older with a short
chin beard and the dark hair under his hat calling attention to his thin
face, and as I leaned forward, listening, I had the strangest feeling
that someone else was leaning forward, watching just as I was. Some
private security operator zooming in to draw a box around Brett's face,
gathering stills and labeling shots with organizational information.
What the group was called, how many appeared to be involved, Brett's
estimated height, weight, eye color, age, ethnicity, any personal details
or key words he used repeatedly.

It really was that kind of a world now, and Brett seemed to
understand.

He had turned to the camera as if peering into that basement
office. "But we don't have to accept that there is nothing we can do to
slow or stop the damage," he said, his rather large, hazel eyes fixed. He
had accepted the role of spokesperson, which meant he could never,
ever get caught in any direct or property-damaging action. The oil
and gas industry would rejoice in making an example out of him.

But now it was Sonya's wide face and her frizzy curls being plastered all over the screen, and the smeary scanned image wasn't making me feel any better. Why no mug shot? Had they already moved her? By eleven o'clock, the drive for drama would have quiet but quizzical Sonya transformed into an ecoterrorist apprehended in the middle of an extensive plot.

There was a time when I was worried about Sonya for other reasons. Early in the semester, when they were all together in that first EcoLit class, she'd missed two weeks without warning and had not kept in touch. It was a small class then, a pilot course I'd just put together. I had purposefully mentioned it to shy Brett and shaky Kate, students I'd had in other classes. Mark had come on his own, a transfer student who had dropped out of engineering school, hoping to find something less exacting. The eight or nine of us in class that day were already deep in discussion, tables pushed to the center of the room to make our small square, when we heard a knock.

I opened the door, still talking about Parsons or Stratton-Porter, one of the lesser known writer-adventurers, and there was Sonya and that smirk. Only that afternoon she didn't appear smug or pensive. She looked tired.

"I didn't know what else to do," she whispered.

There was a tuft of blond hair and a child's perfectly round head sticking out from the sleeping bag she held across her body, and without a word I slipped her and Hank inside.

Just a week before, the provost had sent down an urgent communication. Without exception, there would be no smoking on campus and no children in the classroom. The college had agreed to provide every student with a stainless-steel water bottle and to remove drink dispensers that used plastic bottles, but we still didn't have childcare. So, woman to woman, I slipped Sonya and her then two-year-old son into the classroom, knowing from the look on her face, she wouldn't finish the semester if I didn't.

Sonya, twenty-one at the time, was a single parent who wrote with sensitivity equal to the writers we were studying, and me, I was barely tenured, teaching a pilot class that was barely running with ten students. Together, we silently ushered in a new pact. Hank became part of the class for the next three or four weeks while Sonya worked to find a new job. In the meantime, Brett and Kate and Mark—the four of them had already formed a strong bond—devised a way to watch Hank between classes and get him to daycare when Sonya's workplace refused to adjust her hours.

But Hank on a well site? There was no way Brett, or Kate, or Mark would let Sonya bring Hank anywhere near a well pad. It didn't make sense. Either Thompson was holding back, or it had all happened so quickly that even the authorities weren't sure who or what they had.

What were they up to?

The *Live at Eleven* teaser ran again, and Justin Thompson appeared at left after an initial pan of the darkening field, sweeping his arm over the "northern Michigan frack well site." I searched again and thought I saw a stake, some of the orange and pink flags marking the widening of a road or the entrance to a well pad, but there was no berm or gleaming limestone, no trucks or equipment. Were they trying to stop a new site?

A year ago, I knew who was drilling where and when. I knew why North American Energy was deep into the Utica-Collingwood and why Dillon was poking holes around the edges of the A-1 Carbonate layer. I knew the landscapes before and after, and I was able to guess what the four or five prospectors in Michigan might be up to in the near future. But that was only because I had devoted two years to some intense boots-on-well-sites research.

After two summers of that kind of research, I needed to get back to school, to make teaching a priority again, and the four of them needed the space to plan whatever it was they were planning.

I knew they would do it, didn't I? Something big. I never knew what, exactly, or when, but I always knew they were serious and that anything they decided to do would be done out of reverence, out of love.

I had listened to their ideas on Sonya's mangy back deck and helped them shape their thoughts as they continued to write. There were times when I thought of Mara, when Mara and I were young like they were, when we acted as a pair. Perhaps I should have told Kate and Brett and Sonya and Mark, more. But whatever it was I was becoming, mentor or friend, I had been their professor, and that role stuck. I was worried about influence.

Now the question was: Had I dropped out on them when they needed me most?

Was I wrong, not letting them know that their professor, Rebecca Walton, had once been known as Elizabeth Stone, a rescue climber and writer inside of actions? That I understood, completely, why they needed to keep quiet, because being a good activist was not so different from being a good teacher? I had walked into teaching not knowing that this role, too, would require me to push back my sense of self so I could be a better listener. Both roles, each in their own way, required me to be a good secret keeper.

Ten o'clock. It would be an hour before any real news came in.

The networks would spend the next hour heightening and sensationalizing. Soon enough the "apparent sabotage" would be "Ecoterrorists target frack well site." "Terrorists threaten America's oil independence." *Live at Eleven* would scramble for the perfect sound bite. They'd create a spinning graphic with canned music to herald in their story, since Thompson was the first on site. By eleven, they'd have an exploding drill rig pinned to the map for sure.

I glanced back to the bag of essays slumped on the couch as if they could again lead me to where I needed to be, and that's when I remembered.

Sonya had sent one of her "Hey Teach" emails a week or so ago.

I'd only skimmed it because it was midterms—that time of year when I barely slept or ate or moved, when my eyes became grainy, and my body ached with the reading.

I considered getting a second wine-beer but decided to make a pot of coffee instead.

For all my worry about influence, all I wanted now was a chance to intercept, to stop the messaging train. They had tried. For two years they had tried: with articles, with songs, with videos of the destruction we had witnessed across the state, with carefully crafted speeches and letters, by standing up at auctions and public meetings. Now, they would be labeled.

Anyone who didn't understand how four promising students in a literature class could become "ecoterrorists" should stand at the crest of the twelve-foot-tall mound of earth surrounding a frack well site, a berm swollen with and smelling of still-living roots. Let anyone quick to judge gaze across ten acres of forest floor scraped level and dry. Let them see and hear, smell and feel the screech of the drill rig biting into brain and bone, the chug of diesel engines, the roar of compressors. Let them stand there trying to comprehend the circus of hoses and coils, the tanks and the vats, piles and piles of half-ton cylinders of steel pipe, because there is no such thing as a two-mile-long pipe. The pipes of drilling and fracking thunder end to end as they descend into the well bore, segment following segment, and the drill bit grinds away.

I walked back past those golden yellow walls, hoping—hoping I had not missed something important.

Chapter 2
Eleven O'Clock and All Is Not Well

Sonya's email didn't say much, not about any action, anyway. Instead, it was full of oddly poetic descriptions. She seemed nostalgic, which wasn't unusual, bringing her energy down deep to a place where she knew what she was about to do felt right, whatever it was that she or they were doing.

Maybe one of the older National Lawyers Guild attorneys had advised her to set up a "morally compelled" defense. Especially as a mother, as a woman who had given birth and felt viscerally connected to Earth's future, she could argue that the tragedies she had witnessed compelled her to act. That the people she'd met, the contamination and the suffering they'd been put through was so wrong that nothing but trying to stop it made sense.

I had always thought Kate was the one I'd be bailing out of jail.

Kate was one hundred percent social, a songwriter, a deep listener, and a "verbal nightmare" as Brett and Sonya teased. It wasn't difficult to imagine small, blonde, super verbal Kate walking or talking her way into trouble.

I remember when it was all about the land, Sonya began, referencing a talk we had had after visiting that awful Wheeler well site, a wasteland of scraped, stained earth that left us all stumbling about in a sunburned haze.

We'd spent too much of that first summer moving from site to site, snapping photos and documenting as fast as we could, and we had to remind ourselves why we were there. "For the land," we said, time and time again. What began as class-based research grew into a mission of awareness. Fracking was spreading throughout Michigan's state forests, and there were people, so many people desperate to show the public their stories.

Traveling about the state, getting to know people living with the screech of the drill rig and its hot oily smells, living with them, however briefly, during their most challenging experiences created instant bonds. But it also left you with a terrible lump of guilt when it came time to leave, time to turn their lives into an eight-hundred-word story to get the word out.

We found what the land was supposed to look like, Sonya wrote, and I recognized her descriptions of State-Lexford, the site that would teach us so much about drilling and fracking and security, too. *Cold, dark water pooled alongside the frozen mud road, the shapes of cedars reflected on the water's surface, their boughs drawn down with lavender, dusk-tipped snow.*

Hiking in to State-Lexford, we had found northern woods and wetlands coming to life in a mid-March heat wave. It was eighty degrees, and the snow was melting so fast that it vaporized into the air, rising as a frozen fog that curled around our movements, and we toyed with it, pulling cool, white strands along with us.

But just a few miles away, where State-Lexford's sister well site had been fracked several times and abandoned, there were no fields of melting snow, no puddles reflecting the sky, only dry, brittle-looking trees and depressions in the ground where water had once pooled.

We walk under a broken oak, its trunk purposefully split to mark the turn toward the well pad, and all we can do is pan the site to capture the vastness of the clearing.

Ten acres scraped level and dry, and in the distance, a single row of birches remains, silver against the plantation pine.

What I want to remember is the way the cedars released cool wisps of moisture, surprising us as we walked, and the pheasants that took flight, their wings beating with such a sudden thrum that we jumped with the sound.

Sonya's eloquent dispatches (she had shared plenty of writings with me, but her language, here, was overly lush) ended with an odd error. We had taken a geo-challenge of our own later that summer as we tried to predict where the next few wells would be drilled, and we found one of their secret well sites in the middle of a wetland. The State-Kitfield was being cleared long before the public knew about it. High on our hunches, we had marched right into the excavation.

But even that day we fought back, remember?

Kate charged the tree pincher, shrieking, "Fight! Fight!" as its tongs bit into the trunks of white birches and the operator worked the trees back and forth.

It was Kate's idea to scratch paces into our boots, remember? 1086. 1017. 1084.

That was the detail that had me cocking my head. We had parked the car and hiked toward the rumblings of heavy equipment. When the driver of the tree pincher got on his phone and we decided to retreat, I had picked up a stone and suggested we scratch a notch for every hundred paces. It was an out-in-the-woods way of relocating a campsite or a tree or a piece of equipment you wanted to find again, later.

I was certain, after watching the *Live at Eleven News*, that Thompson knew more than he was reporting. Either that, or he was stalling.

His late-night report didn't offer much more except their location. He confirmed that the arrest had taken place in Crawford county. None of the other sources, not *EcoNotes* or *Terra Now!* had posted any details, which hopefully meant they wanted to stay quiet.

Maybe Thompson was happy with himself for breaking the story, for being where no one else was. But I swore, watching his mouth and his eyes, there was something in his voice that said he knew more. He walked back and forth with the dark, piney night behind him, looking as if he were on the verge of an "I'll be damned" chuckle. There was still some mystery. That's what I caught in his posture and in his face: anticipation. Did they trust this guy?

"So far, if there were others involved, as police suspect," Thompson said, turning to the camera, "no additional suspects have been apprehended."

And then, without much more than a quick flash of that same low-res photo of Sonya, Thompson signed out. "More tomorrow, with daylight's help. This is Justin Thompson, live at eleven."

My old television sizzled down to gray, and suddenly, I felt lonely. Years ago, my living room would have been full of people helping to solve the mystery. Now, when any real planning started, I had to split off alone.

Where were they? What made sense?

Even as students, Kate and Brett and Sonya and tech-entranced Mark, too, when they made him aware, had been incredibly caring and mature. Perhaps that was why they didn't call or text. They knew what midterms were like.

Two years of documentation. Months of quiet.

What did I know last? What was I sure of, in general?

It was Kate's idea to scratch paces into our boots, remember?

We knew our results would be slightly different, but we could average them out. Later.

I pulled the ottoman under my feet and started a list.

I wrote "Check Paces" and put a checkbox next to it. Sonya and I had sat in the back of Kate's pickup that afternoon, noting taped trees and distances as we drove away from the excavation we'd discovered between wetlands, but it wasn't Kate's idea to mark paces on our boots. Sonya knew that. I'd have to look through my journals to see what I had written.

I wrote down the well sites Sonya had noted in the order she mentioned them—State-Lexford, State-Wheeler, State-Kitfield—all on state land.

Sonya had ended her email with an obvious nod to Kate. *Sometimes*, she wrote, *it all depends upon the two-track you turn down.* They were together, all right.

If Sonya was in trouble, it wouldn't take investigators long to connect her to school, and then to Kate and Brett, and eventually, all four of them to one class. I'd keep articles, images, video clips that were strictly factual, but anything that put us together on any well sites had to go.

There was no way I was going to let some private security hack with a film noir sense get his hands on Kate's heartfelt songs or Mark's intricate maps. And no way in hell was I going to let them land on Brett's darker moments regarding civilization and its destructive ways.

I went in search of the twelve-cup coffeemaker I hadn't used since the end of the last semester, when I avoided grading final exams until the bitter end.

Chapter 3
Class Direction

The class could have gone in any direction. We studied the nature writers, the adventurers, the whistleblowers. We investigated water use and abuse, solar and wind energy, mass transportation in the state that bred cars. We struggled with the risks that came with so-called unconventional fossil fuels: the tar sands oil spill in the Kalamazoo River and the aging pipeline under the Straits of Mackinac. It was early in 2012. The public wouldn't know about the decisions that led to the poisoning of Flint's water until three years later, a year after it began.

It was Kate, dear, shaky Kate, who propelled us toward our first public meeting and those first few well site visits. Sonya was interested but quiet. Mark was skeptical. Michigan would never get "fracked." Brett, with ties to the Ottawa and Chippewa tribes, was highly skeptical of Mark's faith in state regulators. With our legislature, of course Michigan would get fracked.

Kate and Brett found hints of fracking in the state's oil-rich southeast, and their research led us to a series of public meetings.

Downstate, the horsehead pumps of the eighties were being replaced with 60-foot-tall drill rigs that drilled 3,000-4,000 feet into the earth, with lateral borings that extended a mile under wooded ravines and wetlands, but the oil and gas industry held to a "we don't frack" approach. No, they claimed, the blasting of the bedrock with water and sand, with lubricants and "kitchen sink" chemicals, was not fracking. The meetings were so canned that after attending a few, we could recite panel members' responses.

A Michigan Department of Environmental Quality official would offer the "same as the chemicals under your kitchen sink" analogy when audience members expressed concerns about the chemicals used in fracking.

A lobbying arm of the oil and gas industry, posing as an educational organization, supplied colorful brochures that highlighted the steel pipes and cement casings, purportedly ample protection for water as drilling fluids and chemicals moved through underground aquifers and on to the shale layers below.

But no, what they were doing was not fracking.

At one meeting, we heard, "We don't frack" fifty-eight times.

We were in a hotel conference room packed with hundreds of people holding signs that read, "Hands off our land" and "Ban Fracking Now!" New rigs were moving in daily. Flames from gas flares had been burning for weeks, and a purple-brown haze hung heavy in the sky. The community had been notified that several deep injection wells were coming, but instead of the EPA hearing the audience expected, they were treated to what turned out to be, in Brett's words, another "shit show."

"Why do you need deep injection wells if you're not fracking?" one woman asked.

The drilling supervisor leaned into his mic. "We don't frack."

A pediatrician reported that the children in her practice were presenting with nosebleeds and asthma at an alarming rate. "You're drilling way too close to schools, and you know it."

The supervisor responded, "We don't frack."

Waterkeepers asked, "How deep are you drilling? Under what rivers? What lakes?" and the oil company CEO took the mic.

"We don't frack." The shale layer they were drilling into was like

Swiss cheese, he explained, full of pockets. "All we need is a bit of acid to loosen things up."

"You're using hydrochloric acid in these wetlands, and you want us to calm down?"

An aging farmer and his wife quieted the room with their concern for neighbors, an elderly couple who had been misled, they said, by one of the many landmen knocking on doors. The couple had signed a lease, and their land had been turned into one of the processing pads that came with fracking.

"Tank farms," the farmer called them. Muddy plats with twenty-some huts lined in two parallel rows, with gas flares rising from rusty metal cylinders at each end.

We had driven by such a site as we toured the area's hills and lakes and farms. We saw signs of poverty, too. Farmhouses left unpainted and outbuildings leaning with neglect.

"And that gas is burning right next to their house," the farmer said.

The oil company supervisor leaned into his mic. "We don't frack."

Back in the car, it took awhile for the conversation to cool.

"The fricking DEQ," Kate said. Strands of blonde hair hung from her bun and shook. "So much misinformation. That's what we get for protection?"

"Might as well enjoy the profits." Brett sighed.

Near the end of the meeting, as landowners opposed to the drilling expressed the fear that they were being surrounded by neighbors who had signed leases, that frack wells could end up within hundreds of feet from their homes, the DEQ official had leaned into his mic and said, "The wells are coming. You might as well enjoy the profits."

"What they're doing is fracking." Mark's usually golden-toned face and the wave of his black bangs were lit by the blue glow of his screen. He had typed away during the meeting, fact checking. "Look," he held his phone out toward us. "Their own definition says so. Acid fracturing."

I merged onto the expressway and told them a story.

One of my friends from college had worked for the Michigan Department of Natural Resources as a land steward. He helped landowners care for parcels of land in the best ways possible, even if that included acknowledging human changes, much to hardliners' dismay.

When he started, he roamed three counties and knew the public officials in every township. Then came downsizing, and he was given eight counties to manage. By the time he quit because he couldn't handle the pressure of pretending to do a job that no one was capable of doing, he had twenty counties assigned to his care. Instead of walking the land and talking to the people of each place, he was supposed to manage land from a desk using satellite imagery.

"Twenty counties," I reiterated. "I try to remember that people go into the DNR and the DEQ because they care. Which is very different than the directors who get appointed. The agency has been gutted. Any agency that's trying to conserve and protect is being gutted."

"We know, Teach, we know." Kate shook her hands in the air. "It's just maddening!"

It was maddening, being forced to sit quietly and participate in their shit show.

"Fifty-eight," Sonya said. Her frizzy curls were backlit by the headlights behind us. "Fifty-eight 'we don't fracks.'"

Fifty-eight times the oil company and their accomplices publicly denied the obvious as their contempt for the public became clear. It certainly piqued our curiosity. What, exactly, was this process they were so afraid to let us see and understand? And what plans were they trying to wordsmith away, albeit very badly, with their "we don't frack" semantics?

Chapter 4
Soaking In

State-Lexford was a site we returned to often. There, we saw the 120-foot-tall Redding 120 drill rig in operation, its mechanized rack lowering sixty-foot segments of steel pipe into the hole, pipe after pipe thundering into place. State-Lexford was our education in color and purpose. We learned to recognize the orange, triple-coned trailers of drilling fluids, the tall navy-blue glycol dehydrators, yellow acid pylons, and bright red battery cars. The site became central to our understanding of fracking's stages. First, they drilled a pilot hole to explore production capacity with the first fracked horizontal, then they left the freshly fracked well to soak in as we found State-Lexford the first time we visited, with the wellhead sitting idle and monitored by gauges welded to a skinny copper pipe. State-Lexford taught us all of these things and more because it was so easy to access. We could duck into the trees and walk around its edges or walk right onto the well pad if we wanted to, as we had that first day.

Later that summer, we would see the Redding 120 walk, the long legs of the rig retracted, wheels lowered as slowly, inch by inch, the rig was rolled a few hundred feet over to drill the next well bore. By fall, we'd record months of road widening and pipeline soldering as State-Lexford was connected to its older, processing-intensive sister, State-Eleanor. The four-mile span between the two well pads introduced us to the pipelines needed to pump fracked oil and gas to more rectangles of scraped earth, to processing stations with their own tanks and compressors and coils.

But that first time, State-Lexford was surprisingly empty.

We parked about a mile down the road at the first available trailhead. Kate got out and narrated nearby hiking trails and an old Civilian Conservation Corps bridge. The creek it crossed joined with waterways to form the headwaters of the Manistee River.

Easy access to water. That was why North American Energy, NorA as the international conglomerate was called, was here.

We planned as we walked. I would get whole-site pictures, pans that gave the wide-angle view. Sonya would get close-ups on equipment so we could begin to put together all the sights and sounds with the purpose of each piece. Kate would videotape the land, the general health or distress of the environment.

Standing at the peak of the earth berm that surrounded the well pad, the site looked pristine in an earthy, scraped-back way, edged as it was in quiet and snow. The dirt was dark and wet, and wherever shrinking piles of snow remained, the air was thick with a cool mist. An early heat wave had us all in T-shirts as we stepped through the chill.

A trio of condensate tanks rose from a mini berm in the corner. There was a trailer that looked like a typical supervisor's office and a mobile light rack parked at center, but most of the site sat flat and brown and empty. The next time we visited, when the Redding 120 drill rig returned, every bit of scraped earth would be covered with piles of pipe and truck trailers and chemical vats.

Kate and Sonya suited up, straightening their long sleeves and stretching their hoods up over baseball caps.

"The bastards aren't getting my picture." Kate nodded, stuffing long strands of hair into her hood. "You got handkerchiefs?" Sonya often tied a handkerchief or a twist of cloth around her face to hold back her hair.

There was a sour, vinegary smell in the air, and the longer we sat on the berm and walked the peak of its perimeter, the more we could taste it.

"It's the tanks," Sonya said, handing me the close-ups she'd taken on her camera. "They've got off-gassing valves at the top."

There was a camera mounted on one corner of the trailer, but after moving from one spot to another to test it, we saw no movement. The lens seemed to be positioned downward, focused on the wellhead.

"It's so fricking small," Kate remarked. "And what the hell's with those drip pans?"

"The deer," Sonya said, "any of the wildlife. They could walk right up and drink."

In its resting state, the wellhead resembled a skinny hydrant. A household-sized copper pipe extended from the top of the well, then curved toward some pressure gauges. There were soldering marks and drip pans at each juncture. On the body of the well were three red wheel valves strung together with a lightweight chain.

"I'm going to get a closer look," I said.

I made it around the berm, climbing up now and then to take wide, slow pans of the red-brown breadth of the well pad, keeping an eye on Kate and Sonya. We'd decided that if anyone showed up and we needed to communicate, Kate would cheep like a chickadee, Sonya said she'd caw like a crow, and I chose the coo of a mourning dove. I'd always loved the gentle birds, knowing they were what was left of the larger pigeons.

Our get-the-hell-out call would be, "Bear!"

"It's hikeworthy." I nodded when Sonya proposed it. It was early spring, well before berry season, when hungry black bears could be grumpy.

If we noticed someone approaching, if the camera mounted on the top of that trailer started to move, if by chance a bear did appear, we were to holler, "Bear!" and get to the car as fast as we could. "No waiting for each other," I said. "Trust each other to get there."

Kate wandered off to videotape the forest in its normal, healthy state, bringing back the bright green of new ferns and the papery peach of last year's young beech leaves being replaced with tight new buds. She also found a still, round lake with overturned canoes rimming its shore.

"Fracking, next to a campground," Sonya smirked.

"Healthy pines there," Kate bobbed. "None of those gray bulges and cracks."

All of the trees closest to the well pad seemed brittle.

In my own photos, the bold blue of the sky made the equipment seem all the more dramatic and out of place: the iridescent purple of welding scars on those huge rusty condensate tanks, the zigzag of yellow coils creating foliage-like shadows across the dirt, and the glint of metal from the trailer throwing hot tin light beams.

Sonya was kneeling at the entrance gate, angling her camera up toward the condensate tanks. "Look. The valves are open," she said, and when I stopped to see, I caught the movement of the camera.

"Step back," I whispered. The camera was pointed right at her.

"What's up?" Kate moved closer, recognizing my tone.

I picked up a handful of stones and backed behind the tanks so the camera, if it did follow, could not see us. "Don't react other than to admire these lovely stones, but I think the camera's moving."

We watched the camera pan toward us then slowly scan the perimeter.

"It followed our voices," Sonya said.

"Maybe." I felt the swell of stupidity expanding in my chest.

While Kate and Sonya were crouching along the berm, I had checked the camera, and when it didn't move in response, I had walked across the well pad to photograph the chained red wheels on the wellhead. We were on state land, which meant NorA couldn't prevent us from observing from the gates, but anything inside the berm was their territory. Someone could have been watching us all along, from the trailer or anywhere.

"We need to separate to see if the camera follows us."

"Shit," Kate said. "You mean someone's watching, like, right now?"

"Francine!" I called, walking and waving. "One of those pink granites you've been looking for."

Sure enough, as Sonya and Kate walked toward me, the camera followed. "Damn it." Sonya handed me a rock. "The thing's right on us."

I laughed to hide my next line. "We'll just keep walking and talking rocks until we get past the site."

Once we were out of range of the camera, we broke into a run.

Kate's fair skin brightened. "Shit, I gotta get in shape!"

I laughed, but my heart was also pounding. We didn't need one of those white trucks full of oil and gas thugs to catch us on a forest road. We were two miles in with nothing but mud and ruts in either direction.

"What's our story?" We slowed to a jog. "What are we out here for?"

"Hiking!" Kate hollered out.

"An environmental writing project for my honors thesis," Sonya said.

"And I'm your advisor."

"As soon as we make it to the car"—I could see my silver-green hatchback through the trees—"we're hightailing it down the road."

I hit the remote, and we threw our bags in.

"Buckle up!" My heartbeat thumped in my ears. "Let's hope to hell my nearly bald tires can handle this."

We drove past the site, and I was about to slow down for a hill when we saw the white truck coming.

"Fricking hell." Kate's voice was close. Her hands gripped my headrest.

"Hang on," I said. Slowing down would give the driver a chance to pull toward us and make us stop. "Just driving out after a great hike!"

"Should we wave?" Kate said, but it was too late. We'd already driven past.

"Secure Tek," Sonya shouted above the sound of gravel pinging the car. "T-e-k."

I could see Kate turn to watch as the white truck slowed.

"Still looking forward," I said, and Kate turned back.

"Fricking hell, he's turning around!"

"He's blocking the road," Sonya watched in the side mirror. "He's not turning around. He's parked all the way across it."

I saw white again as we crested the next hill.

"Shit," Kate said.

Thankfully, the driver of the second white truck was accelerating uphill and didn't have time to stop.

"Straight ahead," I said. "Straight ahead."

"Two men," Sonya said.

I could feel their faces turn toward us as they slowed.

We watched their brake lights until we dipped into a muddy curve, and I hit the gas.

My balding tires started to skid and the car headed a bit sideways. I could see the end of the mud, far ahead, where gravel met a two-lane highway. "I'm not going to stop, so hold on."

"Washboards," Sonya said. "Watch the washboards!"

I tapped the brakes and angled my way toward the blacktop so as not to hit the pavement abruptly. "Are they following us?"

"No," Sonya said. "But they sure took a good, hard look."

I floored it, heading east, in the opposite direction of the campground where we had pitched our tents.

"Go, Teach!" Kate cackled from the back.

"You were going sideways down that last hill," Sonya smirked.

"Yup," I patted the dash. "But the old car held on."

—

I backed the car into the corner of a trailhead lot several miles up the road, where we could watch the cars zoom by.

Back at the Lexford site, Kate and Sonya had shimmied up the berm, hoods up and pointed like elves. They had covered every bit of skin and any recognizable features. I had chuckled and taken a few candids as they peeked over the berm, binoculars and cameras pointed at the equipment. But I'd also felt uncomfortable. Hiding under hoods and scarves, we could appear more suspicious than our actual motive, to observe.

I had forgotten too much. We made three obvious mistakes in rapid succession, and any one of them could have ended our boots-on-well-sites research right then and there.

One: We vacillated between being undercover and overt. First, climbing up the backside of the berm with scarves tied around our faces. But then, after thinking about our approach, we were on state forest land after all, we decided that sneaking around would make us look like we were up to no good, so we came back in broad daylight, showing ourselves.

Two: We let them see us vacillating, which would tell them we were inexperienced amateurs thinking we were up to no good.

And three: We had taken pictures and video that placed us on site, and then we had walked around with those incriminating images in our cameras.

We had made it all too easy for someone to use our own stupidity against us.

The next time we went out, I would keep my professor card, as Kate called it, close. Kate and Sonya were students at the college, working on an environmental writing project, and I was their advisor. If someone really started pressing, Sonya would give them the whole spiel about her honors thesis on the environmental history of Michigan's state forests, because she did a great job of dead-panning the explanation. Kate shook and smiled too much when she was nervous.

I would stay cool and observe. Let them speak for themselves and step in only if I needed to pull the professor card.

"Or get nasty," Kate snickered. "'Cause we know you can do that too."

"And hold on pretty good to a sideways slide down a hill," Sonya teased.

Chapter 5

Fen Preserve

Fifteen Years Earlier

Fen Preserve. Such a beautiful place. Even as David walked away from our efforts to save its purple-green wetlands and glacier-carved ridges, it was the beauty of the place that I wanted to remember: the violet mist of its mornings, the hot white-silver of its moonlight, the prehistoric trumpeting of cranes at dawn and dusk. Fen's was a place where the landscape was inextricably intertwined with the wildlife and the people who roamed it. To separate the wetlands from the hills and prairies, to separate the geology of the place and its stories from the humans who researched—who set up easels and painted, who tagged plants and tallied flights—such separations were impossible.

The herons and the cranes, they may have sensed the human drama of our fight to save their habitat, but their routines, as long as Benten Development was held at bay, had not yet changed.

"Why are you doing this *now*?" I asked David.

It was escalation time, and David was leaving. I was no leader. I was a stage setter, an observer. And the worst of it? He knew why they wanted him.

The Big Greens were in trouble. After growing their funding and distancing themselves from any real action, they were losing the support of people who had watched hard-fought gains of the 70s deregulated and then purchased away in the 80s and 90s. And the 2000s? Nothing but a backlash of "drill, baby, drill!"

David would be their real protestor, their new "face of activism." He would organize mountaintop removal protests in West Virginia, get handcuffed in front of the White House calling for an end to the myth of clean coal. He'd cross small lines over and over while an expert legal team sprung him in minutes so he could write eloquent emails calling for justice and contributions.

I was counting out supplies, filling backpacks with rope, prusiks, and carabiners. Throw lines would be set the day before when each team would complete a run-through. David and I had been following each other all morning, trying to keep the tension between us a secret, which was a joke. We walked into a clearing and everyone cleared out.

"If you go through with this," he said, as if the twenty-some students, researchers, and locals united in the fight were mine, all mine, "I can't support you."

"Support?" I all out laughed. He was standing and watching as I dragged pole pine trunks under the bridge. "This is your idea of support?"

"You know what I mean," he said. "Come on."

I yanked at the heaviest log. "Levi!" I glared at David as he watched.

Levi was a door-sized young man who worked as a research tech, an equipment manager who got people the appropriate boats and oars, flags of all colors for marking plants.

At some point, David had decided he would not lay a finger on the action. He couldn't, if he was going to take Big Green's deal.

"Levi!" I shouted, insanely frustrated as David watched.

Levi and I stacked the three trunks, packed rope and loops into a gear bag, and tucked everything under the riser. Levi shook his head at David as he backed out from under the bridge.

"Can't believe you're leaving, man. Can't believe it."

I couldn't either. In weeks, they had changed him.

"You're not going to grow your influence, David. You're not going to *do* anything."

"Everything's changing, Beck. Everything. These small, targeted actions aren't going to work anymore. They've got people everywhere, and I mean everywhere."

"Yeah? Well now they've got you too."

For a year, Benten Development had been actively destroying the wetlands that were an integral part of Fen Preserve, a four-thousand-acre miracle of lakes and prairies and the glacial esker that rose like the backbone of some ancient, sleeping creature above the creek and the wetlands below.

Petition after petition, meeting after meeting, regardless and in spite of public input Benten marched on, buying up adjacent wetland areas and surrounding the park. When Benten started secretly building up junk concrete walls to try to separate and dry out adjacent wetlands, we set up around-the-clock surveillance, photographing the illegal work. Trucks dumped and then buried broken concrete in three-foot-high walls between waterways. Earthmovers pulled down hills when Benten had only a topsoil permit.

We had all the documentation necessary to stop the midnight dredging and pumping raids, but every official, it seemed, had grown numb and dumb. Benten had spun gold in their ears. Job creation. Tax roll. Prosperity.

So, we decided to act. The director, summer researchers, locals who couldn't believe the lack of oversight—they were all taking this risk. And now, the only thing I could do to protect myself and everything we had worked for was to get away from David and the lack of faith that had gotten into him.

He was the one.

"First rule of advocacy, David. Never take money from the industry or group that you're trying to regulate or destroy."

They wanted him because he was smart, safe. But he was also half wild with his shaggy hair and intense gray eyes, the way his smile seemed to surprise his face, creating deep lines from his cheekbones to his chin.

"There's nothing else we can do, Beck. Either we get in the game and look legit, or we're all going down, one by one."

I knew there was truth in what he was saying. I just didn't want to hear him saying it.

"They'll water you down until you can't do any good. You know that."

Not one single tree sitter, not one of the people who clipped wrists inside metal-clad PVC pipes or locked themselves to a dozer, not one person who climbed onto an earthmover and poured a gallon of water and sand into the oil intake thought their actions would actually stop so-called progress. Not for long. But we could call attention to horrific wrongs, get a numbed and passive public to respond. If we kept the faith, maybe, just maybe, so would the public.

"You'll have an office and a nice photo signature on your emails. So what? That's as good as it's going to get."

"Beck!" he hollered as I headed back to camp to do what I'd seen him do so many times before: organize, inspire, smile with knowing. Someone had to be that person who knew, without a doubt, that spreading out and preventing a dozen earthmovers and tree pinchers from starting up in the morning was not only doable but the right thing to do.

"Beck!"

I turned around, deciding that he could see my mad-as-hell face, because I was supremely pissed off at myself, really, for thinking that I could change his course.

We had shared so many moments. That full moon night in October when his face turned up to the sky had looked so skeletal, his cheekbones flat and gleaming and his eye sockets so deep and dark, that I had wondered out loud if that's how the All Hallows traditions began. If fall's intense moonlight made living faces reminiscent of the dead walking among us. There, on the bridge over the narrows of the wetland, we watched the moonlight turn the lily pads and the twisted brush that edged the water into a world both eerily frozen and hot silver-white, a land between life and death. And now he was leaving for a pastel office and a four-color laser printer.

"David, if this is about income, about being able to survive, tell me." No one but the Big Greens could afford to pay a livable salary. "Tell me now and I'll understand."

But he didn't tell me. He didn't explain. So I turned and went back to the group, back to drilling plywood and tying knots, back to making sure everyone who would soon raise tripods and bury tack strips across dirt roads had everything they needed to stay strong.

"David!" I ran after him just once. "What if we can?"

"What if we can what, Beck? What?" His face was red in the morning chill and colored, too, with the exertion of our extended argument.

I quieted my voice. "What if we really can stop them?" What I meant was, what if we could stop *this* them, *this* developer, and *this* project, right here, right now?

None of us dared to think that stopping an industry as huge as suburban sprawl or as powerful as oil and gas was possible. Slowing them down, kicking them in the shins—that was the best we could hope for.

I wanted him to stay for all of our sakes. For Levi and for Sharon, the director, for the superintendent and her husband, for the college students who researched at the preserve and were putting their freedom on the line, many of them because they were in love with David too. The young men wanted to be around him, the young women wanted their men to be like him, and now I was stuck defending him. What was "being like David" going to look like now?

He grabbed me by the elbow. "You have to be rock solid. Completely committed and ready." Others were taking notice. He dropped his grip. "Walk with me. Please."

Down the trail, he paced. "You have to ask yourself, Beck, really ask yourself, are you ready right now, and tomorrow too, to risk years?"

The chicken shit! He was trying to get me to leave with him.

"Why are you doing this?"

He spread his arms out to the trees, the huge old maples and the muscular beeches with their soft-etched eyes watching over the ridge and its inhabitants as they had for hundreds of years. "Could you survive without this?"

That's when I understood. He was one of them, already, on the sell.

I watched him walk off, thinking he couldn't have given me a more ridiculously romantic movie ending, except I didn't believe that we were ending. Our almost-relationship, years before, had ended without a moment of closure, after Mara and the canyon and all that came after. But David and I had been reunited at Fen's. We were together, truly together.

There was always a mist over the wetland, and that morning as the sun rose, illuminating the golden greens and rosy blues that arched over the water, the sun's bolder rays raced across the esker, that ancient backbone ridge, striking the crest just as David reached the top of the hill, and he disappeared into a burst of violet.

"You can call me anytime, Beck. Always."

What a crappy last line to leave me with.

I was six or seven years older than Kate and Sonya the last time I saw him, though unlike Kate and Sonya, I was embarrassingly idealistic. But, as Brett said during one of our last meetings on Sonya's back deck, "That's how they get people to conform, by getting us to believe idealism is immature."

Fifteen years. A lifetime ago, for both of us. Would David and I be able to talk?

For a moment, I thought through the time difference. What time was it on the West Coast? What on earth would I say? Yeah, it's been a lifetime. But hey, anything that legal team of yours could do to spring one of my former students?

How would I begin? David wouldn't even know that I had students.

Chapter 6

Taste of Organizing

I told them the stories I was able to tell. Sometimes Brett would tilt his head my way or Sonya would smirk, but I did my best to stay back and observe.

Until the auction protest.

Who could forget the oddity of sitting in a pale green room listening to an auctioneer prattle "Ho!" and "Ha!" as the right to drill into the geological record of life below us was sold to forty-some middle-aged men wearing khakis and plaid button-downs?

By the time the spring and fall mineral rights auctions came to our attention, the oil and gas industry had already leased over a million acres of state forest land. We had witnessed the Redding 120's third walk as NorA repositioned it for a third 8,000-foot-deep vertical on the State-Lexford well pad. And from each of those 8,000-foot borings, they drilled three horizontal legs, a total of nine laterals extending out two miles in spoke-like fashion, each leg using twenty million gallons of fresh water. Water that would never return to the Great Lakes Basin. It couldn't. It was too toxic. The only place flowback could go was deep underground, into deep injection wells.

The thought of that level of industrial might spreading throughout the state forests sent them all to Kate's whiteboard, and I was proud of their vision.

They filled the downtown DNR building with layers of color

and noise and commotion. Protestors lined the hall where land-men entered and registered to bid. Hundreds more gathered in the courtyard outside the basement auction room, chanting and pressing their signs to the windows. One young woman ran the length of the room, pounding on the glass, and inside, each time the auctioneer proclaimed a parcel, "Sold!" protestors hollered back, "Stolen!"

Brett positioned himself by the windows. I sat up front, by the auctioneers, and Mark was videotaping from the back of the room. Sonya was home with Hank, waiting for news coverage.

I wasn't sure what Kate's role would be until she strolled up the center aisle dressed in a bold blue skirt and a ruffled blouse, her long blonde hair pinned up with curls draping to her neck. She and the tall female environmental lawyer who walked in with her were going to bid.

The lawyer represented a nature education center that had offered to be a gathering place for people and groups concerned about the threat of fracking, and their concerns had proven correct. Every acre of the state recreation land around the center was up for auction.

"Gonna be quite the ride, Teach," Kate had told me. "There's some people riled up. Money's coming in."

At first I was caught up in the process, watching bidders silently raise their numbered cards. The auctioneer prattled and his assistant did a lot of pointing, calling out, "Ho!" and "Ha!" as he recognized bids. There were moments of faked competition, but by and by, it became clear that the big boys, NorA and Dillon and a few in-state players working for them, all knew what parcels they each needed, and there was no challenge to their bids. For a long half hour, we watched forests, lakes, and riverbeds go for the minimum bid of $10 per acre.

The disruptions began when a voice from the hallway wailed, "How can we sit by when they're selling off public lands?"

Each person who stood up laid down one piece of protest next to the other. "Fracking poisons the water for our grandchildren, for you and your grandchildren too. Would you have them drink your flowback water?"

One young woman stood before the bidders and raised her hands in testimony. People in chairs raised their hands to receive her words. "This is my homeland, where my family has raised food for the community for generations. This is land that I love.

"Where are your sacred places?" she called to the bidders as the only conservation officer in the room escorted her out.

"Where are your homes?" came a room-wide echo.

A young man surprised us all when he jumped from his seat onto one of the bidder's tables, hollering, "Billion-dollar corporations poison us for pennies!" and the four landmen sitting at the table pushed back their chairs. A tall, rather imposing man in khakis and a pale blue shirt—an officer, we assumed—yanked the young man from the table.

Outside, in the hall, protestors took up the call. "Poison us for pennies! Poison us for pennies!" and both officers started to haul vocal protestors away.

When the environmental lawyer raised her card, bidding on parcels near the nature center, suddenly land that had been going for $10 to $20 per acre jumped to $200, then $300, then $500 per acre.

The auctioneers went into high gear, their gestures robust. "I've got $325 from bidder number 108. Do I hear $350?"

Bidders from all over the room drove up the bids until one bidder called out, "I'll give you $500 for every acre on the page." Each time Kate and the lawyer got up to $400 per acre, he outbid them. "Five hundred for the page!"

Kate hugged the lawyer when they won two small parcels, and the $500 bidder shook his head. "Come on," he said, presumably to the DNR manager sitting up front. "Get these people outta here."

When most of the public seating was empty and the last few protestors had gone limp, forcing the officers to drag them out, a young woman stood up and delivered a quiet plea. "Ban fracking now." Her words were borrowed from the sign she held, and her long dark hair seemed to accentuate her thinness, but she spoke with such quiet honesty, such necessity, that a hush fell over the room.

She had resolved to do something, even when it seemed too late for hope. The whole room seemed to be reviewing her words when Kate and Brett ended the protest with one last surge.

Kate rose from her bidder's table and swaggered up the aisle, looking over the bidders as she clapped in time with her walk. "How about that DEQ? Huh? How about that DNR?

"Come on." She cooed at the bidders, and they began to smile along with her. I thought some of them might start to clap. "Come on, fellas." She gestured to the DNR staff at their front table. "Where would Big Oil be without your buddies at the DNR and the DEQ?"

The plain-clothed officer hurried her out, and Kate winked my way.

"Well!" the auctioneer smiled, and the bidders shook their heads with him.

They had been caught enjoying, and underestimating, a young woman's presence.

Brett crossed the room to follow Kate, and I thought it was over. Protestors had been working in pairs all morning, which was smart. Each time a protestor was escorted out, a bystander would follow to observe. But suddenly, Brett's lanky body came soaring in from the hall. His feet landed with a stomp. "Woo-hoo, wildcatters!"

I fumbled with my camera. Shy Brett was putting on a show?

"Hell, yes!" he hollered, swinging his arms back and forth. "Let's frack the hell out of the land before they know what hit 'em, fellas.

"Make all the money we can before they can't drink the water! Woo-hoo!"

The stand-ups had gotten more and more theatrical, and by the time Brett rocked his arms back and forth, making fun of the bidders to the point where a few of them were laughing at his guffawing humor, the tall officer in khakis didn't seem like he had any patience left.

Brett's "let's gouge it all out, dig it all up, blow it all up as fast as we can!" antics brought the officer in with a rush.

He dragged Brett out, wrenching one arm up to the middle of his back, and though I saw Brett wince, he kept up the show. He was absolutely swooning as he laid his head on the beefy man's shoulder. "Now, you know that turns me on when you get all forceful like that, Mr. Officer."

The bidders chuckled, and the officer reddened with rage.

Mark followed, and I hurried out after, just in time to catch the plain-clothed officer pulling both of Brett's hands behind him and leading him to the elevator.

"Are you an officer?" Mark asked, his video camera up and rolling.

Brett did not turn around or look back. He stood facing the elevators, silent.

"Yes," the man responded.

But I wanted to make sure. "Can we see your badge?"

Mark nodded. "Can we see your badge?"

The man had entered the auction room and immediately started hauling protestors out. Dressed in khakis with his pale blue shirt untucked, he could have been with oil and gas for all we knew.

He held out his badge, and I steadied it in front of Mark's camera.

"So you're a DNR officer then?" I said to let Brett know.

Mark tried to step into the elevator with them, but the officer motioned down the hall. "Public elevators."

"Is he being arrested?" I asked.

The elevator doors shut, and the officer did not answer.

Outside, later, Kate playfully punched Brett in the arm. "Come on, wild man. We gotta talk about what comes next and watch Marko's footage."

"You coming?" Brett asked.

"It's been quite a day," I said.

I was feeling a bit raw after watching what I thought was going to be Brett's arrest. It was clear that the forces of progress—the DNR, the oil and gas industry, regulators at the DEQ—were working together. And our legislators? They were calling for all manner of unconventional oil and gas development: tar sands pipelines, fracking, natural gas–powered electric plants around the Great Lakes. But it was equally clear that these young people had managed some multilayered, intentional organizing. They had rattled the DNR, which meant they were not going to get away with disrupting an auction so easily next time. Especially Kate and Brett, who would be on their radar for sure.

"Thanks for handling the big guy in there," Mark said. "I froze for a moment."

"You did fine. You all did. You did great."

I hugged each one of them, hanging on to Brett a bit longer, and watched them walk together toward Kate's old pickup.

Chapter 7

Visits

We spent the rest of that first summer visiting every one of the dozen or so frack well sites in the state, or so we thought. Soon enough, a tall, booming-voiced man named Del revealed another side to the story, the secret side—well sites operating within wetlands and forests that weren't showing up on anyone's maps.

Mark kept his eyes on the DEQ's database and permit lists. Sonya, who was busy raising Hank and working, took our visit notes and photos and turned them into an ongoing series of updates from each site, while Brett and Kate and I and occasionally Mark, when he could pull away from the books he was studying for his legal college admissions test, visited well sites as often as we could. We dreamed of being able to document every stage of the process: well pad prep, drilling, and fracking, so people could see what we were seeing.

We returned, over and over, to State-Lexford. NorA's drill rig crews lived on site in two-week shifts, and we learned a lot about the drilling process from the supervisors who rotated in and out with their crews. Getting photos of the actual fracking process was another matter. No one seemed to want the full frontal ugliness of fracking to get out to the public.

Charlie, a stocky older man with stubbles of gray hair and a folder full of annotated plat maps, accompanied us on several tours of "pipeline central," as he called it, where NorA had constructed its first pipeline corridor. Charlie had served as a volunteer Waterkeeper on the Manistee River for decades. He kept a close watch on NorA's progress. Starting with State-Lexford and its sister site State-Eleanor, NorA had cut two parallel paths through the center of the north country, adding well pad after well pad as they zigzagged down that corridor. After two decades without work, the people of struggling northern towns accepted the excavation and security jobs NorA offered, hoping for more. Bad-mouthing the oil and gas revenue that built high school ice rinks and stadiums wasn't well tolerated. We felt safer when Charlie was with us. He had a history in the area that none of the drill rig supervisors had, so they left us alone when Charlie was around. But the more informed we became with our questions, even the nice guys at NorA began to claim new rules. Stakes and flags marked wider and wider clearings, and supervisors who at first tolerated us walking directly up to the gates claimed that their easements extended well beyond the berms. More than once, our raised lenses captured images of their cameras pointed back at us.

We met Tammy and Del in the mid-north where two cold glacial lakes, Higgins and Houghton, and the miles of marshlands between them gave rise to the Manistee and Muskegon Rivers; and their wetlands, of course, communicated with the wetlands of the forked Au Sable. The rivers drew the people together.

The Amish farm community, anglers, and members of small-town lake associations had been showing up at township meetings armed with questions about water use and chemicals, and when they asked for an EPA hearing, they got the same shit show we had witnessed downstate.

We were in a packed high school auditorium surrounded by armed police and conservation officers. Kate bobbed next to me. "Uh-oh. People of color are showin' up. Now the man's going to get nasty."

A Black woman wearing a dress and a lab coat walked down the aisle, her dark hair smoothed back and pulled into a bun just above her collar. Her gaze and her posture looked serious. I was glad to see

Frank, director of a Native American Cultural Center that my classes visited often, following behind her. He was dressed in jeans and a casual blazer, a holdover from his years in academia. His graying hair was tied back in a ponytail, and he held the canister of maps he carried into every meeting. Frank had been speaking often, framing the argument that oil and gas development of any kind, without securing tribal permission, was a violation of the 1836 treaty. He nodded as he passed by me and Brett and Kate. I didn't notice immediately the tall, silver-haired White man in a T-shirt and baggy shorts who followed.

My relief at seeing Frank had to do with what was not addressed at public meetings, when it came to land rights and justice. Throughout our country's industrial history, the privileged barely paid attention to the placement of chemical plants and refineries. People living in poverty and communities of color bore the brunt of cheap oil's burdens. But fracking and its pipelines could go anywhere. Into state forests, between schools, behind upscale suburban neighborhoods, and with that proximity, white middle class America was finally reacting to the destruction and the toxins and the loss of safety at home.

In my classes, I could bring larger issues before my students, but in public meetings, I felt unqualified. Who was I to stand up and speak about land rights?

"You're not," Frank said to me the last time we had spoken. "And I'm not either."

Frank's dialogue could be gruff, and his eyes were deep set beneath bushy, graying eyebrows. It had taken me a while to recognize his wide, flat grin.

We weren't protecting rights *to* land, Frank would say. We were standing up *for* land. For water, sky, for the nonhuman world and its right to be. Recognizing tribal rights to manage treaty lands was the first step, he said, toward something much more brave and smart— toward healing.

Brett returned to the seat next to me in the auditorium. "Frankie's badass," he said, spreading out the 1836 treaty lands map he and Frank passed out, row by row. "We've got to get this on the website."

For some reason, Brett's smile sparked a memory. We were not meant to live each other's histories, a professor of mine used to say, but we could listen. Instead of fearing each other's stories, we could listen.

Frank leaned toward me, patting the back of my chair before he sat a few rows up. "Wait until you hear Tammy give them hell."

Tammy's poise was obvious when she stood up to talk about air quality. The lab coat and her healthcare bun (as she called it) didn't hurt. She had worked as the director of a downriver Detroit clinic for years, she explained, where they were no stranger to refinery asthma.

She was small in stature, but when she gripped the sides of the podium and demanded answers, her voice was direct. Wherever fracking went, she began, the health story was the same. "Kids with nosebleeds, rising asthma rates, people with ear canals that swell shut, and hot, hurtful skin rashes.

"When, in this meeting," she asked, "will we discuss public health? Who on this panel is qualified to assess air quality and health risks?"

Del stood, motioning toward the officers that rimmed the auditorium. "Why all the officers? What are you doing that makes you afraid of the people who live here?"

The COs moved quickly once Del stood. He was tall and broad, and his voice was filled with confrontation.

Tammy, a county health official, seemed to command respect, but the moment Del stood up, the big guy had to go. A pair of conservation officers escorted him out while the crowd booed. "Let him speak!"

From the back of the auditorium, Del's booming voice called out, "Anyone who really wants to talk about fracking, meet outside."

"My hunting shorts," he laughed later, gesturing to the camouflage print as we talked after the meeting. "My up north getup, you know what I mean?"

At times I had to work to hide my frustration with Kate's

scheduling, the hopping from well site to well site as Kate called yet another one of our local contacts and promised them we'd stop by, but I was glad that she kept us in touch.

Tammy and Del, and Frank too, became special to us.

A week after the Gladwin auditorium meeting, Del gave Kate and Brett and me our first Jeep tour of the local state park. We bumped along miles and miles of sandy two-tracks where pink and orange flags were tied to stakes, wrapped around trees, hanging from the branches of saplings, and red metal gates locked people out of equestrian areas.

"They're talking trail maintenance, but you know that's got to be cover." Del grinned, turning his face half to us and half to the road. "The DNR's got a skeleton crew, and suddenly they're going to clean up Gladwin's horse trails, you know what I mean?"

We knew, as we bounced in Del's Jeep, that we had met someone important. He was tall and bright, a friendly man who would stand over the devastated clearings we came upon and move us all to tears. Most times, not without some wisecrack to bring us back.

At one particularly aching point in the late afternoon, we stood at the summit of a rolling hill that had been clear cut for miles. The slope ribboned away, tufted with drying brush and tree stumps, resembling an adventure slide bordered by the sandy two-tracks running up both sides. Two-tracks that had been invisible to each other, separated by a dense young forest, until they cut it down. Del figured a pipeline was coming.

I must have moaned out loud, because Del turned to me and said, "How's the despair index now, Beck?"

I noticed that he had started calling me "Beck," but coming from Del, the shortening of my name was a sign of endearment. We had been talking about the trees, how the mix of maples and birches and beeches, and most recently the oaks and the return of white pines, were good signs. So, though Kate raised her eyebrows and giggled when Brett mimicked him, "Hey, Beck, check this out," I let it go.

We rounded the backside of that slow, graceful hill, and Del pushed in the clutch, silencing the Jeep's effort. The wall of tree trunks before us was, at first, incomprehensible. We all leaned forward, straining to understand the ridiculously high pile of stripped trunks that went on for what must have been a quarter of a mile.

We touched the cut maples and pines, the apricot-colored pulp of the beeches. "I knew you'd want to see this," Del said.

He pointed to a lone pole pine, one tree left standing in the middle of the field. "Why do they do that?" he wondered out loud, and we all tilted our heads. Almost always, in the middle of a clear cut, loggers left one stripped tree trunk behind—never a whole tree—and the birds, most likely bewildered as we were, would come to rest at the top of the beheaded trunk, peering out at the emptiness.

A pileated woodpecker sat staring back at us.

"Looks like some kind of sick punishment, you know what I mean?"

Chapter 8

And More Visits

The next time we met up with Del, he led us on a whirlwind tour of frack well sites that were not showing up on anyone's maps. Not the industry's, not the DEQ's, and as Kate said, "Even Marko can't find them."

"Confidential," Del told us. "When they first start drilling, they ask for confidential status. Course, around here, they've been drilling for half a year and no reports."

Brett shook his head. "How insane is that? After they've drilled and fracked, then the public gets to know?"

The well sites Del showed us that day were in a shale layer we hadn't yet heard of, the A-1 Carbonate layer, which carried a new risk: hydrogen sulfide.

On the phone on the way up, Del had joked with Kate, telling her we would get a kick out of the parking lot where he asked us to meet. His voice boomed from Kate's phone. "Tammy said to make sure you tell Beck, it's not my kind of place."

"Topless beats Jobless," the marquee at the junction read. The words ran under a silhouette of a pole dancer with upturned breasts. Below, a second line read, "See Manager for Audition."

"I bet," Kate huffed. She posed beneath the sign, jumping into the landscaping box that had been built around the sign's base. Brett took his turn, grabbing his chest and pursing his lips in an exaggerated kiss.

Del rolled by in his Jeep. "Great sign, isn't it?" Framed by his silver hair, his summer face was a deep red-tan. "Job growth, you know what I'm saying?"

Brett pinked. "Sorry. We were just joking around."

"You kidding me?" Del patted Brett's back and pulled him out of the gravel box. "That sign's the biggest news around."

Kate stood on her tiptoes to give him a hug, and Del reached out to me. "Come on, Teach." It was August, temps in the nineties, yet Del was wearing his signature black T-shirt and baggy camo shorts. Kate had kept in close touch with Tammy and Del since our first visit, and they always seemed glad to see us.

"Good country folk," Kate joked, though Del and Tammy had both come from Detroit. Del had worked as an investment manager for a state pension fund, a job he had quit with the takeover of public schools. Placing schools under emergency management, the privatization of public water, it was all a warm-up to shutting the public out of public decisions. That's what concerned Del the most. "Getting us ready for the takeover," he would say.

Del elbowed Kate, gesturing to the sign. "Done with school yet? Job prospects are picking up around here."

Minutes later we were in my hatchback, following Del's Jeep, when he slowed as the pavement dipped to dirt. "Smell that?" his voice boomed from Kate's phone.

"Oh, I do," I said, reacting to the sour, greasy smell filling the car. It felt hot. "Is that brine? Is it on the road?" Some of drilling's by-products were legal to spread on roads, to slick the dust down.

"Nope," Del said. "Meet your culprit, State-Wheeler."

We rolled past a flat, open well pad, where a huge spool of coiled tubing was being fed into the well. Prep work or clean-out pipe, Del figured. They were at the beginning or the end of a fracking stage. There were several trucks backed into place around the wellhead, and with layer upon layer of bold blue rings and red metal valves adding to its height, it towered over the workers around it.

We photographed another new sight that day: hydrogen sulfide warning flags.

At the entrance gate was a plastic sawhorse sectioned with three bars of color: green at top, yellow in the middle, and red at the bottom.

"Gee," Brett joked. "I wonder what happens on a red day."

The green band read "SAFE" for safe levels of hydrogen sulfide. A yellow flag sat in a flag cup attached to the sawhorse, and we could smell why. Yellow meant there was a "MODERATE" risk of exposure. I would find out later that hydrogen sulfide gas, heavier than air, can travel in pockets, undetected, floating between the monitors that are supposed to pick up its presence.

Red was "HIGH RISK" with the addition of "DANGER!"

How sad it was, looking out at the dry, sun-bleached dirt beyond the entrance gate, that Michigan had courted the industry with free water. This well pad had been scraped from a tract of woods across from farmers' fields. They had cleared enough land for two well pads, leaving the ground bare to the sun. For the most part, hydrogen sulfide or anything else escaping from State-Wheeler was free to roam.

The sun beat down on the truck trailers backed around the wellhead, their back panels full of spigots and valves and hoses hanging limp. Rows of tall, boxy compressors and more coils and hoses were connected to the roar of effort that went into the giant blue tension arm feeding some kind of flexible pipe into the well bore.

The man who stepped out from the Secure Tek trailer wore minimal protection, a hard hat and boots, and I wondered, noticing the oils and powders that stained the dirt, if he wore those boots home. Did he have children? But these weren't questions to begin with.

Kate and Brett gathered photos as I tried to talk us on site.

"We're researching the natural gas boom in Michigan," I said. "Can I ask you a few questions about what's happening here today?"

"That's proprietary," he said, but I asked anyway, and as he and I stood sweating in the sunshine, I could taste puffs of sour vapor on the breeze.

I asked Brett and Kate to move up the road a bit, to see if they could get pictures of the back ends of the trucks. I wasn't sure if the heat or the oily puffs that blew over us were getting to me, but I felt dizzy and wanted them to move away. Del had already driven away and sat waiting beyond the next cross street.

"I get the hell out now when that stuff starts to affect me," he said. "Get out after you get the shots you want, you got it?"

Later, we walked through the ferns that covered the forest floor behind Tammy and Del's home, taking pictures of survey stakes tipped with pink and orange flags. Their property bordered what had always been undevelopable state forest land. But now, just a hundred or so feet into the woods, were red and blue flags tied to a stake with the words "WELL PAD CORNER" written in permanent black marker. Their future neighbor would be named State-Miralette.

"Unfortunately," Del said. "We've got one more place to go."

That place was Randy and Diane's.

The rig had not yet arrived, but the vast rectangle of peach dirt and bright white limestone was ready. We walked the State-Rudmond site for over an hour, smelling the freshness of excavation.

Randy was slight of build and rather soft spoken, his thin brown hair pulled back in a ponytail. Such a contrast to Diane, a tall, square-shouldered woman with a rasp in her voice and bright blonde hair. The two of them ran a music store and sold vintage guitars. Diane walked us to the site, then squeezed Randy's hand and turned toward home.

"She's been fighting the DNR for over a year," Randy told us. "Fighting to keep state land from being leased. Now there's nothing to do but wait."

Sunlight angled strong and amber-white over the tree line to the west, making the well pad's smoothed peach floor and its central square of limestone sparkle. A silvery dust rose as we walked.

Randy shared what he and Diane had been told. State-Rudmond was a pilot hole, due for a 14,000-foot horizontal to explore what the shale might produce. Dillon's rig would be set just a thousand feet from Randy and Diane's backyard deck, so they would see and hear it all—trucks coming and going, compressors roaring, plumes of black smoke rising from the rig.

We knelt on the grating, peering through the open weave of metal to get a closer look at the buried silo of rippled metal where two pipes came up from below.

"The big round pipe sticking up," Randy explained, "that's the casing they have to do when they drill through the water aquifer." The square pipe off to the side, he said, had something to do with the blowout preventer.

Brett and Kate and I traded knowing glances. Randy had heard the DEQ's explanation of what to expect, which never clearly addressed the scale of the operation. Within weeks, the entire well pad would be covered with pipes and tanks, and the drill rig would be screeching away.

Brett and Del and Randy seemed to be enjoying each other's company, so Kate and I left the "boys" as Kate called them, standing between two bulldozers, joking about driving them off into the woods. The heaped dirt of the berm warmed to a bold orange-brown in the evening sun, and the smell of understory, of dampness not meant to be turned over and exposed, hung in the air.

I watched Del scan the site, his tall frame turning to face each side of the berm—north, east, south, and west—before he turned back to the car where Randy and Brett stood nodding and smiling.

Something about the way Del leaned toward Randy, the way his hand moved along the top of my car, seeking comfort, took me back to Fen Preserve, to the first time we felt the repercussions of acting out, and I, specifically, felt the sting of knowing my own words had pushed someone to act.

Levi and I were walking Fen Creek, tying flags to trees on the edge of the preserve, flagging boundaries that no one had felt a need to mark before, when we felt a deep rumble under our feet.

Levi put his hand on my shoulder. "That sounded like an explosion."

"The research lab," I said, and we took off running.

Levi, his long legs covering ground much faster than I could, glanced back, and I waved him on. "Go! Go! Just get there and help!"

At the research station, I found Levi and the staff standing along the ridge that fell to the preserve's property line, and I knew by the way Levi reached back to me that I wasn't going to be all right. Benten's dozers were working below in two lines. Small Bobcats backed up and accelerated forward, slamming into the trunks of trees. The heads of the huge maples and beeches shook wildly, branches flailing, and as their movements slowed, a second line of larger dozers came in, and their drivers wrapped the loosened trunks with chains.

With my whole body, I felt responsible.

I was usually quiet at meetings. I took pictures. I took notes. I didn't stand up or ask to speak. But at the last meeting, Benten's cockiness had gotten to me so badly that I had fired back when he made fun of one of the locals who noted that removing trees would cause erosion and runoff for years.

"Dead trees don't soak up water," Benten had scoffed at her.

"They most certainly do." I stood and faced him, tired of his ignorance. "Trees hold hills, they hold dunes. Even roots left in the ground. Of course they soak up water."

He had waved me off, and I shot back. "You rip out those trees and you're going to destabilize those hills."

Scientifically, we know that whole groves live as interconnected systems. Trees share water and warnings with their kin, and thanks to my impassioned lecture ("This isn't the 1950s. Any decent developer knows not to rip up trees and fill in wetlands!"), I felt responsible for Benten's payback.

There was a watchful, crass old grandmother of a tree that we called Mildred, a maple whose branches spread over the younger maples and beeches and the tamaracks that grew near her. I knew, after sitting with her so many mornings, that Mildred loved those tamaracks and their crazy cornflower-like blooms, and in turn the tamaracks flourished under her beech-maple sky. The tamaracks must have felt Mildred's death that day too.

Wetland trees do not snap, after all. Wetland trees are moist and interwoven. They bend and whine with such long-drawn tension that when David came striding toward me, I grabbed his hands and pressed them over my ears.

The trees around Mildred stood stiff, their branches braced against hers as two dozers chained her and chugged in reverse, straining with an outpouring of blue-black diesel power, and Mildred's trunk began to slide. The ground around her kinked up in long, earthen ropes that rose and stretched taut until the earth split open, dirt flying as her roots snapped and recoiled in tiny explosions that we could feel as we watched.

Kate's voice brought me back to State-Rudmond.

"Man, you are cooked today, aren't you?"

The gleam of the limestone had mellowed to a cool lavender, and Del's posture, as he leaned over Randy, his hand still feeling the roof of my car for a good place, was full of grief. The uproar over the proposed well site near Tammy and Del's home had chased Dillon Industries north to Randy and Diane's, where a more agreeable township welcomed the road widening and the jobs, even the new strip club at the county cross-roads. Tammy and Del's win had become Randy and Diane's loss.

Kate pulled me over to the corner of the pad where three perfectly apexed piles of peach sand sat ready to be spread.

Your sins will follow you, she had written across the well pad floor.

We headed toward Randy and Diane's, and I turned back to pan the site. A doe and her fawn nosed around the corners, trying to get their bearings within the new landscape.

Chapter 9

Meetings at Sonya's

For a while, DEQ geologists suffered through the public's desire to know about fracking. They fielded questions about water and chemicals, bearing the comparisons to Pennsylvania and Colorado where water wells had been contaminated with methane. They nodded through talk of Ohio, where injection wells around Youngstown set off a year of earthquakes in an area not known for seismic activity. But when the public became more insistent, less willing to sit quietly for canned "Safe Fracking" presentations, what we saw in a mid-north high school auditorium became the norm. Armed officers and signs directed the public to be silent.

Kate swore off the fake meetings, and we all stopped showing up to some extent. It was time, most of the people and groups they were meeting with agreed, to organize local resistance.

Kate and Mark and Brett and Sonya moved to Sonya's backyard where the ideas began to fly week by week, month by month. The four of them and occasionally me or a member of one of the groups they worked with would gather on the worn wooden deck off the back of Sonya's farmhouse-style kitchen turning over damp cushions on an assortment of folding chairs. Starts and stops of Sonya's gardening efforts edged the deck, and a rather broken down—or listening in, as Brett suggested—old tulip tree brushed the shoulders of anyone sitting close. A young sycamore lent its rusty mauves and lavender grays, its leaves blossoming over the deck like a head of hair.

Everything in Sonya's yard seemed to bloom and gather in the most organic way, as if her own frizzy curls with their chaotic and somehow balanced flare had influenced her surroundings. I often wondered how Sonya, working as an aide in an assisted living facility and raising Hank on her own, afforded the rent, but I never asked. The house was full of Hank's creative clutter and, after a time, Kate's diagrams and lists.

Some nights we simply shared information. Mark updated everyone on the latest studies and permits, Kate would return from an action camp and share strategies, and Brett and Sonya would brainstorm. Sometimes we joked about sharpening tree branches and plunging them into tires, the very trees the industry had brought down, of course.

"Spook them off, you know?" Kate said, her head bobbing.

"Like the old Sherwood Forest," Mark added.

"Little forest hoodlums!" Kate reached across the table as if to grab hold of what Mark had said. "Make them think about what they're doing, you know? Like they're being watched.

"That's why we gotta stick close to the people," Kate said. "Know their places, so we can hear what's going on."

Watching Brett find his voice was one of the most enjoyable parts of meetings at Sonya's. He often texted to ask if I was coming. In the early days, I was a source of support when it came to Brett daring to speak to Kate's shrieking and Sonya's quiet knowing.

In class, he had often held back. When he did speak, everyone would give him the time and space to work up what he wanted to say, which only made his uneasiness worse. His light olive skin would pink, and he would finger comb the then long, black strands of his hair.

"You play with your hair like a girl," Kate often teased him. "Just spit it out, bud. We're with you."

As summer came on hot and strong and we talked deeper into the nights and sometimes into those muggy summer mornings, Brett became the Brett who appeared on the news segment that aired from their Winter Campout: ready to speak with an easy, steady confidence.

He became an equal, especially when it came to funneling ideas into doable plans. Brett and Kate were a natural team, wrangling the group's ideas into strategy. Mark mapped out each task, Kate thought on her whiteboard, and Sonya was the quiet force that pulled them all together. Sonya had come to college and to our class, she said, seeking a restart, and maybe, I thought, community. Sometimes her gaze held such a strong desire for connection that few of us, other than Kate, could hold it.

"You okay with the Sherwood Forest antics?" I asked Sonya when I arrived early one night, hoping to get a chance to catch up. Their last deck conversation had them raining pea gravel down upon site surveyors from the trees.

"I'm the safe place with food," she smiled, chopping tomatillos for salsa. "I'm okay with that for now."

"Not unlike a classroom," I said, raising a cold beer and opening one for her.

"I'm a parent. I can't afford to do anything that would get me arrested." She smirked. "But I can be the person who knows what to do when it happens."

Hank smirked like Sonya. He had the same sand-beige skin, and his sandy brown hair still shined golden in the sun, but his eyes were a deep blue, not red-brown like Sonya's, and his face was much more narrow. Sonya never talked about Hank's father, not in my presence, but I had the distinct feeling that she and Kate were talking about a lot more than tar sands and fracking.

When Kate dragged in the whiteboard, Mark, Sonya, Brett, and I were all in the kitchen. Mark was cutting carrots and green peppers, and Hank was standing on a stool, arms reaching under the tap, rinsing vegetables.

We were joking about Kate's late sense of timing.

"Well, hello!" Hank snorted, "Late Kate!" He had given us all nicknames. Hairy Mark for the dark hair that covered Mark's forearms and calves. Brett was Bubble Head, Hank said, because he was always thinking, and I had become, much to both Sonya's and my dismay, Aunty Becky. Oh, how Hank would laugh at the sound.

We all turned when Mark, who had backed out of the kitchen when we heard a car door slam, said, "Jesus. What is she doing now?"

His expression was so free that it took on an affectionate tone. At least I thought I heard affection. We all loved Kate. We loved her deeply for her passion and her flaws, and her outward sense of knowing her passions and flaws. And it made so much sense that Mark's go-to expression would be "Jesus!" He had grown up in a Christian household and struggled to understand what he called his mixed-up Zeitgeist. Adopted from an Indian orphanage, he could have been born to Buddhist, Hindu, Muslim, or Christian parents.

"Holy fricking hell," Mark mocked Kate's phrase. "She stole a piece of school."

We watched as Kate lifted a huge whiteboard out of the back of her truck, and she and Brett carried it up Sonya's driveway, struggling to balance their difference in height.

"Where the heck did you get that?" Mark held open the door. It had an aluminum marker tray mounted along the bottom, like a classroom board.

"I have my ways," she said. Brett eased the board into a lean against the wall, and Kate smiled. "See. It fits. It fits just fine."

"Markers!" Hank hollered out, throwing his arms around Kate. "Markers. Markers. Markers!"

In class, Kate had always been the one to grab several colors and start drawing and outlining what we talked about. Whenever I set a marker down, she would ask if she could continue.

"So this is what you meant when you said everyone should have a whiteboard at home."

"I always mean what I say," she said.

She was right. Kate said what she meant and she meant what she said, even if her expressions sometimes burst out at inappropriate or fleeting times.

If I had read Sonya's email on time, I could have gone to Kate and found out exactly what they were planning. Unless Kate had planned it. She had the surprising ability to be patient when she was working with her own secrets.

Her whiteboard way, as Mark had coined it.

"We have to visualize what we want to happen," Kate said that night. "Move it all about until it feels right."

"Create a vision," Brett added.

"Exactly," Kate had bobbed as she started partitioning the whiteboard. "We gotta be tangible. Keep working toward something we can see."

Oh, what that whiteboard could tell me if I could get to it. They had dreamed up action camps, a coordinated spray-painting mission to stencil smoky drill rigs on the state's summer tourism billboards, and Late Kate had proposed the Winter Campout.

"Why winter?" Brett had asked.

"Because," Kate answered. "Seeing people freezing their asses off in the middle of winter makes it all the more obvious how much they care."

"We could call for a land occupation," Mark said. "The spectacle factor would certainly be there."

"Spectacle, my ass." Kate had slapped his arm. "I'm talking about caring. True, freeze-your-ass-off caring here!"

Hopefully, they had gotten rid of Kate's lists before they left. If they had left.

Activism was always better received if the public thought it was an act of moral outrage. Something a young man or a grandmother felt compelled to do. Losing your cool for a short time? Fine. But planning to have a real, lasting effect, to change even one industrial project or outcome? That kind of patience was the stuff of revolutions.

I knew about Mark's parents. I knew Kate had grown up with her mom, and they had a good relationship. Brett and his family had moved to Traverse City when he was young. They had ties with the Grand Traverse Band.

Who were Sonya's people?

Somewhere, a parent or a significant other might be watching the news. Or worse, they might not know at all.

Chapter 10
Deeply Unsettled

It was early in the second summer, spring really, and none of us were sure we wanted to spend another summer visiting well sites. We had photographed, so many times, the Redding 120 in action. We had crawled over the backside of berms, where pallets of cement mixes and huge plastic vats full of chemicals sat at the periphery. We were tired of the hot, oily winds that made our skin feel sandpapered by the sun. But when Charlie the Waterkeeper called, Kate and I jumped in the car. NorA was fracking near gorgeously aqua-blue Higgins Lake.

Unfortunately, unprepared as we were, we drove straight into the unmarked access drive. We rounded an abrupt curve in the road and suddenly we could see the trucks in the distance, metal and windshields gleaming in the midafternoon sun.

The summer before we had driven directly onto one of their secret well sites with one of the roughneck's out-of-state license plates borrowed and clamped over mine as Kate circled the wellhead and I photographed, as quickly as possible, the giant tension arm cranked back and feeding perforated pipe down into the well bore as chemical trucks idled nearby.

We had surprised them then, but that was early in the game when very few people knew there were frack well sites in Michigan. A summer later, there were guard trailers, gates, and cameras.

I stopped the car, and we debated. Should we keep driving? Act as if we didn't realize we had turned off the road, because we hadn't, actually. The industry built raised gravel roads over two-tracks and trails, widening all the way, so when their road banked, so had we. We'd be turned back at the gate, examined suspiciously, but Kate could ask some of her signature questions. "We're looking for an old township cemetery." Or, "You wouldn't happen to have seen a land for sale sign, driving in and out of here, have you?"

We decided to ease our way back along the curve, hoping they hadn't spotted us.

Kate leaned out the open window. "Did you hear that?"

I stopped, thinking I had heard a long, strange twinge.

"Did you hear that crack?"

Later, we would talk about it, ask others, wonder if we had heard the crack of one of those huge valves being pried apart or if Kate truly had, as she believed, heard the ground crack. Folks she worked with in Ohio told her it was real. Sometimes you could hear the ground crack.

The original road was evident once we backed up to face it. Narrow and arched over with trees, it was a car-sized bear trail. We drove a mile or so down the sandy two-track, and I backed my little green hatchback into a snarl of bushes. Still, I fretted about whether or not the car was hidden. Should I back it deeper into the bushes? Was the license plate covered? Could we pull out fast if we needed to?

Something hadn't felt right since I'd turned into that long graded curve.

The whole day had gone off track, from my being over an hour late to pick up Kate, to Kate taking her dear, sweet time packing us a healthy lunch. How could I complain? By the time we gassed up and hit the highway, we arrived much later in the afternoon than we'd hoped to, which left us no time to get our bearings. Neither one of us had downloaded the permit or familiarized ourselves with the site plan.

Several paths led away from the grassy clearing where we parked, so we took the path most traveled. We were only vaguely certain that the angled path would lead us to the well site. Still, I calmed myself, knowing we would hear the site long before we saw it. If nothing else, we could follow the sounds.

Kate's hiking stick clumped on the ground, its rubbery echo bouncing up from the dirt, and we fell in with its rhythm. She lifted her face to the sun, and I did my best to be with the land.

With the sun up and temperatures in the seventies, May was coming in warm, but in the north woods there was a shadow over spring's awakening.

The long grasses in the fields were straw-like and pale, bent over with the weight of winter winds and melt. New growth, underneath, was just beginning to green. Young birches and maples, their numbers growing as we walked, seemed to be blooming with caution, their leaves still cinched and jagged. Only the youngest saplings were showing their leaves, yellow-greens that caught the sun and the slightest breeze.

We had felt the pounding and the screeching of plenty of rigs, tasted the greasy heat and rumbling winds, but we hadn't yet witnessed a fully functioning frack job as it was happening. This time, on state land, we could walk right up and see the rows of trucks backed up to the well. We would hear the water being sucked out of a million-gallon, spring-formed pool. We would watch the bright orange hoses stiffen with pressure as crew leaders in command trailers watched over it all.

The trail started to grass over, though the indents of four-wheelers and dirt bike tires were evident, and we came to a clump of autumn olive trees—recent growth, judging by the trail's abrupt detour around them. They were a surprise and a distraction. Autumn olive, so far north? I turned back to see their silvery green leaves brighten to a hot white-green in a sudden show of full sun, and I forgot for a moment the growing sense of unease coming over me.

Dis-ease, I thought, noticing the beeches and maples that pocked the fields around us, the dryness of the pines.

And then we came upon that first pile of stumps, a long, dark mound ahead of us.

Kate's head shook. "What is that? A logjam?"

There were hundreds of huge, old, goofy-footed red oak stumps piled into a wall, a mass of stumps and mangled roots that had been bulldozed into a grub-like bulge that blocked the path. Some of the yanked roots reached out from the mound, their hair-like projections fanning out as if to take hold on the air.

We fingered the still-living soil in the grooves of bark, patted the huge, footed stumps.

"What kind of person could do this? Use the trees this way?" Kate asked.

The crown of a young white pine had been tossed, upright, on the top of the blockade. Normally, a white pine's whispering hush was comforting, full of a sense of the ages in the wind's silver-green voice, but hearing that hush from the top of that pile of ripped roots and trunks, I realized what I had been feeling as I walked and stopped and listened.

Something was wrong with the trees.

The maples, the beeches, the paper birches, the pines—they were all on high alert, and I went on high alert with them.

Spring trees should look and feel alive, branches reaching and leaves opening to gather the sun. But the farther we walked, the more I sensed a prickly tautness coming from the trees, worsened by the X-ray whiteness of the sky.

Kate was getting more and more pumped, expecting me to forge ahead with new purpose. "I'm just ready for the confrontation, you know? Got the video camera rolling. Let them try to mess with us."

We began to hear what sounded like the whir of vacuums, a steady series of thunks and clunks. NorA's subsidiary HydraCore was on site, just starting the frack job, and HydraCore's presence meant heightened security. But even as I began to feel a powerful urge to turn around, I knew it wasn't the confrontation I was worried about.

By the time we came to the second pile of stumps, I was in deep trouble.

The trees thinned (bashed down and out of the way) and we could hear the clanging of metal, feel the weight of the equipment reverberating through the air. We were close—seconds away if we kept walking across the sunken, grassy clearing where we could see the bright red battery cars and the bold blue of the water tank, patches of color between the few scraggly trees that remained—and I was breaking down, losing a battle I could not explain.

"I just need to stay put for a few minutes," I told Kate.

The pines, especially, appeared sickly and gray. Sure, there had been browning and die-off, but even the young trees were way too dry. Something pure and strong was emanating from the trees, and I could feel it.

I had the strangest feeling that we were in actual physical peril.

Kate tried to talk me into giving the feeling its due and moving on—my own advice—but even as I listened and understood, I started to visualize the car. Escaping.

The trees, the ground, the oddly cool but scalding white of the sun, everything seemed to be vibrating with a warning. Get out!

I stopped and started, came and went, tried to square up with the trail and push on.

I stalled, touching bark. What was it that a national forest study had found? Leaves dying two and three days after exposure to fracking chemicals, trees dead in a month? But the more I acknowledged the trees, the more I could feel them.

I moved into the coolness of the pines that flanked us, a last tuft of trees where the ground mounded up slightly, and there, on the pine loam, I bent over my legs and asked: *What is this? What are you doing?*

I stared at my dirt-brown boots, feeling the soles of my feet. I could focus on them, make my mind enter them, but there was no moving them.

The soles of my feet were listening to the ground.

When I stood still, I could live with the feeling. But so much as begin to peel a foot free and I felt exposed all over again, as if to step into the clearing that lay ahead of us was to step off into some undetectable range of nothingness, something treacherous.

I was jelly and bones, and so was the ground.

If it is possible to come apart from the inside, to have your muscles and organs crowd around without your permission, that was what I was feeling. My innards were weighty and my bones flimsy with their pull. The very core of me, that steel ball center of gravity that we know to be our center, had begun to move on its own.

I returned to the sound of revved compressors, that steady roar of wind that feels like an unnaturally strong, hot breath, and from far behind I heard the screech of a hawk. I scanned the open clearing, realizing I had lost Kate.

"Kate!" I whispered. "Kate!"

"What?" She emerged from the pines, slightly ahead of me. She hadn't gone on to the site as I feared. "What fricking hell, you scared me."

"I can't go any farther," I admitted.

She was annoyed.

"I can't explain it, but I literally, physically, cannot make myself go any farther."

For Kate's sake, I tried.

We pushed together into the clearing, crouching under one particularly dry, V-trunked pine standing alone and close to the well pad. I pressed my back to its trunk, trying to normalize the chug of diesel motors, the thunks and metallic clangs.

Kate shouldered me for comfort. She smirked like Sonya, and I had the strongest feeling that Sonya would have felt it too, whatever I was feeling. Sonya would have given in long before I had.

I tried to talk myself into diving toward the next clump of trees, thin sticks of trunks, all of them brittle. I tried to tell myself that photographing through those scraggly adolescents would bring us some useful photos, but all we could capture were bands of bright reds and blues and shards of glare off windshields.

Kate shook with missed opportunity. "We're so-so-so-so close. I just want to walk right up, you know? We're so close."

We were on site at a brand new frack job. Quick, simple steps from the documentation that Charlie—dear old Charlie who had shown us so many of the places he loved—was counting on us to get. If there was one thing I had learned and relearned, it was this: If we took a deep breath and approached boldly, they had a hard time pushing us off balance.

We'd be met by the site supervisor, of course. We had experienced intimidation. The white trucks that followed us from site to site. The clenched fists of a guard when we refused to back down. We had felt our vulnerability, especially as women isolated in the presence of so many men. But what I was feeling was a different, deeper fear, and I knew I would hate every minute of remembering how I had blown it.

In the end, I got no farther than that V-trunked pine. As long as I was sitting, pressed against it for support, I could consider moving closer. But once standing, the same unbearable sense of vulnerability returned, and all I could do was sink back.

When it was clear that the sun was setting, that our chance to cut back into the woods and approach the well pad from a different angle was gone, I made it one tree closer, to a sadly skinny maple that was peeling so profusely it could have been a shag bark.

Later, when we took the time to print out the site plans and read over the permit, we found that we had been walking directly over the first horizontal leg of the well site, a mile-long boring on the same angle we had traveled.

We were walking on ground that was being actively fracked 8,000 feet below.

Knowing what we knew about the way they frack, starting at the end of each boring, then plugging and blasting their way back toward the well pad, it all became clear. We had been hiking a route that had been fracked just days and hours before, approaching closer and closer to that place, 8,000 feet below, where they were setting their plugs, zapping a new four-hundred-foot segment of ancient geological shale with electricity, and then blasting the freshly shocked rock with a 12,000 psi wash of water, sand, and chemicals—horribly toxic chemicals. Then they would pull the pipe back, set the next plug, and repeat.

Plug. Blast. Pressurize. Repeat. And somehow, I had felt it.

The ground, the sky, the trees—together we had all experienced something deeply, deeply unsettling.

Something the rooted beings and the rock could not escape.

Chapter 11
Sonya's Last Meeting

When I described the feeling to Sonya a few days later, her response was immediate and affirming. The shame I was feeling wasn't my own, she assured me. I was feeling the very human shame of knowing what our species could do—and then justify.

Unfortunately for Sonya, when she reached her breaking point, I wasn't there for her. The thugs got a two-for-one that night. They threatened Sonya out, and poor Quinn, a young geologist, was schooled in.

We were at a particularly contentious meeting at a rural township hall in northern Kent county. We knew what to expect. A DEQ geologist would begin with an informative presentation about the geology of the Great Lakes basin, then move quickly through the drilling and fracking process using industry photos. A state college educator would encourage landowners to negotiate their own lease terms, and finally, a lawyer familiar with the Farm Bureau would discuss leasing options.

The hall was packed when we arrived. Kate and I sat near each other on one side of the room. Sonya and Brett sat on the opposite side. A woman next to us told us, "The whole county's crawling with landmen." Parks and recreation areas, even banks of the Grand River, were going up for auction.

The irony was hard to escape. Grand Rapids was one of the greenest cities in the country, but there might soon be pumping stations and processing plants operating north of town. As Brett had joked in the car, "The industry's got a vision for every body of water."

We had sworn off meetings, but this was Kate's homeland. I encouraged them to speak out. They'd done their research. They were ready.

Unfortunately, so was the industry. There were just as many landmen in pale plaid shirts as there were men in overalls and muck boots—aging farmers, mostly, and their wives. Kate knew the local character. "Still a place where the man runs the business and the woman runs the house."

The meeting began like many others. Steve Quinland, Quinn as he introduced himself, was younger than other DEQ geologists we had met. He had, as Kate noted, dressed for the farm folk, standing before us in jeans, a flannel shirt, and a John Deere cap. He ran through slides labeled "Horizontal Hydraulic Fracturing," though he made sure to minimize the danger of the chemicals used. "Out of millions of gallons of fracking fluid, only 1 or 2 percent are chemicals." He neglected to complete the math. Two percent of 20 million gallons of water meant there could be up to 400,000 gallons of chemicals in the mix.

An elderly farmer asked, "But this type of fracking, this deep shale fracking, it's different than the old vertical wells, isn't it?"

Kate, a few rows up from me, rolled her eyes when Quinn gave the standard answer. "We've been safely fracking in Michigan for fifty years."

"How often do you go out to inspect these wells?" a woman with a sharp voice asked.

"Me, personally?" Quinn responded.

"Yes, you," she said. "How many people like yourself does the DEQ have out there to inspect these wells?"

First, he tried the DEQ standard. "Careful now. The geology in Michigan is different than the geology in Pennsylvania. Fracking isn't the same everywhere."

"Fine," she said. "How often are you out there, keeping an eye on things?"

Next came the generalities. "The industry has to report everything. Every bit of the drilling process."

She pushed. "How many of there are you, for the state? I'm asking how many and how much time do you spend at each well?"

"There's seven of us," he answered, and the crowd sighed. Seven inspectors for the entire state? They were on site, Quinn guessed, "about half an hour."

"A day?" she countered.

"A day?" he chuckled. "We don't have time to sit on these sites every day. Once a week, once a month."

A young woman stood and talked about her grandparents' farm. How the landmen had been back six or seven times and were pressuring her grandparents to sign a lease. She sounded nervous. "What can you do if the wells leak, or if methane gets into people's water supply?"

Predictably, Quinn responded to her concerns by saying Michigan's regulations were the best. Kate turned toward me, holding up her notebook. She had written in big letters, *Best Pizza in Town!*

We had met an ecologist who restored ecosystems that had been damaged, in one way or another, by oil and gas exploration. Now, she was fighting to educate the public about fracking's well pads and pipelines, about the fragmentation that forever changed the forest.

"It's like pizza boxes," Bev would say. "The 'Best Pizza in Town' slogan is on every box, but we don't believe it. They can't all be the best."

"It's a load of crap!" she said. "The regulations are the same everywhere because they're written by the industry."

I waited for Brett or Sonya or Kate to stand up, but when it was clear that the landmen and the suits behind us were getting fed up with the slightest challenge, I stood up and held my hand in the air.

Brett moved toward grumbling in the back of the room. Sonya remained seated, staring ahead. I checked for Kate and saw her readying her pen to take notes.

I knew I would get only one chance to speak, so I decided to pack it all in.

"Mr. Quinland," I began, "you mentioned, briefly, that there were environmental concerns. Can you tell us more about the chemicals used in hydraulic fracturing, about the known carcinogens and neurotoxins? Can we talk about methane migration, which several studies verified in the Marcellus Shale, and what about the extreme water use in Michigan? Will the people here have a chance to hear about these issues?"

By the time I mentioned methane migration, the shouting had begun. Male voices yelled, "Sit down!" "Next question!"

Quinn, for his part, tried to answer, but the chorus of retaliation was too loud.

There was a final, "Go on home!" and the state college educator stepped in front of Quinn. "No more questions," he said. "We're not going to waste time with someone's agenda."

Sonya appeared, her eyes trying to say something important, but Quinn walked up to me, his hand extended to shake mine. Sonya tucked a note into my journal and slipped away, but hands clutched together as Quinn and I were, I didn't read it. I moved with Quinn to the back of the room to finish the conversation.

Quinn's own difficult position became clear when one of the suited men came to his elbow, suggesting that our discussion was interfering with the presentation. Quinn motioned for me to follow him into the kitchen to carry on the conversation. I went back for my bag and watched as three suits swept the young geologist into the back room, and the door that had been open all evening was closed.

I sat outside the door and listened to Quinn being admonished.

"It don't matter what you know," one voice said. "You can't answer their questions."

As soon as the meeting was adjourned, an older man beelined straight for me, his eyes bright with anger.

"How many acres do you have?" He was shaking, and he stood way too close.

"I'm not sure what you mean," I said, more deliberately than I needed to, hoping for support.

He glared at me, his eyes full of fear. "How many acres do you have to lease?"

Kate and Brett appeared.

"He's scared," I said as we watched him hurry away. Scared to lease and scared not to.

Kate laughed nervously. "Fricking hell, I am too!"

I surveyed our tiny circle. "Where's Sonya?"

"I think she went out to the parking lot," Brett said.

"Alone?" I asked.

Outside, four men moved away from my car, throwing us shoulders and awful smiles. Oil and gas thugs, by the looks of the white trucks they climbed into.

Sonya was sitting in the back seat, and I remembered her note. Later, I would find her plea. *Time to leave. Please.*

She had been startled, so she ran to the car, she said. She didn't want to give the thugs the satisfaction of knowing they had gotten to her.

We sat in the car, watching the thugs pull away.

"They knew we were together. They were talking about getting our names off the sign-in sheet."

So much for journalistic integrity. In the old days, if I was going to write about a public meeting, I had to be me, straight up. But what place did integrity have when the thugs were taking names? We hadn't signed in.

"Sonya, what did they say to you?"

I drove, glancing at her in my rearview mirror. I had learned, over time, that when something got to Sonya, really got to her, she looked worn.

"They were making snide comments about you and your group of women."

"Fuck that," Kate said. "Fricking fuck those assholes!"

Brett turned in his seat, trying to lighten things up. "What the hell am I, then?"

Sonya turned away, and Brett turned pink.

"They pushed their chairs right up against mine. And then the big guy, the one who started all the hollering, leaned up behind me, and I could feel his breath."

"'Tree huggers,' he said, 'They're always women.' One of the other guys kicked my chair and I couldn't help it, I jumped."

"Fricking assholes!" Kate said. Her voice was shaking.

Brett was quiet, listening.

"The big guy, he started playing up his accent, and then he leaned in really close. 'Give me a rope and I'll show you what I can do with a tree and a woman,' he said."

Brett's head sunk.

"What happened next, Sonya?" I knew there was more.

"He touched the back of my neck with a wet finger, something wet, and I shot up. I had to." Her voice tightened.

Brett rubbed his hands, and I could feel his anger. My own, too. Kate was silent.

Later, after we dropped Sonya off at home, Kate confided in me.

"When I first ran out," she said, "they were leaning on the hood of the car, staring at her."

I saw Brett's eyes close. "I should have followed her out, but I didn't want to treat her like she couldn't handle it."

Kate leaned forward, shaking. "We gotta find out who that big guy was. The big fricking thug who started yelling, 'Sit down!' when you were up there." She pulled at my headrest. "We gotta get those fricking assholes."

"I did my best to ignore them," Sonya had said, staring out the window on the way home. "But that rope business."

"Should I call her?" I asked Kate.

"No." Kate shook. "She won't say much anyhow."

When Sonya stepped out of the car, Brett got out too. He tried to reach out to her, but she motioned him off and leaned back into the car, looking straight at me. "That's the last meeting I go to."

And then she slammed the door shut, leaving Brett standing on the sidewalk.

"She wasn't scared, you know," Kate said. "She was mad as hell that they were able to pull that shit off in the middle of a crowded room."

Through that sliver in the back door I had listened to Quinn being coached. The tall guy in the suit had faced him. "You don't let them shape the questions."

Quinn had said something about valid questions, and the suit stepped closer. "You stick to the phrases we talked about. Stick to proven knowledge."

Before he shut the door tight, I heard, "You let them wrangle these meetings and they'll bring up all sorts of whacky crap."

Where were Quinn's superiors? Not one DEQ supervisor was in the room. There was no one to help the young geologist as the door closed and they surrounded him.

Sonya's face had remained turned toward the fields as she told us what the thugs had said and done. What woman didn't know that feeling? Searching for rebearing in the world after being harassed. Being a woman who spoke for trees and animals and water brought out a particularly nasty brand of misogyny.

Three men. Some of them had wives and daughters. But to get what they wanted, to get farmland signed quick and cheap, they would do anything. They had probably breathed their hateful breath across the back of Sonya's neck specifically because they had daughters. They understood their ability to do harm.

Chapter 12
The Ultimate Out of Balance

We came to know that fracking can look uglier and uglier depending on who, ultimately, is in charge. From the rusty sheet metal welded to the framework of their 136-foot-tall monster of a drill rig to the messes they left behind, Dillon sites, we soon discovered, were pure carelessness and slop.

When we returned to the State-Wheeler well site that Del had introduced us to weeks before, the gates were wide open and the security trailer gone. The last time we'd visited, the wellhead had been surrounded by trucks, hoses dangling, limp, as a huge tension arm fed flexible tubing down into the well bore. Clean-out pipe, the supervisor had told us. Now, the long triangular gates were wide open and everything was gone. No metal coils snaking across the floor, no compressors or diesel engines or light racks, nothing but a vast, flat swath of limestone and sun-bleached dirt.

Sonya appeared at my side. "It's a wasteland," she said.

"Fricking *the Waste Land*," Kate bobbed.

It's possible that T. S. Eliot himself wouldn't have been able to imagine such a thing. The black plastic liner torn and lying in clumps, the mustard yellow and rust-colored stains wherever the dirt was exposed, the waxy sheen on the surface of the drought-dry earth, and all of it sat across the road from the Amish farm where the family's oldest son drove a horse-drawn rake through the field. He stopped to say hello and told us that just that morning a slew of trucks had come and hauled everything away. Everything except the chemical barrels and jugs left here and there, the hoses left open to the ground where evidence of their contents fanned out in salty stains, and our favorite find, a plastic toolbox labeled *Five Minute Escape Pack*.

It was an ecological apocalypse on a ten-acre scale.

It was August, late in a summer drought that had been scorching crops with temperatures in the nineties, and the sky above was roiling with cold blue clouds that refused to let go of their moisture. Sonya and I knelt in front of chemical barrels, photographing labels and tearing off any packing slips we found. Kate replenished the soaked handkerchiefs covering our noses and mouths and wandered about the site, taking video of the frogs that blended in with the pasty green water pooled around the entrance gate.

Three plastic barrels, each with their own hazardous symbols, were left sitting out in the hot August sun, even though the symbols indicated various degrees of combustibility when exposed to heat and sunlight. These were chemicals that could eat through the soft tissue linings of the lungs or the esophagus. Left out in full sun, for how long? For how much longer?

But nothing prepared us for the sewage-like moat around the pit that spanned the back of the well pad.

The black plastic liner that was supposed to be cleanly draped over the edges of the pit was torn in too many places to photograph. Shredded pieces of black plastic laced the piles of crusted dirt that had been pushed beyond the pit.

DEQ presenters always made a point to laud Michigan's storage regulations, which did not allow flowback to be stored and evaporated from open pits.

"That's one thing Michigan got right," they always said. "Flowback has to be stored in tanks. There's no open flowback pits here."

But when the flowback came back up quickly, during those first few stages of fracking, it had to go somewhere, and this pit, obviously, had held flowback or gelling agents or acids and chemicals at some point. The signs were everywhere, especially in the watery moat that surrounded us.

Oily, organic-looking shapes floated in clumps that coagulated like sewage on the surface of the water. In the middle of a drought, there was a moat several feet deep with a current that rippled in the wind. Yet those puffy, sewage-like shapes held their form. Layers of purple-brown and pasty yellow clumps covered the moat bottom, and where the edges of the moat met the scalded earth, the dirt curled up like layers of carved balsa wood. Supposedly plain old dirt and water stood in stiff, curled wisps.

What we saw all over that site—rust and mustard powders, combustion symbols on the barrels and jugs left behind, ripples of oily organic waste floating and sculpting the depths of that awful moat—there was nothing natural or safe or supervised about State-Wheeler.

It was a wasteland—the Wheeler Wasteland, as we came to call it.

Kate cooed at the frogs submerged in the pasty green puddles. "Oh, buddies, you gotta get out of there."

"The frogs," she shook her head, "they're always the first sign."

After several long minutes of watching them, one of the frogs that clung to the edge of the mud sank away, sliding down into the milky green water.

Kate was still talking about the frogs when I steered the car into the long, banked curve that took us past the State-Rudmond site and Dillon's monster of a rig rising over the trees of the Au Sable State Forest.

The specter of that drill rig towering over Spring Lake and Randy and Diane's struck me with awe and despair, and as we made our way up the access drive, past the guard shack, I knew the guard would be after us. But I also knew on state land, our land, we could walk right up to the gate and we could not be arrested.

After what we had experienced at State-Wheeler, all three of us were bold with the need to document and share.

The well site was bathed in exaltingly hot orange light, a wrong light that lit up each metal rung and each bulbous tank head and the towering upward climb of the rig itself with a glow of brilliant color. Hot whites, bold yellows, pure blues—all set against the most turquoise sky. How could a sky so bold and beautiful offer itself as a backdrop to such a circus of rust and metal and noise?

I was sun-bleached myself, dulled and taxed after our disturbing work at Wheeler, which made the spread of color and noise difficult to process. The drill rig rose from a tumult of rusting rounds and valves, navy blue glycol tanks, and orange, cone-shaped vats. Gray scaffolding made up the structure around the base of the rig, which, seeing it from the side where we were, we could see right down into the hole. The legs of the rig splayed out like the base of the Eiffel Tower, and we watched the drill housing rise and fall, trailing its bright yellow coil.

I stood, trying to comprehend the screech of the rig, the drill bit grinding through the rock below us, the blazing yellows and blues and rusted joints of it all, and all of that color and sound seemed to meld together to create a shimmer of a man walking toward me.

I knew the guard was behind me. I knew Sonya and Kate had stepped in to give me time to photograph. I heard Sonya's voice, calm and steady. "Put your fist down and we'll answer you."

I turned back for a moment to see the guard's dark hair and his hunched shoulders, his face close to Sonya's, his fist lowering but still clenched. I heard the whole conversation, but at that point, I was mesmerized by the vision.

There was a man rising from the base of the drill rig, and I lowered my camera to watch. His long fire-retardant jacket wavered in slices, yet I knew he was real. I watched him take shape as if he had been blown up and out of that well bore, as if he was now blown forward by the intense whisper-screams of the rock.

I glanced down at my camera and back up, and he was gone.

Later, we wondered if the heat and fumes had somehow created the wavering mirage of a man that neither Kate nor Sonya saw. With the sun shining down at a severe, golden angle on two stories of sheet metal and stairways and bright colored tanks, the base of the rig had turned into a kaleidoscope of colors. Smears of bold blues and yellows began to blend and breathe and move, and overwhelmed by the grinding screech of the drill, I wondered if my own sunburned eyes had assembled a man of mirage as I tried to resolve foreground from background and the unbearable noise.

We had all had experiences before. We had tasted puffs of vinegar on the wind the first time we visited State-Wheeler. We knew the smell was getting to us, but we were getting great pictures. Later, standing downwind from the well pad, I was aware that I was breathing in too much hydrogen sulfide. The flags had been up at yellow that day, and in the heat and humidity, I could taste pockets of concentrated presence on the wind. We left abruptly when our lips and fingertips began to tingle.

For days my skin felt as if it had been sandpapered with pure heat. As if the sun mixed with that oily, sulfury smell was abrasive itself. That's when Kate started soaking our handkerchiefs in water of various acidities, water treatments the Japanese used for radiation and chemical exposure.

Then, there was the night Sonya said she would never forget.

Sonya and Kate and I had been out on the State-Lexford site for hours, and I had been so determined to capture the mess behind the drill rig that I crawled through the vine-laced ferns, sneaking up over the berm to get shots from all angles.

When I was discovered by the drill rig supervisor, I decided to stay and talk, to be exactly who and what I was. I leveled with him, and we had a conversation about drill rigs he'd worked on in Louisiana, Pennsylvania, in the Middle East, and in Ukraine, where the people were some of the friendliest he'd ever met.

He was the one who told me about the guys on the floor, how they had the real shit jobs. He didn't go so far as to talk about the lost fingers and mangled hands, but he expressed real human empathy, at least for his crew, and as the western horizon cooled to periwinkle, we shook hands.

Later that evening, Kate and Sonya reviewed what we'd seen and done that day, and I stared into the fire and sighed. I felt sadness, true sadness, and I admitted it.

The two of them were laughing at me for coming clean with the guy, for admitting my intent to share what I was seeing and smelling and learning. When he came toward us as we crouched down and worked our way through the woods, Kate and Sonya had angled away and I had stayed, giving them time to sneak off.

But as he and I stood together and talked, the feeling that people who believed in their work—and others who were stuck in such work—were blasting the earth below us with horrible chemicals and sand mined at great cost brought on that awful sense that there was no stopping the process.

And so, as we talked about his wife being a physician's assistant, how she'd gone to Ukraine with him and spent a year working in an orphanage, we bonded, in the most momentary way. We were all doing a job, doing the best we could.

Of course, he also tried to tell me they were painting the rig, getting it ready for a visit from investors, and that's what was causing the pungent smell that was making me feel light-headed. But as night fell, I knew I wasn't feeling right.

"I think you got gassed, Teach," Kate said.

Time passed in slow and quick spurts, and I couldn't find a deep, satisfying breath. Sonya seemed to understand that something more than a slight exposure problem was going on. "Maybe we should all sleep in one tent tonight."

We'd brought two tents—Kate's four-person and my tiny two-person that was so short you had to crawl into it. I zipped myself in, telling them, "Nah, I'll be fine." But I wasn't.

I was gripped by currents of irrational fear. My tent was tucked into a flat spot surrounded by huge old oak trees, but I kept imagining, each time I started to drift off to sleep, that a pickup was careening through the park, headed straight for me. When I sat up and peered through the tent fabric, another camper's light was shining in the distance. Perhaps I had felt that light through my closed eyelids and imagined being run over. But as soon as I tucked myself back into my sleeping bag and closed my eyes, the truck would head right for me again.

I crawled out of my tent and paced the campsite. My tent seemed a tragedy away from Kate and Sonya. I tried lying on the picnic table, my sleeping bag under me, my wool throw over me. I tried to enjoy being comforted by the stars, but then the picnic table wasn't close enough either. Sonya appeared when I started dragging the heavy wood table closer to her and Kate's tent.

The next morning, Sonya said I was frighteningly focused on moving that picnic table. I seemed entranced by the idea. Eventually, I agreed to let her get her blankets and go back to my tent with me.

Once Sonya rolled herself up against the outer rim of my tent and told me to get some sleep, I did. I slept hard. Dumb. I didn't dream or stir or wake until after she and Kate had cleared breakfast and gone down to the lake for a swim.

Even then, until I showered and drank some of Kate's strong coffee, until we took a walk in the woods that had nothing to do with well sites, that feeling of deep worry didn't leave me.

Kate teased me relentlessly, though she'd slept through my picnic table antics.

"You were really messed up." She shook her head. "You can't stay on site that long anymore. You gotta stop spilling your guts."

Sonya, however, seemed to regard me in a new way. I had become less of a mentor and more of a friend. She had recognized that I needed someone else to be stronger, to know what to do, and she'd stepped in and mothered me.

Later, when we were safe on her mangy back deck and the experience was enough in the past not to hurt, she enjoyed recounting the scene, how I had dragged the picnic table across the campsite and then draped my sleeping bag over me like a lead vest. But she always told the story with respect.

She had mothered me, and that made us equals.

"You'd have a terrible time with motherhood," she said, smirking in that sarcastic but knowing way. "That kind of worry is so much a part of being a mom."

Chapter 13

From Way Down Below

I sat up with the word *murder*, feeling it pass over my lips and out into the dark, silver air. Lights from a well pad bathe everything in artificial shadows—light shadows.

We were sleeping on mats spread across the floor of the lake house, one thousand feet from Dillon's newly set drill rig, when a screech, a sudden change on the well pad, had Sonya and me sitting straight up, facing each other.

Sonya's face was flat as it broke the light, and when her gaze shifted to Hank, asleep on the inflatable mattress between us, mine followed. One of Hank's skinny boy legs was sticking out from the blanket that he and Brett shared. His white crew sock was glowing.

We walked outside together to listen, leaving Brett and Hank inside, asleep. Somehow, they had not heard the screech, the long moan of compressors winding down, the series of bell tones that followed. We found Randy and Diane outside. Randy aimed his binoculars at the upper portion of the drill rig, and he drifted toward the well site, his feet indistinguishable from the gleaming sand of the two-track.

"I can't hear the birds anymore," Diane said. Her blonde hair was silver in the light. "The screech of a jay, sometimes a hawk." She gestured toward Randy. "He's never going to get any sleep."

Another series of bell tones sounded, and Diane hollered into the darkness where the thickness of low pines blocked the light. "Randy!"

Floodlights on the rig's latticed metal tower sent beams of gold and blue-white light into the night, lighting the rising vapors and dust so that the sky itself appeared to be recoiling, agitated by the disturbance below.

I reached out to touch Diane's arm. "Everything is out of balance," she said. "Everything." She hollered into the darkness. "Randy!"

We waited for Randy to return before we headed back to the lake house, the cabin Randy and Diane had lived in while they built their retirement home up the hill, a modest home with a deck that jutted out into the air, surrounded by oaks and pines and now, the drill rig that towered over the tree line. We compared what we had each heard: a screech, something that sounded like the drill bit backpedaling, a repeating succession of bell tones. Maybe they had hit a gas pocket or ground down the bit trying to chew through an especially tough vein.

Back at the lake house, I couldn't sleep so I built a fire, outside, listening to the bell tones that continued to sound. I opened my journal, and I remembered.

I thought about Randy's first call. How he believed maybe we could do something, if people understood how state land, public land, was being leased with no input from the public. "We're in the middle of a network of wetlands," he had said. "Spring-fed lakes in the Au Sable River watershed. That's not sensitive enough?"

I liked Randy from the start. He was smart and calm, even with his intense distrust of what he called the new DNR and its Imperial Storm Troopers, fully armed conservation officers who had started to show up at public meetings.

"The final frontier," Randy often said, mixing his galactic references. "The marriage between corporation and state." His round, light eyes were so cheery, even his deep cynicism was delivered with a smile.

It was Randy who called to let us know the drilling had begun, so we packed a cooler full of food and headed up to share their grief. What else could we do?

Wisps of smoke rose to join a moving, glowing sky that at times brought with it that vinegary, sulfur smell, and I sat, watching.

Near daylight, Brett handed me a cup of coffee and stoked the fire. I barely noticed him, other than the dark short hairs that poked out from his hat, like sideburns. The logs hissed with the persistent mist. The three of them, Brett and Sonya and Hank, wove through the long grasses and reeds edging the lake, making their way to Randy's fishing dock. In their green rain ponchos they resembled hooded gnomes trekking across a lush, purple-edged shire.

Just weeks before, Kate and I had stood in the middle of the newly excavated well pad talking about how oddly alive the earth berm seemed. So much life scraped and shaved, modeled like a factory floor.

A bee had clung to my video camera that day, facing me as I panned the site. No matter how many times I changed position or set the camera down on the dusty peach dirt to allow the bee its space to leave, the bee stayed.

Kate and I had lain, bellies to the berm, dreaming of ways to get the public's attention. We envisioned a zombie walk, people from all over the state walking along the top of that berm, shuffling and moaning the walk of the dead, announcing another frack well on state land. We might get an hour or two on tape before we were yanked off the berm, but it would certainly draw attention.

Wouldn't Rachel Carson be heartbroken, we sighed, to know that sharing the science and the poetry, the chemistry and its burdens, was no longer enough. People wanted spectacle.

The hooded gnomes returned with a bucket of bluegill, cleaning them on an oak stump, and I envisioned what was to come: the gleam of silica sand tanks, chemical trucks, pressure dials and clamps, the hulking orange hoses that stiffened and strained.

The wind gusted, bringing real rain, and I decided this would be my last frack well visit, because the sharpness of Diane's fear and the softness of Hank's hurt from the night before was still with me.

We were all out on Randy and Diane's deck. Del was there, thankfully, or we might not have recovered. A plume of diesel smoke floated over the tree line, and the drill rig's screech whined higher. Diane came out, setting a pitcher of lemonade at the center of the table, and then she turned—we all did—toward a deep, vibrating *thunk*. Brett reached for the pitcher as Hank, next to him, extended his glass. Warmed air drifted over us, black-blue with diesel, and Diane turned back with it, shouting at Hank, "No!"

She gazed up at the sky, then down at Hank, and ran into the house.

Hank's eyes teared up and he asked Brett, softly, "What did I do?"

We all knew enough about fracking to know that the most dangerous time for water contamination comes during the initial phases of drilling and fracking, when they're first pumping fluids through the aquifer, but until that very moment, none of us had internalized that fear—viewed a glass of water or the lemonade sitting in the pitcher before us as dangerous.

Sonya grabbed the pitcher and leaned into Hank's shoulder. "She was looking out for you, bud. It's okay," and I followed Sonya into the house.

Del's big voice tried to smooth things over. "That damned screeching is getting on my nerves too, you know what I mean?"

Diane and Sonya hugged, Diane apologizing over and over, with Sonya repeating, "I know. I know," and I scrounged through the refrigerator. The three of us reemerged with club soda, lemons, cranberry juice, and several bottles of beer.

Del sat upright, pretending to lecture Hank. "You see what I'm seeing, big guy? Until that damned thing stops screeching away, we're on juice and beer."

Brett poured juice and soda, and they raised their glasses. "To juice and beer!" they joked, and Hank giggled, "To juice and beer!"

Diane moved behind Hank's chair and gave him a long, hearty hug over his shoulders. Hank and Del rolled their eyes, and quickly, Hank wiped away a tear.

Brett nodded to Randy, who sat with his head in his hands, rubbing his forehead.

"To solidarity and self-medication!" Del toasted, and for one brief moment, Randy stopped rubbing his forehead to giggle with Hank.

I stayed outside until the acorns hurt, until I was dripping wet and too many of the nuts were dropping from the oaks all around me, and even then, I stayed a bit more, because I was taken by the feeling of being an observer when what I really wanted to do was strap on Randy's Kevlar vest (we joked that he had one) and charge up the access drive, screaming with the knowledge that I could take out one rig. One, which would never be enough, because the whispered word that moved up through me, the rush that pushed my body upright to listen, was not my own.

Chapter 14

More Than One Death at Fen's

Sonya asked me, after that day at the lake house, "What are you doing with your writing?" and I wanted to tell her about the rumbling voice of the bedrock that had moved up through me, drilling pipe to windpipe, how of course that made sense because the wind is breath. We breathe and speak on Earth's wind.

And I almost confessed—about writing from the inside of actions for years, about the difficulty of being an observer, never a doer, never that person who gets to lock down and holler out with all her might, "No more!"

But I couldn't. So I told her, "I write for me."

Levi and I were lying on our bellies, squeezing each other's forearms, silently celebrating "Yes!" as we recorded Benten's dozer crews sinking into the moist black dirt of the wetland they supposedly had not dredged and filled.

We didn't know that across the preserve, someone was about to pay the biggest price for that temporary victory. All we knew then was that after two hours of bone-shaking chill, we had it all on tape.

With the sky just beginning to pink, the Bobcats and dozers sat idling as their drivers waited on the light. They talked about the drinking escapades of their Friday nights as lavender spread over the trees. I thought of David but quickly put his image away. One of the drivers lit up a joint. Our local guy passed, thankfully. There might be drug tests once the insurance companies got involved.

One by one, the men climbed into their dozers and headed toward the red-black soil they had spread over what used to be standing water. The Bobcats made it past our first heavily reinforced holes as we hoped they would. We wanted them to get caught beyond the first wetland and into the second to illustrate, clearly, Benten's disregard for the law. Our guy drove up onto the bank and the other two followed, all three avoiding the dark, fertile soil they had dredged from the floor of the wetland and spread as topsoil. The air was still pungent with mold and fungus.

Beyond the junk concrete walls, the Bobcats started to experience some troubles.

The first Bobcat, driven by our local guy, took a sudden nosedive, the front end sinking up to its cage. The driver hopped out and back-pedaled away, but the other two, as they crested the hill and slowed to figure out what they were seeing, sat in their Bobcats, idling.

And then, something spectacular happened. Both Bobcats looked as if they were idling on quicksand. Just about the time their engines started to sputter and choke, the small dozers started to sink, as if the ground was sucking them down. Their drivers hopped out and ran for higher ground, hollering what sounded like, "Sinkhole! Sinkhole!"

Back in the field, the earthmovers began to roll along the roadway they had built to access the second wetland, but as soon as they hit that wetland soil, their tracks and rollers slowed. They dipped and shuddered, the undersides of the huge machines sliding side to side as if they were trying to cross a bed of marbles, and their tracks dug in, throwing up dirt. And then the ground, which we had been preparing all week, gave way.

We had gotten the idea from Benten's own illegal work. They had pumped and dredged, then scooped out fertile wetland bottom soil and piled it up like coal tailings, replacing it with fill sand. Finally, they used the dark sediment as topsoil, spreading it in thick black layers that the Bobcats and dozers had trouble moving over. The soil was still acting as a wetland, and it would, for months.

Night after night, using the preserve's and some locally donated equipment, we had pulled back the freshly spread soil and layered, underneath it, tree limbs and branches and stumps Benten's crews had yanked from the ground. Carefully, we stacked and layered branches into mini bridges, floors over small open pits. We didn't need big pits to sink the brutes, our local guy told us. Tiny rolling obstacles would best jam them up. Their huge belts and tires would struggle to gain a grip.

The pit bridges were working, and more than that, the preserve played its role perfectly. When the site was inspected, only the roots and trunks and pieces of trees that had been illegally yanked from the ground would be found—Benten's own mess.

Levi and I hugged and hooted and took a rash of photos.

Earth 6—Benten 0. All six of the dozers and Bobcats in the first wetland area were either sunk or ground to a chugging halt, and on Caleb and Stephanie's site, three out of four of the machines were disabled. Only one, Stephanie outright giggled into the radio, was still up and running, coughing and sputtering as it circled the others and picked up rattled drivers.

Nine out of ten caught in action. Not bad. Benten had to have spent a fortune on that many dozers, hurrying before he got stopped. Levi radioed Sharon, the preserve's director, and told her to start making calls. Sharon would alert the news networks and get them there quickly. We had contractors jumping out of sinking dozers. Contractors who might talk to save their own asses if the reporters got to them before Benten.

Levi had special plans for Benten: the Benten Bully Catcher, a sprung system of bungees and cargo nets that would have Benten and his truck embraced by the trees before he knew what happened.

—

Levi and I made our way to the canoes at Fen Creek, setting off in opposite directions, Levi to help with the main blockade while I headed deeper into the woods to make sure the tree sitters were in place.

The first team's tree sitters were safely up, and I was testing ropes, traversing all the tie-offs, when I got the call. Stephanie and Caleb were raising the second team's tripod and something had gone wrong.

"Beck," Stephanie barked, "Caleb's in trouble. He's hanging flat in his harness."

I clipped the radio to my neck guard and started to transfer my weight.

"Caleb." No response. "Caleb, if you can hear me, you've got to reach up and pull on your chest prusik, now. Get your head up. Now."

I skipped the wrapping of my thigh and descended fast, letting the palm of my hand burn. Something was wrong, very wrong.

"Steph! Get someone under him. Get his weight off the rope so you can raise his chest. Get him upright."

I radioed Levi as I ran.

As soon as I saw Caleb, I knew. Steph had gotten under him and managed to push his torso up, but his legs dangled, heavy. His feet looked huge in his boots, hanging there flat.

I was up in a minute, two at most. The others had already pulled a rope. I had learned in rescue training that it was quicker to glide, to ease back and push up without yanking. If I sat back too hard, the prusiks would tighten, adding hitches of time that Caleb didn't have while I fumbled with overly tightened knots.

I came up under Caleb, and I could feel the warmth leaving his body. The very vapor of his being was airing out into the huge old beech he was climbing.

"Damn it, Caleb." His ivory face was too pale. Losing color. "We need you. Sit your damned ass up. Don't you dare go to sleep on me."

He was warm, but the undersides of his arms were already starting to redden. His blood wasn't circulating.

"You have to sit up, Caleb. Help us now."

I heaved his chest prusik up the line and, with Steph cradling his back, I tried a few quick puffs and pumps, but only getting him down would allow me to work through some real CPR.

What did I know about Caleb? He had researched at Fen's during his undergraduate years, studying hog peanuts and some other plant that was codependent. What a funny word when applied to plants. I knew that he was close to his family. Just the night before, he had told us that his mom and his sister were coming to join the blockade.

"Caleb, your mom and your sister are coming." His lips were cold. "You've got to be here for them." Between pumps and puffs, I checked his hands, his gear, his neck. No knots, no tangles, his radio was working. Nothing had pierced his clothing. What the hell had gone wrong?

Down on the ground, it was clear that he was already gone. Stephanie held her hand over her mouth as I lifted his arms to be sure. The undersides of his long forearms and the pads of his fingers were a deep red-purple. His blood was pooling with gravity.

Levi ran up as I held Caleb's hand. No pulse. "His heart stopped before I got to him."

I kept at him for several minutes. Too long, but after a while, beating on his chest made no sense. Stephanie had cradled him, held his face, told him how much we all loved him as I brought him down. Caleb kept his dark hair pulled back in a ponytail, and his lips were the kind that curled up at the ends, giving his face a perpetually amused look.

Levi bent close to tell him he was the best climber on site, a good friend. I brushed stray hairs from his cheek and noticed that his lips, even as their color began to drain, were still upturned.

At the hospital, the attending physician called Caleb's parents while I was questioned by the police.

"Who was in charge?"

"No one." I answered the expected questions automatically, running, in my mind, the ABCs. What had happened? His carabiners, his harness, the rope—everything seemed fine. Fine.

"There had to be someone."

"It was a team effort. Organic." The authorities hated that word. Like the news, they wanted a leader, a group to investigate.

"Who's on the team?" The sheriff stood ready to write.

I gave the names that I knew. "Ash. Buzz. Lumberjack. Billy Jeans."

He frowned. "Those aren't names."

"They're the names I know," I said.

"Who was in charge of Caleb's team?"

My honest and unchecked answer was, "Caleb."

"He planned the protest?"

"No one planned a protest."

"He directed his team?"

I saw Caleb's curled smile, his white, white face. "He's a great climber."

"So you were in charge."

"I'm an observer," I said, recognizing how utterly pitiful I sounded. Caleb's mother and sister were on their way, and all I could do, all I had done all along, was watch. "I observe, and I write."

Just hours before, I had decided I could push through without David. Levi and I and Steph and Caleb, we knew exactly how to handle each part of the action. The initial equipment failures, the blockade that would keep Benten's people and tow trucks out but let the news in, the tree-sitting teams that would keep Benten from getting into the next two wetland areas while the staff at the preserve pressed for time and charges. We were relieved to be able to fight after months of watching. So even then, when the sheriff left to file a report and I sat alone asking myself what I had missed, I was glad I had not known.

There would be no writing about the action at Fen Preserve, not from me.

These things just didn't work if Ash became Stephanie Dearing and Buzz the Arborist became Matt Bird from Minnesota. When I climbed into that ambulance as Rebecca Walton and gave the EMT the details she needed, my days of writing as Elizabeth Stone, of being Stone the rescue climber, were over. There were simply too many connections that could be made if Rebecca Walton and Elizabeth Stone became one. Too many people to be harmed.

Eight years before, Mara was the actor no one could talk to or speak of, the friend I could not apologize to or forgive.

Now, I was the person others would train themselves to forget.

For everyone, especially for those huge old beeches that Caleb loved, I walked away.

Why didn't I know more about Sonya?

She had mentioned living in or at least being around Seattle once, when the war protests flared up. She had had a short relationship with a man Brett referred to as the hipster named Henry. Then, at the age of twenty-one, she showed up at Great Lakes College and joined my EcoLit class at the urging of another instructor.

Chapter 15
Winter Campout

I may never have missed the old days more than the day I hiked into a snow-covered clearing along the south branch of the Au Sable River, close to where we first toured those awful clear cuts with Del, and stood overlooking a field of orange and green tents wiggling over the snow. So many tents! They were pitched in rows around a central big top, a huge red-and-white tent that had been donated from a rental shop, and coming upon the sight as I had near dusk, the field appeared to be a cold weather incubator, a gathering place where lantern light set the thin-skinned forms aglow, and the hum of battery-powered heaters cycled up and back like a collective purr. It was exactly as Kate had hoped. Colorful fabrics, human scents and sounds, camaraderie thick as the cold and snow, and all of it coexisting under the whisper of the pines and the clattering of dry leaves that still clung to adolescent oaks. The field, the tents, that ridiculous red-and-white big top at center where the whiteboard held each day's lists and sketches—it was a full-scale land occupation, and it just kept growing.

People showed up from Muskegon, from Kalamazoo, from Detroit, and Traverse City. One group came down from the Upper Peninsula to give and gather support. They were staging their own fight against mining in the Bay de Noc wilderness. Add uranium on Lake Superior's shoreline to the dangers posed to the Great Lakes by the sixty-year-old pipes lying open to the water at the bottom of the Straits. None of the threats discussed at Winter Campout seemed beyond the oil and gas industry's purview. It didn't matter if extracting methane was proving to be as dirty as coal. It didn't matter if fracking ever proved to be economical. The oil and gas industry had its end times eyes set on Michigan, and its bullying nature didn't allow for concession.

I timed my visit not with the freak thundersnows that rolled in, but with Thompson's and his news crew's visit. When Thompson arrived, I told Kate and Brett and Mark and Sonya (who was week-ending with Hank) that I was going to fade back, take photos from the periphery. Once the story hit the news, private security would be around, hoping to pump someone in the fifty or so tents in that snowy field for information.

I suggested to the four of them that they ask Thompson to talk off camera for the first hour or so, and to his credit, he agreed. He stayed for an entire day with a crew that he didn't put to work until later that afternoon, interviewing people who had come from all over to join in.

Campers from Kalamazoo talked about the oil spill in the Kalamazoo River and how the pipeline expansion would push twice as much tar sands oil—and perhaps liquid natural gas and fracking chemicals too—through an area that still hadn't been properly cleaned up. There were "No Swimming" signs on the riverbanks, and people seized on their kitchen floors. Residents were dealing with health problems that no official dared to relate to the original spill or the toxic dispersants used in the ongoing cleanup.

Ban petitioners and musicians from Grand Rapids and Traverse City talked about the risks to water, and the people from Detroit and Flint warned of the state's desire to put our most poverty-stressed communities under emergency financial management so water could be privatized. Did we really want our right to fresh water sold for cor-porate profit?

Donations started to come in—money, food, messages of

support—and when Thompson's special aired the following weekend, he included some of Kate's "Silent Spring" lyrics, text rolling as her voice accompanied scenes from camp.

No frogs, no birds left to sing
No mold to break down, lay down the foundations of everything
Progress signs roll over the joyful splash of spring
Rachel Carson told us stories of just this thing

The report was beautiful, really, even with splices of industry speak, quotes Thompson had to include to uphold journalistic integrity. A regional executive from NorA spoke of the misguided actions of American youth. "Their concern for the environment is NorA's concern too. They've been misinformed, and that misinformation is what they're acting upon."

The chair of Michigan's business circle adamantly claimed, "There hasn't been a single accident from fracking in the state of Michigan. Not one."

I laughed from the warmth of my apartment. Even my first-year students would spot the unsupportable nature of that claim. How could one man or his small group of colleagues claim to have access to the history of every well site in Michigan?

There was a shot of Frank fixing a laminated 1836 treaty statement and a map to the stake that identified the clearing as State-Avery. In a colorful knit cap and scarf, he marked the location on the map then turned to face the camera with a sweeping gesture to the land, and I thought of his students. It must have taken them weeks to get used to his blend of seriousness and sarcasm.

Thompson's last segment captured a field of people standing outside their tents, late in the evening, watching a flash of pink light spread across the sky and seep into the snow. For two nights we stood outside, arching our backs to follow and sometimes walk along underneath as pink and red flashes lit up the sky and then stayed, magnified by the moisture in the air. Thundersnow, the TV weather announcers called it, as if the flashes of pink-red light and the rumbles of thunder that stretched on the wind were phenomenon any of us had ever experienced.

Kate's voice closed out the show:

> *Wetlands become wastelands, in no time at all*
> *Together we stand, or thirsty we fall*

Thompson's report captured the incredible sense of purpose in the campout. People spoke through clouds of frozen breath about what it was like to be out there in near-zero temperatures, twenty-four hours a day, with a polar "vortex" (another meteorologist's favorite) blasting down upon the camp. The snow was constant. Icy powder colored the air with such a dense, palpable white-gray that even out in the middle of that clear-cut field it was possible to feel claustrophobic, as if you were never going to get out of the grip of the snow. Some weekends another twenty or thirty campers arrived to support the core group of fifty who stayed until spring. Local restaurants came in with hot food and coffee. A plumbing company brought a restroom on wheels with a composting toilet and a tiny stainless-steel sink.

A local radio station hosted Kate and Brett or Mark for a daily show, with members of the public calling in to ask questions and to make comments. It was, as Kate had first suggested, the campers' determination to stay even with the cold that captured the public's attention.

"It's certainly a testimony to how much you all care," one elderly woman said when Kate and Sonya were on the air, hailing as Marge and Peggy. "Someone's got to stand up to all this nonsense."

A caller who introduced himself as working for the industry said,

"I think I may have met a few of you. You've been checking out sites, taking pictures, right?"

"Mm-hmm," Kate answered. I imagined her head shaking and her eyes widening at Sonya. "We've talked to a lot of industry folk over the last year or so."

"I get what you're doing," the man said. His voice sounded older, worn. "I wish things were different, but you have to know. This industry has a two-hundred-year history of getting what it wants, no matter who stands in its way."

"What about the public?" Kate asked. "Doesn't the public have a right to push back?"

The man on the line had sighed. "I wish you luck," he said. "I hope you all survive the cold. Keep the soup coming, right?"

Sonya had surprised me. "Bring a pot of soup with you and come out and see us."

"Oh," he chuckled, "I don't think I'd fit in."

"Hey," Kate bounced back. "A job's a job, right? We've learned a lot from people in the industry. What we all need is a new type of job."

Mark, it seemed, was a sensation on the airwaves. Nearly nonverbal in person, with a mic and a set of headphones, he was "downright chatty," Kate said. He reported on well sites and read stories of the people living near them, and listeners from Canada, from Ireland, from France, and groups around the country started to ask where they could send money and supplies.

There were some tense moments, too. One night toward the end of the campout, a band of men in ten or twelve trucks drove the perimeter of the camp, honking and hollering and shooting off guns. I was having trouble falling asleep, standing outside my tent, when I heard the sound of engines climbing the hills. Years in the woods had taught me that the last sound you wanted to hear was a convoy of trucks or ATVs laced with the voices of men.

The sound of shots preceded them, and people began to scramble out of their tents. "They're shooting! They're shooting!"

"They're blanks!" I shouted, hoping to keep people calm as the lights of several trucks crested the slope. Cap guns or starter pistols, some kind of blanks people figured later, but the desire to instill fear was clear.

I cupped my hands and hollered, "Get to the big top!"

"Check the tents around you!" someone else shouted, and we repeated both calls as we ran.

Hank was along for the weekend, and the thought of one of those trucks accidentally or purposefully driving over someone still in their tent scared everyone.

We gathered under the big top, where Mark instructed everyone to make sure each group's members and neighbors were safe. Brett and Kate kept everyone in a circle, facing outward.

The trucks stayed in a line for the most part. Occasionally, a few of them would engage in a mock race, pulling up next to each other as they rode the dirt slopes that rimmed the field. They drove past the big top in one last wild surge, revving their engines and honking before they turned to climb the path out of the clearing. One of the trucks, as the line retreated, swerved into camp, running over the edges of tents on the way out. The nylon, waving under its taillights, curled up like flames in the truck's wake.

Mark and a few others ran from tent to tent, lifting fabric and hollering, "Anyone in there? Anyone in there?"

Hank was pressed against Sonya, his hands over his ears, and when he saw Mark sprinting across the field, he cried out, "Mom! Mom!"

A stainless steel cooler was overturned and dented, its hinges mangled and its contents dumped in the snow, but no one was hurt, not directly. We relocated the tents that had been run over, to try to ease the minds of the people camping in them. Kate, smartly, asked everyone to gather around the firepit. She let everyone know that it was all right to leave if they felt threatened, but most of us, though keeping our ears open for that whining engine sound, were determined not to let the scare tactics work.

The DNR came out on several occasions, conservation officers advising everyone that they would be arrested for trespassing and perhaps interfering with commerce, a charge that, according to a National Lawyers Guild lawyer, was a bluff. The campers were on state land. They were safe, as far as the NLG was concerned, until the spring thaw came and the oil and gas industry actually laid claim to their right to excavate. At that point, with a signed, paid mineral rights lease, there was no way the campers could legally protect the land.

Some in camp began putting tripods together, asking the trees for help. Kate showed me the poles and platforms stacked where pink and orange flags marked State-Avery's perimeter. But the rig never came.

Instead, NorA moved their Redding 120 back to the spot deep in the woods west of Higgins Lake where Kate and I had walked over ground being actively fracked, and I had clung to the trunk of a brittle pine, asking the trees and the ground to help me make sense of what was happening.

Chapter 16
Knowing Your Threshold

It was Brett who first articulated the concept of knowing your threshold, something he said in class that I asked him to repeat.

"For some people, it might mean sitting outside their senator's door and refusing to leave until they are heard. For others, it might mean locking down to a bulldozer.

"The idea is to know what will push you to act. Know what will make you go into action before it happens."

We had been talking about schemes to withdraw water from the Great Lakes. Supertankers running giant flexible containers through the lakes and then across the ocean.

"You're talking about a threshold," I said in class that day. "Knowing your threshold."

We were hanging out on Sonya's back deck, talking about Robin Hood and a forest full of troublemakers. It was late and muggy. We'd all had a few beers, which were fueling our ideas.

Kate brought up the legend of Sherwood Forest, how medieval Europe's fear of nature and women was probably responsible for the original story of Maid Marian and all those orphaned children. Perhaps there had been an original gang charged with keeping the story alive, making sure anyone who entered the forest felt its spirits.

Most likely, it was the women and children themselves who created mischief from the trees to keep the knights at bay.

"Uncontrollable lot that we are," Kate growled.

"Some rustling in the trees and branches falling down upon the horses might have scared armored knights off for a while," Mark said, "but it wouldn't work forever. After they'd been robbed and duped a few times, the sheriff would have ordered them deeper into the forest."

"True," Brett said. "At some point, there must have been those in the forest who were willing to go all the way with the story."

We imagined the woods turned into a booby-trapped, nightmarish place to keep excavators and contractors away.

"At some point someone would have to pick 'em off," Kate said.

"What do you mean?" Brett said. "Climb up into the trees and shoot pea gravel at them?"

"Paintball," Mark said.

"People have gone to jail for throwing stuffed bunnies," Sonya said.

"Oh, holy fricking hell!" Kate squealed. "A tranquilizer gun! When the pea gravel stops working, every time another drill rig rolls in, ping!"

Brett and Kate kicked the tranquilizer idea back and forth, ending up, once again, at strapping the tranquilized trespasser to a raft and setting them afloat in the nearest body of water.

"Wouldn't that be a right good morning!" Kate shrieked.

Sonya, who had been staring at her beer bottle, spoke up. "You wouldn't do half the shit you spout off about."

She took a swig of beer and looked straight at Brett as if there was something she was saying only to him with the rest of us watching.

"Fricking pick 'em off," Kate bobbed. She mimicked a shot at Brett.

Sonya's hand came down firmly on the table. "You can't say shit like that, ever. Ever!"

Brett sat forward. "She's right."

"No!" Sonya lashed out at no one in particular, and Mark pushed back from the table.

"I'm not talking about being careful." Sonya let out a sarcastic laugh. "That's a given. At least it should be."

"I didn't mean it," Kate said.

"That's the problem," Sonya said. "What good is 'I didn't mean it' when someone ends up paying for your mouth?"

Mark set his hands on his thighs. "Maybe we've talked enough for tonight."

"You think so, Marko?" Sonya said. "Really. You think so? I'm sorry, but sometimes all the talk gets old. It gets really fricking old."

Kate whispered more to the table than to Sonya, and I knew it wasn't going to be good. Kate had a habit of mumbling when she knew she should be quiet. "Just because I can't do everything we talk about doesn't mean I can't—"

We all jumped when Sonya slammed her beer down and stood with such force that her chair flipped over behind her.

"Great! So you'd champion the big fricking pick-'em-off idea and then when someone actually does it, when someone offs a contractor with a tranquilizer gun and gets locked away for good, you're going to run right up and support them, right? Right?"

"Hey, Son." Brett tried to reach toward her, but she was already moving away and mimicking Kate.

"Run right up and tell the authorities, I support her. I support what she did because it was right. Let her go, 'kay?"

Sonya stopped to say something else, but when I caught her eye and gestured toward Kate, whose head was down, she reached across the table, grabbing at empties. Then, she walked into the kitchen where she set each bottle down with a great deal of noise, slammed the slider, and locked it.

"What just happened?" Mark said.

Brett started toward the slider, but I stopped him.

"Let me try to talk to her for a minute."

I walked around the house, entering through the front door, thinking that was an oddly immature gesture coming from Sonya, her locking us out.

She was at the sink, rinsing tomatillos and glaring at each one fiercely before setting it down on a plate. She saw me approach but kept her eyes on the tiny green tomatoes.

"She's way too loose-lipped," she said as she sliced into one.

I picked up another and started slicing. "I know."

"People with children have to make much more difficult decisions."

"I know. Ideas aren't as easy to play with when you have a child to consider."

She stopped chopping and looked straight at me. "Maybe it's fun for you all to joke about this and that mayhem, but when a parent gets arrested, everything changes. Everything."

Her eyes were intense, so vividly brown that I had to glance away.

"I know," I said. She seemed hurt. Maybe surprised that I hadn't picked up on her hurt.

"None of the rest of us have that deeper sense of responsibility running in the background all day. But I know Kate didn't mean the pick-'em-off thing seriously. None of us did."

She stilled for a moment, then grabbed another tomatillo.

"Sometimes we're insensitive shitheads," I said. "We forget."

"Well, I can't," she said, staring into the bowl she was quickly filling with the next load of salsa. "And yes, you are."

I leaned in and put my arm around her shoulder for a quick hug. "Hank's an incredible kid," I said. "We all adore that little guy, and no one expects you to put yourself in the pick-'em-off spot. Literally or figuratively."

She tapped her knife against the bowl, and I saw out of the corner of my eye that Brett had walked in. His tall frame was bending down, not for the kitchen's rounded archway or the low-hanging lamp, but in a move of subtle supplication.

"That's just it, though," she said. "Hank is exactly why someone would have to do it."

"Hey." Brett straightened.

Sonya shoved the bowl of tomatillo sauce into Brett's stomach and grabbed a bag of pita bread, unlocking the slider and throwing it open.

When Kate stood and automatically grabbed the pita bag and started slicing, Sonya reached out to her and they hugged.

"I'm sorry," Sonya said. "But you have to shut up. You do."

"I know." Kate's head bobbed on Sonya's shoulder. "I get all passionate and start shootin' off, but I'm harmless."

"No." Sonya pulled back and looked at her. "With your mouth, you're nowhere near harmless."

"Sorry." Kate's eyes were glossy. "It's just fun, sometimes, to talk with my besties."

Mark fidgeted. "Are we okay now? Because you know I can't stand this kind of grief. I'm way too much of a lightweight."

"Cheers to us for making it through our first fight," Brett said, putting out his beer.

Sonya threw him a look but put her bottle up with the rest of us.

"It happens," I said. "Like band drama."

Chapter 17

The Last Few Visits

Three warnings came in rapid succession.

First, Sonya and I had a run-in with security in the middle of a farmer's bean field.

Someone called to say NorA was fracking downstate, which was a surprise. NorA had been fracking solely in their northern pipeline corridor, on state land. This well was on private land, which made it tricky to observe.

Sonya and I drove the country roads that bordered several working farms, catching glimpses of a crane positioning a bright blue perforating gun on a towering wellhead. We parked as close as we could and zoomed in from a great distance. On the ground below the bold blue cage of the perforating gun was quite a show of red, yellow, and white hazmat suits moving about. Workers dressed in full hazmat gear, including hoods that appeared to have face shields stitched into them, moved through a series of choreographed movements and hand signals. Red would deliver some object to Yellow. Yellow would move into position, back-to-back with White, then the two of them moved through a series of bent arm signals as they opened and closed a hatch on a long white trailer that was covered with all sorts of points and projections. Explosives? We wondered.

Whatever they were doing, it all occurred a few hundred feet from the white farmhouse with black shutters that appeared as the backdrop in all our pixelated, wiggly photos.

Sonya and I knew that driving across private land was a bad idea, but the Red-Yellow-White show had us curious, so when we found an overgrown trail, an old two-track bordering a farm fence that would get us close to the well pad, we took it.

We drove slowly, watchfully down that fence line, right into a trap. NorA had security at the end of the two-track, and the security guard stationed there was in communication with a pair of security officers sitting in a black SUV on the well pad.

I talked us out of trespassing charges, claiming that we were trying to get to the drainage stream that ran between farms. I'm sure our State Ag hats helped. Did the officer want to see my plat map?

When we got back to pavement and hurried away, Sonya turned to me. "We're supposed to be the careful ones. I think we're done now. Don't you? We're done now."

Yes, there were groups eager to see our pictures and listen to our research. But every time we left a new find—chemical vats left out in the open, blackened water filters, kids with blisters outlining their lips and noses—we experienced a new level of exhaustion. Kate would shake and say, "I need three days to sit and fricking stare at the air."

Then, we met the Sheradays.

We were at a Common Ground meeting, a gathering of people and groups from across the state who were working to protect land, air, and water, and Julia of Frack No! begged us to make one more visit. "You've got to meet Hettie and Merle. They're such a sweet old couple, and it's terrible. The noise is deafening. Their house is shaking. They'd be so glad to have you come."

Brett was the first to cave. "Julia and Emma, they're doing so much. How can we not support them?" And Kate nodded along.

So, although we had all agreed that we had witnessed enough,

Kate and Brett and I made one more trip up north to meet an elderly couple living between a frack well site and a sand mine.

Merle had a tall man's stoop, and his gestures were animated as he talked. Hettie's round face was a bit more serious. Her white hair highlighted a strong gaze, and she was angry. First, the kitchen tap had started to spit and cough. Then, every glass they filled was topped with an inch or two of suds that took ten minutes to settle. Finally, on that Saturday morning in June, their water well had run dry.

"Pump's been sucking air all day." Merle shook his head.

"And they're trying to tell us that the trucks rumbling on the road are doing it," Hettie scoffed. "I guess the ground water's just too upset to come back up."

Hettie had just turned eighty, Merle was headed for eighty that winter, but both of them looked young when they smiled. After a lifetime of moves around the country for work, they had resettled. "Our last settle," Hettie said, was to the farm where she had spent her childhood.

"We saved what was left," Hettie said, speaking of the family's once 640-acre farm. All but the forty acres they lived on had been sold to the state for safe keeping. She swept her hand toward the sand mine across the street, where loops of bright yellow conduit looked like giant tubas buried in the sand. "I guess that's the ultimate lesson here," she nodded. "Hold on to the land."

Hettie and Merle had survived the arrival of the sand mine. They had comforted family members when the drill rig arrived. But when the fracking started, they were startled from sleep by a "god-awful" screeching that vibrated their walls and shook their cupboard doors open. The last straw, for Hettie and Merle and their neighbors, was the silica sand.

"That's what got hot shot, here, hauled off the other day." Hettie sent Merle a sour grin.

Standing in their front yard, we watched a plume of silica sand drift up and away from a bank of stainless steel truck trailers that lined the outer edge of the well pad just down the street. The neighbors living downwind had been relocated when their house was covered in the creamy yellow dust.

"They put them up in a motel outside of town," Merle said.

"They never claimed responsibility, of course," Hettie said. "A big wig came to see them after Susan gave the site supervisor an earful. He wiped dust off the kids' playset and told them the dust wasn't a threat to their children."

"Two weeks," Merle added. "They told Susan and Don the dust would be gone in two weeks."

Hettie's eyes softened. "Can you imagine? Having small children there with that dust blowing onto your house for days on end, and then your water well runs dry."

Merle took us to the edge of their property, walking us along the exact border where their land met NorA's access road. He showed us every tree, every patch of ferns, even the lumps of pine loam that defined the border.

"You stay here," he said, stretching his long arms to designate the property line, "and you'll be fine. If they try to tell you that you can't be here, you tell them I showed you exactly where our property line is, and I'll call the cops on them if they don't stop harassing you."

NorA had cut a temporary access drive between the Sheradays' land and the well pad, the "fake drive" as Hettie and Merle called it. "The only thing they're using it for is to park trucks so we can't get a good look at what's going on."

"But you're in luck today." Merle smiled, pointing to yet another bright blue tanker that rolled past the main gate without stopping. "They're hauling water in and out so fast, no one's parking."

The compressors started to whir, and Merle turned to leave us. "All right. Not a step onto this gravel." He put his hands on Brett's and Kate's shoulders. "Just the same, if they take one step toward you, on our land, you call me. Let them throw this old man in jail."

Through the spindles of young trees, we gazed upon a spread of trucks and hoses and compressors, and men made small as they scurried about, monitoring all of the metal and machinery. The wellhead rose above it all, elevated with bold blue rings and red clamps. A dozen or more trucks were backed up to the well, lined up in two rows, and from the back of each truck, white and orange hoses drooped, hanging limp from the valves and faucets that covered the trucks' back panels. Too many hoses to count lay flat and ribbon-like across the well pad floor, snaking between compressors and vats. At the wellhead, they rose and banded together with even bigger hoses, bright red hoses that knotted them all together in great clots.

The compressors kicked in, roaring up to a level we had never heard before. The lids of the stainless steel tanks blew open and yellow powder shot up from the broken seals. The ground began to shake, and a hot, steady pressure filled the air.

Finally, we understood the pressure, Merle's "god-awful" pressure.

The final circus of it all, after two years of research, came full circle. The hoses that hung limp from the back of every truck began to stiffen. Lumps of pressure raced toward the circle of knots around the well until the entire lot of hoses rose, stiff and stressed, making the twenty-foot-tall wellhead look like an angry scarecrow. The sounds of pressure soared, and the scarecrow's rod-like arms yanked at the trailers and the backs of those trucks.

At every hose and clamp, the chance for an accident was clear.

For the first time in years, I wished for my climbing gear. All it would take to videotape the whole process, unadulterated by the spindles and shadows we had to work around, was to get higher. Brett tried over and over to get beyond the first thick branches of the maples and pines on Hettie and Merle's property line while Kate and I worked between the trees, and I told myself if I ever visited another site, I'd bring gear. Still, crouching and climbing, we got the full frontal ugliness of fracking.

When Merle came back to tell us it was dinnertime at the farm, he turned Brett around and showed us a coating of silica dust on the back of Brett's jacket.

"Brush it off each other," he warned as he swiped his long, knuckley hands across Brett's shoulders and down his back. "You don't want this stuff going home with you. It does god-awful things to a person's lungs."

We said our goodbyes at sunset.

Hettie and Merle walked along with us, arm in arm, as I let the car roll down their long driveway.

"Tell our story if it helps," Hettie said, leaning in to pat my arm.

"You tell it any way you think is right." Merle smiled.

"The screeching and the dust blowing, it's just awful," Julia had said when she begged us to visit. "You'll be glad you made the trip."

Glad? Yes, Brett and Kate and I were grateful for the opportunity to meet Hettie and Merle, who joined in, singing and clapping, when Kate and Brett played their guitars and sang their old-time songs. We were honored that they trusted us with their story. But there was something about meeting Hettie and Merle that also drove us to an end.

Finally, there was Del. The unstoppable jokester was sick, terribly sick. He had had a mild heart attack, and his blood pressure was soaring and plummeting beyond anything the doctors could understand.

Tall, baggy-dressed Del, who had drawn secret well sites on a county map and led us on several tours. Del, who the townsfolk knew as the person who carried clipboards of ban petitions everywhere he went. They found him in the grocery store, at public meetings, at the local bar.

"There are only two kinds of people around here anymore, you know what I mean?" he always said. "The ones who come looking for me to sign, and the ones who come looking for me because their paychecks are coming from Dillon."

Tammy had called, crying. Del was home, on the couch, drawing on a portable oxygen tank and using a walker to get around the house. "He can't even walk the dogs," she said. Their two huskies, Zadie and Rue, paced the house and whined at Del's new equipment. Kate and Brett stopped in to check on Del and Tammy every time a show or a presentation brought them up north, and their reports sounded more and more grim.

"All this trouble damned well better count for something," Del would tell me when he called. Dillon, who had been granted confidential status for every well site they drilled and fracked, seemed to have abandoned their wells within the Gladwin and Au Sable state forests.

I never wanted to tell Tammy and Del or Randy and Diane what I suspected—that Dillon was poking holes to stake out a perimeter. That perhaps they planned to come back and frack the hell out of any land between those holes. Their international stakeholders weren't about to let all that leased land sit as reserves for long. That we had learned from the folks in Texas whose water wells were now officially dry.

Watching loveable, laughable Del go down hard made me worry that I had played a part in his continued contact with those well sites. What if it was hydrogen sulfide poisoning or worse?

We had made several trips to the State-Wheeler wasteland, photographing and writing about the drilling and fracking and that awful day when twelve-year-old Jacob, the eldest son of the Amish family across the road, told us that the trucks had come and hauled everything away.

"Will you take some water to test again?" Jacob had asked.

His mouth was lined with blisters. The whole family, he told us, his mom, his six brothers and sisters, they all had blisters around their mouths and noses. Sometimes their eyelids became irritated with red pinpricks.

Kate had stood alongside the horse-drawn rake, patting the horse's neck, and I went to the car to grab jugs. We had to do something, even if we knew that the water tests the DEQ offered wouldn't look for fracking chemicals. If the family wanted meaningful tests, they would have to hire certified researchers to administer every step and pay thousands of dollars.

And now Del was home, confined to low-level activity as his blood pressure mysteriously rose all night and fell all day. If he so much as tried to take the dogs for a walk to the old spillway where the purple-gold water of the Au Sable pooled into a copper-bottomed reservoir, the monitors on his arms and chest would beep until the dogs whined him back home.

"Ol' Zadie," he would say, ruffling the hair under the old husky's neck as she stared up at him with worried eyes. "She won't let me take another step once these things go off. I think Tammy's got her trained." He winked.

He was still the same Del, his eyes watery with emotion and his booming voice on the verge of laughter, but his gait was unsteady even with the walker.

"He looks tentative," Brett said. "It's hard to see him like that."

"The big guy," Kate started but didn't finish.

Del and I shared reports of people who had become temporarily and even permanently disabled by hydrogen sulfide and other hazardous emissions. The studies were riddled with familiar symptoms: difficulty breathing, tingling lips and fingertips, loss of consciousness, and with repeated exposure, heart attacks and pulmonary distress and bouncing blood pressure that refused to respond to treatment.

"We know what's going on," Del said the last time we visited. "No matter what type of legal limit horseshit they try to pull over on us."

He and Brett had fist-bumped as we sat outside with Zadie and Rue gazing over the woods that still held the "Well Pad Corner" stakes we had first seen over a year before.

"I still want to pull the damned things up." Kate shook. "Pull them all up."

Chapter 18
Suspicious Characters

"So you've been on a lot of well sites too, huh? I'm just an amateur, but you, you're a pro, I can tell." He leans close. "Have you seen the Drill Rig Finder?"

He looks boyish in a baseball cap, and the way he tucks his chin makes his smile seem humble. He plays that up.

"Oh," he winces. "Kind of stupid to say that out loud. Maybe I'm the only person obsessed with this stuff."

Dan Werckz: the only person we'd ever truly suspected as an infiltrator.

In some ways he was way too obvious, but that was just it. Security types could be blatantly obvious. Courting people involved in protests, showing up at meetings with all kinds of passion and active listening skills, promising the time that a roomful of determined but exhausted activists had been trying to carve out from their lives for years.

The first time I saw him, Werckz was in the audience at a presentation given by an outspoken ex-insider. Anti-fracking groups had been tracking activity in the Antrim Shale, but with exploration in deeper layers, with drilling into the Utica-Collingwood and the A-1 Carbonate spreading up and down from the center of the state, people were hungry to know where it was all going, and Ben Gill, a Texas roughneck turned whistleblower, had the answer. Once the industry leased your land, Gill warned, it was highly unlikely that they were going to walk away from undeveloped reserves.

Gill's message could be summed up in one word: density. Slide by slide, he showed us a density of well pads and processing sites that we had not yet fathomed. His satellite images from the Barnett Shale had white pockmarks all over them—well pads sandwiched between schools and farms, pumping stations and refineries butted up to the town's strip mall.

I admired the way he opened his talk, making it clear that he was there for the public, not to have a public debate with the industry folks in the audience. And there were plenty of them, site supervisors in bright red polos and suits with bright red pins on their lapels. "US Energy! US Jobs!"

"If you want to dispute my experiences in Texas," Gill said, "stick around and ask your questions at the end. Until then, I'm not here to dispute your 'safe fracking' claims.

"I'm here to tell the audience what it was like to work with and live with fracking," he said, "and I say *was* because my wife and I decided we couldn't stay and fight anymore." He and his wife had abandoned the house they could not sell when their daughters were continually hospitalized with nosebleeds and breathing difficulties.

"All-night nosebleeds," he said. "And I mean all night."

I ducked out during the Q and A, just after Charlie the Waterkeeper put the industry in its place. "As far as water that's safe to drink, I'll let mothers and grandmothers decide. That's who ought to be writing regulations."

Unfortunately, I walked straight into Big Boyd Blay, an industry PR guy, on the other side of the door. He had his notebook ready.

"You were at the Traverse City presentation. What was your name?"

Brett and Kate had coined the nickname Big Boyd when Blay and his video camera popped up at every meeting we attended. More than once we watched Blay point his camera at anyone who voiced opposition to oil and gas development.

I pretended not to recognize him. "Are you with the local news?"

Werckz walked into the conversation without apology. He stretched his hand toward me, ignoring Blay, which made me wonder if he and Blay were working in tandem. Was Werckz supposed to rescue me?

"Dan," Werckz said, and Blay backed away.

"There's a lot of red shirts in there." Werckz smiled. "I guess that's supposed to make people like us feel intimidated. Sounds like I'm just starting to do what you've been doing."

I made my way toward the restrooms, and Werckz followed.

"What I've been doing?"

"Oh," he grinned, "I heard you talking to Gill before he started. So you've been on a lot of well sites too, huh?"

He threw out every talking point: the industry's discussion forum, NorA's new facility, and he was obviously excited about an online tool called the Rig Finder.

"I can't believe they don't keep that information closer, you know?" He quieted. "All I had to do was create a fake name, and I'm looking at a schedule that shows where every rig across the country is and where it's going next."

With such obvious connections to potential direct action, I didn't respond.

"Well, here I am," I said, walking into the restroom.

As the door swung shut, I saw him shift and smile. "Maybe I'm the only person obsessed with this stuff."

I debated whether or not I should invite Werckz along on the tour. Charlie and I had offered to accompany the state's Big Green chairs to the State-Lexford well site. Together, we would give them a brief history of the drilling and fracking and pipeline expansions. Charlie had asked NorA to give us a tour, but NorA refused.

I had stopped at State-Lexford that morning to find NorA's walking drill rig repositioned and drilling a third vertical hole on the same well pad. How they'd gotten approval to drill so many well bores so close together was a mystery. The chances for communication between wells, for liquids and pressure to migrate from one well to another, seemed ridiculously high. But the current state of the site, the thundering sounds as pipe after pipe was loaded and lowered into the hole, the array of colors and heat and fumes, the sensory details would make a powerful introduction for our visitors.

It was my morning shots of State-Lexford that I'd been showing Ben Gill before his presentation. Apparently, Werckz had been watching and listening too.

Werckz was waiting for me outside the restroom, so I asked him along.

"I might ride out there," he said, "but don't be surprised if I don't." He lowered his head, trying to look pained, I thought. "Being that close, it gets to me. Doesn't it get to you?"

I drove up behind Charlie's van and found Werckz sitting on his motorcycle, Charlie standing next to him, ready with his plat book and a walking stick.

Werckz remained tucked into a side trail as I had done several times to avoid being seen by workers on the well site. Was he afraid someone on site might greet him, not as a foe, but as a friend?

"Glad to see you made it." I smiled as I walked toward him. "You should tell everyone about the history of the site. I'm sure you know a lot more than I do." He had claimed to live nearby.

Our crowd arrived and parked directly in front of the site. The plan was simple. Let the industry see our numbers and our concern. We would introduce ourselves, climb to the crest of the berm to take pictures, but we wouldn't cross over it. Those who were willing to fight their way through brush and vines would scout the perimeter with me.

"You coming?" I asked Werckz.

He repeated the chin tuck, the shy smile. "I'm going to head out."

"You sure?" I pushed. "It would be great to hear from someone living so close."

I had asked for his specific location, but he never varied from "close."

Werckz walked his bike into a turn. "That's just the thing." He stopped. "I'm too close. This stuff gets too emotional for me."

Charlie and I watched him ride away. "Have you ever seen him around?" I asked.

"Nope," Charlie replied. "But he knew his stuff on my plat map."

When Werckz showed up at the first Common Ground meeting, a meeting that brought together environmental groups from across the state, Kate and Brett recognized something disingenuous about him right away.

"It would be easy for someone to think the same of us," Mark said. "We're showing up all over the state, giving everyone the pictures and the stories they need."

But that was exactly what bothered me about Werckz—his photos. There were no people in them. He'd shown me and Kate photos of a well site where the lined pit was being filled with flowback, water gushing in from thick black hoses. In another shot, the photographer would have had to have been standing in the middle of the well pad, level with the vats and tanks, to get such images without obstruction.

"How did you manage to get these shots?" I asked.

"Lots of zoom." He smiled.

"No people," I said. "It's hard to get a shot without workers in it, but you manage to get clean shots all the time."

He came alone to the first Common Ground meeting, listening intently to the roundtable introductions, each of us stating our name, any organization we represented, what we saw ourselves contributing to the overall effort. There were educators, students, artists and musicians, nonprofit and community organizers, a doctor, a water well driller, and petitioners working on a ban effort in Michigan.

When it came time for Werckz to introduce himself, he made nervous (supposedly) comments about how passionate he was about this stuff. He fidgeted with his baseball cap and lowered his head, tearing up, apparently.

"I'm sorry." He shook his head.

Across the table, the Frack No! women shushed him. "Don't apologize for caring. My gosh, we all know."

He stayed for the full day, talking about how the forests around his home were being destroyed. But when Rhonda, the meeting host, set up a projector and asked all the writers and researchers to share with the group after dinner, "Dan? You've taken a lot of photos. Share them with us?" he grinned sheepishly and declined.

"I'd rather let Rebecca show us her photos. She's the pro." He lowered his head, adding an uncomfortable grin. "Maybe later, if there's time."

"We're all amateurs," someone said. "Don't worry about it."

Later, over beers and guitar strumming, Werckz made the rounds before saying goodbye. He used his shy grin a lot, especially as he sidled up to women. He also made sure, during our closing talk, to laud the young people who were organizing actions.

"I may not be the one getting out there. A lot of us aren't. But we've got to support the people who are doing the hard-core stuff. These young people, standing up at auction protests and raising a stink. We've got to support that."

In my journal, I noted every person he named: "Brett here, and Kate, and Mark, isn't it? And the pipeline folks who got arrested down here in the spring, Jared and Christine, we're all in this together. Fracking. Tar sands. Water."

When Werckz showed up at the second Common Ground meeting, delivering everything we all needed, I was sure. He was either a private contractor or, more likely, industry.

At the first meeting, he had played up to Mark pretty hard, asking Mark all sorts of questions about the Frac Tours website. Six months later, Werckz showed up with an old friend, a computer expert named Mike Smart, and they demonstrated their gift to everyone. Their fully functioning website was exactly what Mark had dreamed of building but hadn't had the time to complete.

Smart demonstrated and Werckz narrated their new website's repository of well site permits, environmental assessments, photographs, and videos. He charmed all but a few of us.

But he also slipped up—big time.

At the first meeting, he had shown me a fuzzy Facebook photo of his six-year-old son who, according to him, was cheering Daddy on when he took off on his motorcycle to get those perfect photos. By the second meeting, he seemed to have forgotten that he had a son. Instead, he had a six-month-old baby girl with a fever and a cough, and his concern for his daughter's welfare had the older women swooning. So much so that they allowed him to break the golden rule when bellying up to the Common Ground table. All cell phones had to be off and batteries removed once the meeting began.

Werckz and Carla, a retired hydrologist who was known as one of the state's top citizen researchers, showed up late, together. They had been out on a site all night, they explained, getting photos of water well problems.

"This is big, you guys," Carla said, her eyes glassy with lack of sleep and an investigator's crush. When your adrenaline is pumping and you're out there in the middle of the night on land that you love, sneaking around with someone who is just as passionate about busting the wrongdoers, romances tended to spring up. Hell, bromances sprang up.

Werckz made a show of putting his cell phone out on the table in front of everyone. "I'll try not to be rude," he said, eyes and chin tucked. "I promised my wife, if our baby girl gets worse, I'd get right home."

"He's been gone all night," Carla added. "Even with a sick baby at home."

At regular intervals, he picked up his phone and checked for messages. Once, he even hurried outside to talk. He put on a good show, fidgeting with his phone as if he could barely pay attention as a room full of activists described what they'd been up to since the group's last meeting.

What I saw in his repeated handling of his phone was an opportunity to stop and reset the record button. He was working Carla hard, playing "two of them against the world" to get her to trust him, and clearly, she had bought it. He was a daredevil, an outdoorsy kind of guy the retired hydrogeologist might have wished she had ended up with her whole life.

He smiled, he fumbled with his phone, he made quick exits, whispering, "Hey, how's she doing?" and Carla's eyes followed.

Thankfully, when the roundtable got to Kate and Brett and Mark, Kate, who shared my suspicions about Dan the Man, spoke quickly and briefly. "We observe," she said, eyeing Mark. "We're putting out the sensory story of fracking."

If his courting of Carla wasn't enough to arouse suspicion, the myriad "insty-buddies" he was able to enlist certainly was. I spoke to Rhonda, the nature center's director, and she was beginning to agree. "Who are these people with full-time jobs and families, yet they've got time to create websites and dig up inside shareholder info in their spare time?"

When the guitars and the cold beer came out at the end of the evening, I asked Werckz and Smart, separately, how they'd met. "Me and Mike?" "Dan and I?" They both stalled before answering, "We've known each other for years."

When pressed, Werckz added, "We grew up together, downstate."

When they were together, I tried again. "So, downstate. Where exactly?"

Werckz turned the attention back to me. "Man, with your pictures?" He shook his head. "Mine are so amateurish next to yours." Werckz nodded to Smart, gesturing in my direction. "What do you think, Mike?"

Smart took a sip, smiling and nodding my way. Their eyebrows danced. When I didn't fish as I was supposed to, Werckz leaned close, sharing their secret.

"Mike and I were thinking," he said. "We could let you post directly to the site, to get your pictures out there. We're not going to let anyone else inside, though, just you and your group, so we wouldn't want anyone else to know."

He closed our huddle. "The three of us, together, we'd be coming at them from all corners."

Of course it would be great. They'd have my IP address and access to my hard drive.

"How's your son?" I asked.

He seemed genuinely taken aback. "My daughter," he said. "She's doing okay, from what her mom says."

"Good to hear." I took a swig and glanced at Smart, who wasn't smiling. Then I turned to Werckz. "That's so odd. I was sure you showed me a photo of your son at our last meeting."

Werckz raised his beer to Smart. "Mike's got two boys," and he scooted away.

Time had taught me that there were three definite flags.

One: *Someone who can be tripped up on their personal story.*

Werckz's slip revealed textbook behavior. In a room filled with activist women, many of whom had been taking abuse from oil and gas thugs for decades, not only did he show up with the website we'd all dreamed of creating, but he showed up as father of the year. Could we pardon him if he had to run out quickly to be there for his sick daughter and his tired wife?

Flag number two: *Someone who waxes passionate and disappears (a scout), or someone who shows up and becomes your everything (an infiltrator).*

Werckz was sloppy, true. His repeated use of the number six was probably personal, an old baseball number or an important digit from a dog tag. But he had changed his story to maximize his appeal. First, he had a six-year-old son, then a six-month-old daughter.

And then, of course, there was the movie version of flag number three: *Someone who wears expensive, polished shoes.*

In practice, the faux pas was usually more thematic, like showing up to a slow food meeting with a bag of processed, GMO-laden cookies. Werckz tripped up on water.

"Okay," Kate bobbed as we talked on the ride home, "so he didn't have the shoes, but come on, a fricking case of Great Springs water?"

Werckz brought in jumbo water bottles from the company that had devastated a west Michigan water table. One of the women at the meeting had led the environmental lawsuit. "Grab a water, everybody." He had smiled. "It'll take us a few minutes to set up."

Rhonda had also noticed. "Really? Plastic water bottles? And how about the way he ran that presentation?"

Throughout the first meeting, Werckz had maintained his shy smile. At the second meeting, he was the man in charge. He moved his presentation along with defined accent points and refused to let questions take him off track. He led as Carla assisted, performing like someone who was used to being listened to. Military, I figured. Ex-military turned security.

It didn't take much to put yourself in business. A raised-letter business card. A home office. A few quick tours of well pads and meetings with supervisors, and a rent-a-snoop could make damn good money.

"Marko," Kate had teased. "The techno-bromance is over. Dan the Man is snooping for someone. He has to be."

—

I entered the kitchen, trying not to guess how close it was getting to dawn, when thoughts of David and Sonya and Werckz blended together, arranging themselves in patterns that brought back uncomfortable flags.

Sonya had been present every single time we encountered security. She was there when the Secure Tek truck sped past us and blocked the road. She was the only one who heard the thugs' lynching threats at that awful meeting. She was with me when I drove us into that security trap at the farm.

She had also stopped visiting.

Werckz's face appeared: *This stuff gets too emotional for me.*

Sonya rarely went on well site visits, yet every time she had been there, we ran into trouble. What would that make Hank, a fake kid?

Possibly a child in custody.

No. I had felt Sonya's disgust the night the thugs surrounded her. We'd all seen the way she sank into the back seat.

If you thought too much about security, everyone seemed suspect. You began to recognize patterns in CEO statements, in the bullying comments of a developer, in the questions people asked when they wanted to get close.

Sonya's arrest had brought David back to mind, of course it had. It had also brought back Mara, but I had learned, with time, to let the forever unresolvable guilt and pain of Mara pass quickly. To linger there was to become paralyzed.

Levi and I, all of us at Fen's had put questions about David to bed long ago.

"Ask yourself, Beck," David had pleaded with me before he left. "Ask yourself, really."

He had grabbed my elbow so hard it hurt.

"Are you one hundred percent sure that this is where you want to draw the line?"

Levi and I had hashed that one out, over and over. Why had David been so sure that I was drawing *that* line? The proverbial this-is-what-I'm-willing-to-go-down-for line?

But we had decided, long ago, that David's exit was untimely, horribly so, but he couldn't have gone to the dark side.

If the Big Greens got word of their staff getting truly active, they distanced themselves as quickly as they could, afraid to lose funding. David was preparing us for his exit. He had to.

He was vulnerable. He was in his early thirties, yet he couldn't afford a pair of jeans or a four-dollar coffee. If anything, his relationship with me might have pushed him to leave. He kept talking about stability, how he had no stability to offer.

For a time, I felt sorry for him and for me. The hurt had gone deep, so I sought reasons other than he had simply burned out and he needed money, because I never actually believed that he would leave without me.

I stood, staring at the coffeepot.

The only thing David and Werckz and Sonya had in common was me. And I was way off track. I knew enough not to dismiss hunches when I started to recognize patterns. But I also knew enough to know when the connections I was making were faulty because I was desperate for direction and maybe feeling left out.

The jury was still out on Werckz. Superego or slop security?

But Sonya? Heat rushed to the surface of my face. I was tired, way too tired and reaching for clues. Maybe I was a bit hurt, though they were right to exclude me.

I watched the coffee flow over the spout and into my cup, dark and thick with that overheated smell, and I poured it out, deciding to make a fresh pot.

Chapter 19

What Makes Sense for the Sheradays by Elizabeth Stone
Four Branches: Great Lakes Region

Meet the Sheradays: Hettie and Merle. Sheep farmers. Active octoge-narians with quick wits and infectious smiles. After decades of moving around the country for work, the couple now sleeps in the same bed-room where Hettie was born eighty years ago, in a northern Michigan farmhouse surrounded by state land.

They're also living in fracking's proverbial rock-and-a-hard place: between a frack well site and a sand mine.

The day I met the Sheradays their water well had run dry, yet they were still laughing. Still teasing each other as we talked, convinced that telling me their story would make a difference.

But I didn't tell their story. I didn't know how.

What the Sheradays showed me was more than the water costs of fracking. Theirs was a love story, and they were a couple of the petro-chemical era falling out of love with the story of their time.

As soon as North American Energy (NorA, an international com-pany) started the frack job next door, the Sheradays' walls began to shake and their cupboard doors wouldn't stay closed. Sometimes, no water came out of the tap. Sometimes, bubbles the color of milk filled their glasses.

Thanks to the confidential status the DEQ extends to every new frack well in Michigan, NorA isn't required to tell the Sheradays the truth they could see for themselves. As the Sheradays' well was running dry, NorA was drilling a seventh water well for the frack well pad next door.

"They'll run another one dry," Merle scoffed. "You can tell every time they run out of water. There's a god-awful screech and the shaking stops."

Fracking is a growing concern in Michigan, where NorA operates within the Au Sable and the Pere Marquette state forests.

The Sheradays are not innocent or ignorant of the growth and progress spurred by the "better living through chemistry" era. They're just not buying it anymore. Not the claim of safe fracking. Not job creation. Certainly not the call for energy independence.

"Hell," Merle says, "as soon as they can get a better price elsewhere, they'll ship it right past us."

Merle worked for the chemical industry his whole life. He and Hettie moved state to state, raising their family and keeping a portion of the family's northern Michigan farm intact for decades. Merle started as a truck driver, hauling chemicals and fertilizers until he completed his degree and became, as Hettie teases, a "Mix-ineer," specializing in agrochemical products. He ended his career as an Explosives Specialist. His final job was to implode the center of a southwest desert mountain to make way for a radioactive waste storage facility.

"What we did there wasn't progress," Merle told me, his bright gaze dimming. "And what they're doing here isn't progress either. It's nothing but good old-fashioned pressure."

After two years of visiting frack well sites, you have to expect something to catch you off guard. The first time you see and hear a drill bit screeching as it grinds into the rock below, and you feel that screech come up through your bones. The first time you crawl over the backside of a berm and see the forest floor stained with mustard and rust colored powders.

This time, gazing upon a towering wellhead circled by chemical trucks and command trailers, it was the hoses. The incredible strain and pressure placed on hundreds of hoses.

Each time the water tank filled, the compressors roared. Diesel motors strained to an uncomfortable pitch, and the hoses hanging from the backs of the trucks came alive. Great lumps of pressure filled those bright red hoses and they snapped up from the wellhead, rod-like and angry, pushing back against every truck and clamp that held them.

Hettie and Merle have made their cultural bed, so to speak, and they plan to lie in it. They do not, however, plan to lie down. Instead, they'll remain in the knuckle region of Michigan's north woods, charged with a new purpose.

"Somebody's got to keep an eye on them," Merle smiled.

"This doesn't make sense anymore," Hettie said. "Not for us, but certainly not for our children and grandchildren. I guess that's my role now. Keep saying it."

And then Hettie asks me a question. "What's your vision of home?"

What Hettie is really asking is: does what makes sense for the Sheradays make sense for us all? Do we want our grandparents, our grandchildren, living how and where they are? Hettie asks me to close my eyes and feel it, my vision of home, so I do.

I picture beech maple forests, an old growth of white pines. I see northern Michigan's central inland region where glacial lakes and wetlands connect state-crossing rivers: the Au Sable and the Manistee.

"Now," Hettie says, and her voice is a smile. "What are you willing to do to live it?"

This is Hettie's "call to vision." A call home, and I know, when she asked me that warm, loud day in June, she was hoping I would throw it out.

So, here it is. A Stone's Throw: What is your vision of home?

And what are you willing to do to live it?

Chapter 20

The Holy Fricking Cross
of Super Fracs

The moment I hit the send button, submitting the story that had bothered me for a year, I knew two things. One: submitting a Stone's Throw all these years later was a bit risky but getting some quick attention for their action, whatever it was, seemed worth it. And two: Sonya had left clues for me in her email. Of course, her paces were wrong. They were strategically wrong. There was no way the uniformity of the numbers made sense.

Her numbers were clues, and those eloquent descriptions of cedar boughs and frozen fog were meant to throw others off. She had left clues!

I ran to my room and pulled down the oversized map of Michigan we had blown up and tiled together so we could see the entire state, county lines and townships, any and all active well sites, all in one view. I taped the old map to my golden dinette wall so I could see the entire mitten of the Lower Peninsula, and I opened Sonya's email.

It was Kate's idea to scratch paces into our boots, remember?
1086. 1017. 1084.

Sonya, Kate, and I had notched wildly different counts on our boots the day we found the State-Kitfield well site. With me at five foot seven and Sonya at five foot eight with long legs, we had ended up with counts in the nine hundreds. Kate at five foot two had racked up over 1,100 paces on her duct-taped boots. Sonya and I had recorded our exact counts as we rode in the back of Kate's pickup, drawing landmarks on the way out. And there they were, boxed in hard dark lines, in my journal: 970. 915. 1180.

1086. 1017. 1084. Were the thousands drop-out numbers? What was left was the clue? 86. 17. 84?

I could see 86 and 84. They were longitudinal lines—86 degrees west skirted the dunes of Lake Michigan, and 84 ran down the east side of the state, grazing the thumb. Most of the fracking activity had occurred closer to the 85th, down the center of the state.

Was that where they were pointing me? Midstate, where NorA's pipeline corridor connected the deep Utica-Collingwood drill sites?

But then, what was the 17?

I opened the DEQ's permit site and started marking recent filings on the big map. There were the usual acid fracking permits downstate, under the thumb. But there were also a surprising number of new A-1 Carbonate applications, in the layer Dillon seemed to have abandoned after their pilot hole at Randy and Diane's didn't produce.

NorA had also filed a slew of new site applications riding above the 44th parallel. Following west to east, lake to lake, the permits created the start of a line across the knuckle region of the mitten, with some concentrated activity in a few key areas.

A pair of new sites lay just inside 86 degrees west. One hovered near Ludington, and another sat four miles to the north, toward Manistee.

Then, way over on the east side of the state, the pattern repeated. There was another pair of future sites, one near the 44th parallel and a second site four miles north, just inside longitude 84.

I drew two lines to connect those pairs, creating a four-mile-wide band across northern Michigan, and that's when I saw it. Tammy and Del sat just above the 44th parallel, and four miles north was the lake house at Randy and Diane's.

I pondered the numbers again: 1086. 1017. 1084. The thousands weren't dropout numbers. They were stays-the-same clues, pointing to the 44th parallel and a new strip of land running west to east across the state.

I ran back to the closet, hunting through my milk crate full of journals and found the map Del had made for us, the Gladwin county map of A-1 Carbonate well sites drilled in secrecy, and I found the 17.

The State-Miralette well site, numbered 1-17, was just three hundred feet from Tammy and Del's backyard. That's where I had seen that 17 before. "State-Miralette 1-17" written on one stake and "Corner Well Pad" written on another.

The numbers 86 – 17 – 84 represented the border of a new, four-mile-wide corridor of land stretching across northern Michigan, lake to lake.

What came clear, next, was an awful, bigger plan.

Sonya had lingered on State-Lexford and its sister site, State-Eleanor, NorA's first Michigan wells. Supersites now, both sites sat at the top of the four-mile-wide pipeline corridor that ran north to south through the center of the state, connecting well pads that zigzagged the corridor, top to bottom, ending at State-Kitfield.

If that corridor continued, if NorA headed south and crossed the new horizontal band that Sonya appeared to be pointing me to, if they kept on going to State-Wheeler, there would be two bands of fracking that would form a giant cross—one running vertically in the Utica-Collingwood layer, and the other running across the state, connecting a series of new A-1 Carbonate wells. And where those corridors crossed was a box that held the State-Rudmond site at Randy and Diane's to the north and the future State-Miralette well at Tammy and Del's to the south.

If what I was plotting was correct, our friends were living in the heart of the Super Frac of all Super Fracs. Two layers at a time, fracked simultaneously.

NorA could extend laterals out and down from Randy and Diane's and drill new legs up from Tammy and Del's, and with each of those runs two miles long, they would nearly touch.

The Super Frac. Was NorA actually going to try it? Laterals too close to avoid the traveling of fractures and migrating of liquids from one well to another?

That four-mile square would be turned to geological jelly.

Carla, the retired hydrologist, had first suggested the possibility. She had shown us an oil and gas forum where contributors hailing as "PumpJack" and "Mole" discussed the possibility of a Super Frac, of fracking two shale layers at once to recover a bonanza of oil and gas.

Up in Alberta, NorA had gotten away with something similar, using steam. They'd shot steam down into the shale, knowing it would crack and fissure and steam up from one shale layer to the next, creating multiple channels for oil and gas to flow. The problem was that those multiple channels kept creating new ones. Yes, the gas and oil flowed, but so did the steam and liquids and radioactivity. At last report, the original target area of four hundred acres had grown into a seeping hot mess that had spread across thousands of acres.

When would they learn?

There is no harness that can hold the power or the mystery of nature.

NorA hadn't left Tammy and Del's. They were biding their time—needlepointing a future cross of well sites and pipelines with pumping stations and refineries to follow.

The Super Fuck as Brett had termed it. "If they do that, we're fucked. Super fucked."

"At that point, we'd have to act," Mark had said. "We couldn't sit around waiting for it to get worse. What could be worse?"

By that time Mark was writing his "In These Fracking Times" poems, and Kate was mixing clay into our water bottles to draw out toxins and heavy metals. Mark had read some of his goofier poems one hot summer night up at Randy and Diane's, and we had howled so loudly that we woke the neighbors across the lake. They had paddled over to join us, banking their canoe in the reeds, and Mark had read for them.

Bitches Combat Training

Gray is a lie.
There are absolutes worth fighting for. Worth dying for.
Shit. I need to get in shape.

"We'd have to act," Kate had thrown up her hands. "Can you imagine? They'd frack it all to hell, way before we had time to protect the water, and people started coming up sick.

"The bastards are going to frack and run," she had said, and we had all shaken our heads, trying to believe that the Super Frac was a myth.

I stood before the map, gazing at two bands of land that crossed exactly where Tammy and Del and Randy and Diane were most likely sleeping. If they could sleep. What the oil and gas industry would do to get at all remaining fossil fuels was always unbelievable when expressed as an idea. Blowing the tops off mountains. Boiling bitumen in great gooey toxic pits. Liquefying the bedrock below us. But sooner or later, you had to believe that they intended to do everything possible.

Then, you had to trust that you could stop it.

Chapter 21
Threshold

The sun was not yet rising, the rosy lavender in the east more in my mind than visible, and in the air I felt fall. The sun's path was inching southward, the earth tilting day by day, and with the sun now rising from its more southerly position, I wouldn't see an actual sunrise until our blue marble slowly tilted back next spring. The houses to the south were blocking my view.

Thoreau would roll over in his grave if he saw what development meant to us today. So much for the huckleberries! We were now walling off the sun and the sky from each other depending on the elevation of our lots in life.

I walked north, feeling the grass and ivy slopes of the park next door, my barefoot ritual for welcoming the cold morning dew.

The Super Frac. Were they really going to try it? Is that why Michigan had seemed off the fracking radar lately? A boom and bust industry was hoping Michigan's rare basin geology would save their financial asses. Deliver a quick spike in production even if it couldn't last.

I checked the pockets of my work bag for the extra USB drive I had loaded before formatting my laptop's hard drive, which was no easy task. So different than the old DOS days when you could drop down and start clearing a hard drive in seconds.

Mark and Kate had teased me incessantly about my old flip phone—so old, it struggled to send and receive pictures, but it also had no GPS. They would appreciate that, if they hadn't figured that out already.

On the night of our last EcoLit class meeting, I had listened to Kate and Brett and Mark and Sonya plan to get together as the sun set behind them. Sonya, with her back to the windows, became a frizzy silhouette surrounded by the most incredibly bold fuchsias and mint greens.

Kate, as usual, bypassed the ethics, whether I could or should meet with them outside of class.

"You'll be there too, right?" She had nodded and lifted her chin.

"Maybe after a while," I said.

She studied her notepad, one leg twirling over the other.

"Get a good start without me around."

"Without Teach?" Mark had teased.

"It's the end of the semester tonight, right?" Kate looked up. "So you're not Teach anymore."

"Maybe you don't need me around. I've been the facilitator, here, but it might be good for you to have a chance to say and do whatever you want."

"We have." Brett shrugged and smiled. "We pretty much have." His dark bangs highlighted his eyes, and his grin stayed.

"Keep me in the loop, and I'll show up at some point," I finally said.

"But we want you to stay with us," Sonya had said.

Her glasses were glazed with the colors of sunset. An honest lack of restraint in her voice surprised me.

"Ditto," Mark offered.

"See how you feel after your first few meetings."

"We'll give you till the second one," Kate had said, leg swinging. "Case closed."

There were two forevers we had going for us. I could trust them, and they could trust me. "End of story," as Kate would say.

We had been through so much together. It was hard not to fall in love with the people and places we had come to know. Tammy and Del and Frank, Randy and Diane, and the folks from Common Ground. We became endeared to each other, a league of justice fighters if there ever was one, though we had real lives and real jobs. And unlike comic book characters, we were exhaustible.

I knew, without a doubt, that Tammy and Del would know where they were, but Randy and Diane would be a better start with Tammy and Del's backyard shaping up to be the target of all targets.

Brett had pressed me the day we stated our thresholds on Sonya's back deck. "You haven't told us yours." The pinking around his eyes was what made me speak. It mattered to him.

"You," I said, and they had all looked at me with crinkled looks.

"Us?"

"Yes. You," I had answered, because I was proud of them, because they had inherited a world that needed every one of them, because they continued to work together, even as they understood the urgency and the odds.

I tipped my head back to drink the last of my coffee, noting the walled off but still beautiful sunrise beyond my neighbors' roof lines. If they were planning something big, which I figured they must be, pulling out of the driveway was only the beginning.

From the moment I saw Sonya's picture on the screen, I knew. Just as firmly as my feet had said "No" that day Kate and I had walked over ground being actively fracked 8,000 feet below us, my whole body, everything I had experienced in the past two years said, "Yes."

This arrest of Sonya's was bogus in some way. I didn't know how yet, but I would. If Randy and Diane didn't know exactly where they were, Frank would. He and Brett had become close.

As much as they adored Tammy and Del, they'd stay clear of State-Miralette. Excavation may have started. It had been months since Del's heart attack, blamed on pneumonia and breathing problems and the stress the illness had put on his heart. The doctors still couldn't figure out what was causing his blood pressure to shoot up all night and then plummet every morning.

Thankfully, one doctor had started to listen. The last time I spoke to Del, he and I had reviewed a series of images by phone, and he'd asked me to send more pictures of the State-Wheeler wasteland. We had scoured shots of hazardous labels, chemical lists that he and his new doctor were investigating.

"Bingo!" he had said on the phone, his voice strong with fight. "That's the label that has a chemical list that almost exactly matches my symptoms.

"She's good," he said of the doctor treating him. "She's asking me to get whatever pictures and MSDS sheets I can. Send me whatever you got, okay Beck?"

I threw my backpack, my climbing gear, and a bag of essays in the back of the car, thinking, what a teacher I had become, bringing essays to a showdown with Big Oil, and I closed the hatch. The oil and gas industry knew the science of climate change. Their own scientists were helping them plan for a warming arctic. That's why Michigan was lining up as the perfect southern port. Why the Sheradays' story finally made sense. The thugs knew the public was falling out of love, and they needed to move fast.

The Sheradays' place, between a frack well and a sand mine, was what the oil and gas industry saw for all of Michigan. So much yet to develop. A shoreline for transportation, coasts lined with pipelines, an interior pocked with well pads, pumping stations, and processing facilities. They dreamed of liquid natural gas ports where they could load up and ship out the most toxic oil and gas products ever created over the largest body of fresh surface water on the planet, and from there, haul it out the St. Lawrence Seaway to a gas- and oil–hungry world.

This was their ten-year vision, twenty at most. They knew none of it was going to last. That was the point. Take it now, fast and hard.

"Frack and run," as Kate put it.

I backed out of the driveway, the birds of fall chirping away as morning's rosy pinks stretched overhead, the first yellow hues turning the sky above a creamy orange. I smiled at the thought of Kate's pursed lips, the way her eyes would narrow as she growled.

"Fricking frack and run."

Showdown

Chapter 22

Together Again

It all happened so quickly that David didn't have time to straighten from his crouch before I stepped back into the trees. Mark and I brushed through the cedars—there was David—and Mark walked on without me.

David stared right at me as he rose, wearing his usual jeans and a long sleeved T-shirt, and I couldn't help but notice that his chest, his arms, his stance looked wider. He was David through a wide-angle lens.

More importantly, he didn't seem nearly as surprised to see me as I was to see him.

"Elizabeth Stone," he said.

"David?" I reached for the wall of cedar boughs behind me, which gave way, of course. His eyes still had that intense, lit-up gray.

Kate rose too, annoyed. "Elizabeth? Who the hell is Elizabeth?"

David's eyes stayed on me as I worked to find steadiness in the prickly feel of cedar boughs sliding through my hands.

Mark looked back and forth between us, cocking his head, and I wanted to say something—but nothing about my trip up, not my stop at Randy and Diane's, not the break I took to stretch my legs and try a few texts, nothing and no one had said, as they pointed me toward camp, that David May was here. What on earth were they planning that would draw him in?

"I mean, Professor Walton, right?"

"Wait." Mark turned to David. "Wait. Did you say Elizabeth Stone?"

We all turned to the snaps of twigs and Hank's voice drawing closer. Brett's low voice rumbled around Hank's higher tones.

Kate began to bounce. "Who the hell is Elizabeth Stone?"

David nodded and his face softened. Perhaps he even understood. He may have wooed Kate and Brett and Mark, but they were my people first, not his, though clearly they had let him in on whatever they were planning.

My face must have communicated, when my eyes went to Kate, exactly what I was thinking. *You told him about this, but you didn't tell me?*

She looked to the ground, and her voice came back quiet. "We thought you wanted to be left out."

I did. I had. But this was different.

"Beck." David started to talk, and I put my hand up to stop him. I was honestly having trouble getting a good, deep breath.

"Beck?" Mark repeated. "You two know each other?"

Brett walked up with Hank at his side, the two of them talking about red and white oaks and how their leaves differed. Brett smiled and strode my way, putting his arms around me in a full lanky hug, and I hugged back, reacting with the sheer simple joy of seeing him and Hank, all of them (minus David, of course; what on earth was he doing here?) together and all right.

"So you've met Sonya's dad?" Brett said.

The cedars no longer held me.

Sonya's *dad?*

"Well, sort of. Pretty much."

Brett reached out and held my arm. "Are you all right?"

Sort of?

Hank walked over to David, who picked him up as if Hank were a much younger child.

"Papa D," Hank said, smiling.

"Papa D," I said, trying to keep my voice neutral for Hank's benefit. Trying, but lack of sleep and too much coffee wasn't a good combination for me.

I looked at Kate and Mark and gently pushed off from Brett's grasp. "How long have you all known?"

The question sounded much more vulnerable than I meant it to.

"About him?" Kate motioned toward David. "We just found out about him a week ago, when Sonya called him before our last visit."

And then Kate being Kate, unable to pick up on a vibe and sit quietly with it, bobbed and grinned. "About you and him? I'm just vibing that out fricking right now."

Mark stepped toward me. "Elizabeth Stone. Seriously?" He turned to face David. "And you two know each other?"

"Who is Elizabeth Stone?" Brett asked.

Suddenly, the thoughts and patterns that had been churning all night came together. The familiarity in Sonya's face, her archaic smile, as Mark called it. I could see Mara now, in Sonya's deliberate gaze.

And here, lean-but-filled-out David was smiling at me, knowing. I had been left only with David's esker face, his agonized, last-day esker face. I had forgotten all others.

He shrugged, and I felt myself sinking into the cedars. *Papa D. Papa D in Seattle.* Hank had mentioned him before.

Mara and David had had a child?

I knew David had cheated on me. Well, sort of. But a child? How could they have kept this from me?

"Sonya's okay?" I asked David.

He was holding Hank over one hip, like a baby. "She's okay."

I turned to Brett. "The arrest was a throw off, right?"

Brett seemed uncomfortable, and Mark answered, "Yes."

I looked around the circle at their faces, my hand still up to stop it all, then I ducked into the cedars. This was way too much for them to witness as it happened. I was way too tired, too steeped in worry, and the resolution I thought I was going to find was now terribly complicated. I found a path and stepped quickly.

"Obviously, I missed something," I heard Brett say.

"Yeah, buddy." Kate chuckled. "You sure did."

"Should we go explain?" Brett asked, and in unison, I heard David and Kate answer, "No."

It occurred to me (which pissed me off at my own uncanny ability to be observant and analytical even as my head was pounding with questions) that David and Kate would get along in the same way that Kate and Sonya had.

How long had Sonya known? Did she know? The implications!

I stepped over and around roots and ruts, doing my best to move through the cedars and pines as gently as possible. Sonya was Mara's? All the old hurts came in. David and Mara sleeping together, and Mara telling me, straight out. Me, being young and stupid and leaving because I thought my hurts were justification enough when things started to feel wrong at the canyon. The ground widened between the trees, pine loam giving way to moist, dark dirt, and I was able to take full, hard strides under oaks and maples. David and Mara, again? I was tougher now. Much tougher. But not tough enough for this. Not tough enough for going all the way back to David and Mara, to Mara standing there, so obviously troubled, and me not being big enough to help her.

Still, nothing fit. Except—Fen's. David had left Fen's months before Mara died, in prison.

The air began to darken and I tired myself out on a long, slow rise into white pines. Saplings colored the air above the ground in their delicate silver-green, and I breathed in their dusty sweet vapor. Mara, my dear friend, left alone, so terribly alone. Was this what she had tried to tell me? She was pregnant? I lifted my face to follow the boughs of the oldest trees, their upward, curving, muscular reaches. I had always thought that the sustained *whish* of the wind through white pines was the most beautiful sound in the forest. If I quieted, their sound would guide me.

I found two straight, young trees and wedged myself between them, pressing my arms flat against their bark. When I saw Hank put his skinny arms around David's neck, when Brett approached David with ease, I felt as uncomfortably on to something as I had when I had drawn David and Sonya together in my kitchen the night before.

I knew Mara was in trouble at the canyon, but how could Sonya be David and Mara's? There was no news about a child. How the hell had all of this gone down without me knowing?

Listen to your hunches. Hadn't I learned and relearned that lesson?

Pay attention to twinges of familiarity, sometimes pangs of discomfort, the anxiousness I often felt when something wasn't entirely settled. I had become alarmed in the middle of the night that both David and Sonya could have been plants, which was ridiculous, yet that false epiphany was connected to something I had felt many times and dismissed.

David had disappeared and Sonya had appeared, one without an end, the other without a beginning. And now Mara, the friend I had been forced to turn away from, was both of their stories?

"Beck."

I held on to the young pines behind me, timing my breaths with their slight, slight sway.

I felt David's careful steps. He was placing each foot, searching the ground for tiny saplings. Sonya did not have David's gray, lit-up eyes. Sonya had Mara's eyes. Rich brown eyes that sometimes appeared, in the light, to be topped with a layer of silt, layered like wet clay.

David's long ago dance on the esker. In his own way, he had tried to tell me. Somehow, he had been surprised. He had received a call or a letter, something that said, "Come, be a father." And now, his agitation that day was clear. There had been something he would not or could not say.

He stopped, close. "I didn't know."

He moved into my gaze. "And it's not what you think."

I wanted to say something smart, like, *Well. That doesn't sound cliché.* But what came out was much more honest. "You and Mara." I was too tired to filter out that old, nagging hurt.

His and Mara's relationship, however brief, had always intimidated me. Mara was beautiful. She was legendary. She was so much more than an observer, and she and I had been friends. Long before David, she had been my friend.

"Sonya is not mine," he said. "She's Mara's. Mara's daughter."

His eyes looked tired. I could see that now.

"Why weren't you surprised to see me?"

"I'm going to need some time to explain. I sent Sonya your way."

"My way?" He had kept track? "You mean, to the college?"

He nodded.

"Sonya's okay?"

"She's okay," he said.

"You've seen her?"

"They've got her at the local jail, but they won't be able to keep her much longer. It was a mix-up. Survey flags in Hank's backpack."

"Oh, no." Poor Hank. "You mean, literally?" Using a child's backpack, without the child, was a common trick.

"Literally." He frowned. "They were walking and talking, and no one realized Hank was picking up flags."

The bag of essays in my car came to me, along with the impossibility of going back to work as if none of this had happened. David and Mara, and now Sonya too. I had tried to warn Kate and Brett and Sonya and Mark, whenever I could. When you get arrested, you get arrested alone. "How did this happen?"

David turned up his forearms in a way that was half shrug, half invitation, and I followed. He had been with Mara before me. Yes. And though I had gotten over that, way too late to make proper amends with Mara, the hug still hurt.

It truly, fully hurt. "It's so good to see you," he said, and I echoed it back. "You too."

My worry about Sonya and Kate and Brett and Mark, and Hank, poor Hank, I gave all of my worry to that hug. David had always had a full, solid hug. Something as stable as a great oak root grew up through him.

"Your hair," he said, touching the darker brown strands at the back of my neck. "It's shorter."

"Yours too," I said, and he lifted his cap. The scraggly bangs that he used to shake out after a shower were gone, replaced by a receding hairline and a cut that stayed close.

We sat under the trees, away from everyone, and talked.

"I was so confused, Beck. I didn't want Mara to get into the work at Fen's, to mess you up too."

Mara had gone down in 1991, well before the Green Scare earned its name, yet she had been immortalized as a Green Scare hero. Mara never talked after a canyon development was burned to the ground. Her confession came so quickly that even the authorities figured she was protecting others. We all did.

There was so much going wrong the last time we talked.

Mara loved animals. She couldn't bear how they were caged and tested. She had flourished in the identity of an animal rights activist. She had participated in actions against labs. She had helped to expose corporate farms raising animals for fur. But the canyon was hers—her action to lead—and she was feeling pressure to give all the men pouring into the canyon an opportunity to act. Their prove-it shit had gotten out of control.

The men and all their rooster dancing, that's what I thought she meant when she said she was feeling lost.

"The world. Everything." Mara had spun her hand in the air. "Too much with me."

But we never got the chance to work that out. The word after the canyon fire, for me in particular, was to stay away. Contact with Mara would jeopardize everyone.

"It was Sonya," David said. "Mara found out she was pregnant after the arrest. She was protecting Sonya."

"You saw Mara?"

"Yes."

"You spoke to her?"

"Several times," he said. "During our time at Fen's."

All those trips to Green Watch. The interviews. His leaving.

He sat on a downed trunk, and I remained standing, looking David over as if I could somehow, vicariously find Mara. He had seen her. Often?

"Did she ever contact her mother's family?"

"Just Marjorie."

Marjorie was a cousin and a grandmother. All the women Marjorie introduced Mara to were grandmothers, all that was left of her mother's family.

"Mara wanted Sonya to know Marjorie, to have some contact with family," David said, "but Marjorie was too old for the teen years again."

So Mara had called David.

"Maybe she knew she was sick," he said, "when she torched the canyon. She never said so, but that would explain."

Alone, with all those men, she had gotten tired of the showmanship, that's what I always figured.

"She went through round after round of chemo and radiation during those eight years."

Why had she let me storm off as if my hurts were most important?

Cancer in prison. Childbirth in prison. They couldn't still chain women in labor, could they, like they used to in state penitentiaries?

I thought I knew, so much, after Caleb died at Fen's. But then Mara died in prison, and forever I would know how much I could not know. And now, David was telling me that Mara had had a child. That he had helped Mara when I could not.

"David. You're sure. Sonya isn't yours."

"The feds would have forced a paternity test. I'm sure they did. The infiltrator. It's the only thing that makes sense."

"Gabe." I remembered the tall blond, his watchfulness. "That awful Gabe."

At the canyon, I told Mara I didn't trust him. Gabe was always speaking in Mara's ear, pulling her away from the circle, saying things to her that should have been said to everyone or not spoken at all. And he made sure we knew. He made sure that I knew, especially, that he had Mara's confidence.

"I tried to talk to her," I said, "but I think she actually cared for him."

"That has to be how she worked her deal."

David and I pieced it all together. Mara had agreed to a confession, offering a morally compelled defense. She had seen animals slaughtered, after all. But the terms, when she was convicted, were clear. The baby was to be kept secret from the father and out of the news. She and her child would be allowed regular visits, and the feds had to agree that they would never track her child.

"Never," David said, or she would go public with the story that their infiltrator not only knew about her plan to burn the canyon development, but he was also sleeping with her.

David brushed his hands over the dirt. "She was willing to give the feds their win, but only if they agreed to keep Sonya out of it."

Mara couldn't have known about her pregnancy. She never would have jeopardized her future if she knew there was another to care for.

David never seemed to ask himself this question: Who could get hurt?

He never seemed to worry about who he stirred up. The superintendent who might lose her job and the respect of her community.

The locals who take out second mortgages on their homes to fund the legal fight. The woman who walks the canyon, tossing flaming bottles into stick-built frames that are obscene in size for any setting, let alone one of the last remaining migration paths for the big cats.

Yes. There is a higher purpose than human law and regulation, but it must feel awfully human to pay the price.

"What was she like?"

"In prison?" The redness of his eyes made his irises a vibrant gray.

"When you saw her. How was she?"

"She was calm. Thin, but she was strong. She wanted Sonya to know more when she was old enough."

He looked up. "I had to leave. All three of us being tied together was a bad idea. That kind of tracking, the constant monitoring, it changes people. She didn't want Sonya to have to deal with that, ever."

"And you were safe, at Green Watch."

His eyes returned to the ground. "I was safe, on the West Coast, in a very public position."

"You should have told me. I could have helped."

"Maybe. It just got harder and harder to do."

"Yeah. A lot of things got harder."

He knew I was referring to Caleb. "I'm so sorry."

David's lack of concern about influence had always created a distance between us, but Mara had trusted David completely.

"Why didn't she reach out to me?"

He frowned. "You were all over the action at Fen's."

If she had contacted me, the action at Fen's might have stopped. And many of us, not just Caleb, might have paid a price. That was the frustration of being close to both David and Mara. You could admire the hell out of them and want to throttle them at the same time.

"Mara wanted me to tell Sonya about you two. About the college years, about book club. When Sonya wanted to hear. She left that to me."

"That's how Sonya ended up here?"

He sighed. "Sonya needed to get away from Hank's father, so I sent her your way."

Sonya was Mara's. Suddenly Sonya's smirks, the way she regarded me, made sense. Sonya knew enough to know that some of my story, too, was missing.

"You knew about me?"

David leaned back. "Didn't you google me now and then?"

I had, at first. "I saw your emails."

"Yeah. You were right. I send a lot of emails."

"Hank's father. You said she needed to get away."

"I'll let her tell you about that."

I waited.

"Drugs," he finally said. "He was going down hard."

Mara never had good judgment when it came to men, either. Even David was a mistake.

It was obvious, once I got back to the canyon, that the two of them had something going on. When I asked her, she straight out told me. Yes, they had slept together. They had shared a tent for a week. She wanted to tell me face-to-face, she said.

I thought then that seeing the big rocks detonated with explosives to cut roads, watching the big cats' migratory paths obliterated, had changed her. She seemed so wounded.

"We didn't hate each other," I told David. "It wasn't like that. I was hurt. You and I hadn't been together yet, and I felt like both of you had used my absence. But Mara, she was in bad shape."

Revisiting our last conversation was nothing I was proud of. Mara had looked at me, obviously in trouble. "Sometimes you just don't know, you know?"

And I had responded. "You should have. You both should have."

"I left because I was mad at you," I told David. "You and all the men on site, ramping up the competition. And that awful Gabe. He preyed on her. I know he did."

David looked up, and I stared straight back. "I blamed you. You and all the rooster dancing."

"I know," he said.

But these were hurts we would have to work through later. Old hurts that no longer mattered. Sonya mattered. Sonya was Mara's daughter.

"You are one hundred percent sure Sonya is not yours."

His gaze was serious. "One hundred percent. After you left, Mara and I didn't touch each other again. She was with him. Gabe. Really with him. I tried to tell her, too."

"Of course he was the informant."

David nodded. "Something happened between him and Mara. She called us all together and said, 'Go home. Spread out. Don't say a word.' But he stayed."

"What happened to him? Where did he go?"

"No idea. The feds must have shipped him off. I think Mara made that part of the deal. No dad. No contact."

Maybe Gabe made our last conversation make sense. Maybe he told Mara the feds were coming. Mara knew she had one last chance to rid a sacred place of something profane. "There is so much about Mara that you couldn't know. She was comfortable like that. With not knowing."

"Like Sonya," David said. With a twig, he picked at the dirt.

"I felt like I owed Mara something," he said. "I know I was part of the problem, at the canyon. I was young. And poor Sonya. She was eight when I met her. She'd grown up in dayrooms, Beck."

"What was it that Mara wanted you to do?"

"She asked me to be an uncle or a godfather. Marjorie liked the sound of that. Someone to help. I took Sonya back and forth to Mara on the weekends. She wanted Sonya to know me, before she was gone."

Mara had endured chemotherapy and radiation, alone, in prison. She had lost her beautiful red-black hair, that huge wavy hair of hers. Day by day, she had witnessed her own leaving.

I understood, now. David had witnessed this too.

During one of David's last trips back and forth from Fen's, he had dragged me out to the wetland boardwalk and indirectly asked me about marriage.

"If I said I wanted to get married and have a child right now, what would you say?"

"No," I had answered. A child? He was yelling at me about marriage. Obviously a "yes" wasn't what he wanted.

"At Fen's. You were thinking you and I could raise Sonya."

"I don't know." He tried to smile. "We were all friends. And you and I, we loved each other, that's how I saw it at the time. I knew I had to help, but I was scared."

He shook his head. "I don't know what it was about Mara."

Oh, I do! I wanted to say. Mara was absolutely magnetic. A wise, old soul if there ever was one. But there was also something missing. Something empty inside her, once you got close.

"No wonder Sonya is so incredibly restrained," I said.

"Hell of a way to grow up, isn't it?" He dug his fingers into the hard, dark dirt. "I still can't imagine what Mara must have gone through."

Sonya's maturity, her devotion to Hank. It all made so much sense. Sonya must have been everything, pure light and its absence, in Mara's life.

There was a noise, a car door noise.

"How big are things going to get?" I asked him.

Again, the outsider quality I had imposed on myself smarted. I was asking David what my former students were up to.

"Big," he said.

"How big?" I didn't want to get knocked off balance again.

"Bigger than anything we ever did."

"I thought so."

Big questions had a way of making you look up and out, especially when you weren't sure what to ask for. So I looked to the trees, to the silver-green saplings with their delicate stems and huge needles, to the hope expressed from the ground up.

David stood and brushed his hands on his jeans. "From what Brett and Kate and Mark have been telling me, the whole state's going to light up in a big green cross."

I grabbed his arm. "I saw it."

I could feel the density of his bones and for a second he must have felt it too, because when he looked up, his eyes had softened. "It?"

"The crisscross of land they're going to frack. I saw it last night. Tar sands meets fracking meets liquid natural gas plants, and it's all pointing to Michigan, exactly as we feared. Michigan as a huge central processing and transport zone."

"That's pretty much the plan," he said.

I stopped in front of him. "Shit."

"Yeah. It's different when they're your kids." But then he smiled. "It's so good to see you," he said. "So good."

I heard Brett's crow caw, and I grabbed David's hands.

"Away from them. Tell me. Who are you expecting?"

I saw his eyes look past me, to Brett's long footsteps.

"At least one group of climbers for sure, but I think there's going to be a lot of people coming in." He nodded in the direction of the footfalls. "Brett and Kate, they've got a lot of friends.

"What about you?" he said.

"All four are still up, but only Ken, in the east, is still active." Mara, me, Kyle, and Ken, the original Four Branches. Now there was a whole new crop of writer-activists keeping the network alive. Reporting from the inside of actions, putting out calls for help.

I had given Ken the okay to post my Sheraday article as a "Stone's Throw."

"I didn't tell them about the Branches," David said. "I figured you'd want to tell them yourself."

Brett came crashing into the clearing. "Del's Jeep! They're here!"

Brett's smile so transformed our space that I let go of David's hands and ran after Brett, and when I saw Tammy and Del and Randy and Diane climbing out of Del's Jeep, I didn't restrain my howl or my hugs. None of us did.

Del looked older, much older than he had just a year ago. His hair was completely silver, and his red-tan face was so thin! But his grin, the way he grabbed me by the shoulders and held me off to deliver that grin, was strong and full of teasing.

My smile felt shaky, and I didn't care.

Tall, broad Del boomed David's way. "Looks like you have some 'splainin' to do, Teach." He winked, knowing that would get Kate going.

"My people!" Kate hollered as she barreled into Tammy and Randy and Diane. Del let go of me and steadied himself over his cane. Tammy and Kate spun in a wild hug, and Tammy's always pulled-back hair, her rounded bun, bounced with them.

Randy pulled me close. "You made it," he chanted. "You made it."

"Together again." Diane smiled. She put her arm around my shoulder. "The kids are all right." She hollered into the air. "The kids are all right!"

Kate's "Fricking hell!" rose as we parted, hugs and clasps rippling outward.

Diane cocked her head toward David, her eyebrows up and asking, and I glanced back to see David standing alone, waiting to be invited in.

Chapter 23
Sonya's Release

We spent the rest of the day setting up camp, minus David and Del, who went into town hoping to return with Sonya. It was impossible to avoid the old flush of guilt, knowing I would face Sonya as Mara's child. It was awful, what Mara and I had been forced to do—cut ties completely. For a long time, I mailed cards and letters and small packages whenever I could get to another city's post office. I shipped packages to a Chicago office where volunteers boxed books for women in prison, but there was so much more I could have done. I never stopped, not completely, but I didn't do as much as I should have, not because I didn't care or because I forgot. I went back to school. I took any teaching and editing gigs I could get. I busied myself with my own life. What could I possibly say to Sonya to make that all right?

There were no right words, so I made work of learning about camp.

Kate and Brett had scouted the area well. We were in the sandy center of the state that most hikers and campers passed by for the beaches and big lakes of Michigan's coasts. The trees were second and third growth, post logging, so we had a central clearing and an old two-track that ran along the river and looped back.

Camp, as Mark had mapped it, would have three camping areas, and for each camping circle, we needed one or two bucket toilets. We needed signs, too. Temporary signs we could paint on scrap wood and pound into the ground to direct campers to workshop circles we had yet to organize.

The land was perfect, really. A branch of the North Sable River followed the easy hills, and the young forest was full of what the mystics used to call spirit green, an enchanting mix of the yellow greens of maples and birches with an understory of lime and deep green ferns. I followed an overgrown logging trail toward higher ground and there, among a stand of oaks and pines, I found the perfect place for Climbing School.

Mark and Randy set off to make sure the route in was clearly flagged before they sent directions to all who were coming.

Brett and Kate and the friends who began to arrive lugged water and dug toilets—buckets buried into the sand then filled with compost and peat that each of us would be responsible for turning.

Diane and Tammy and I painted signs, and they filled me in on the Showdown that was Green Cross. Up at the top, at the Straits, the Oil Out of Water people were planning a boat blockade and a fake oil spill under the Mackinac Bridge. There was so much support, especially from the merchants and hotel owners on the island, that they were expecting a hundred boats big enough to withstand the Strait's currents. At west and east cross points, near Manistee and Ogemaw, there would be demonstrations calling attention to future well sites and water withdrawals. And downstate, near the bean field where Sonya and I had photographed that bold, blue perforating gun operating way too close to a farmhouse, they were planning some kind of hazmat suit spectacle.

The main actions—blockades and a tree sit and a pile of rusty cars—would occur at the center of the cross, at Tammy and Del's and Randy and Diane's.

Tammy held her brush in the air as she faced me, her eyes turned up and her mouth tense. "You know what that means." Her heart-shaped face, cheekbones high and golden-taupe, accentuated her dark eyes.

"Kate and Brett?"

She shook her head, a lot, and Diane patted my back.

Under our new Art tent, the three of us painted a large piece of masonite, drilled for hanging at the corners. Diane proved to be quite talented with white shoe polish daubers and a supply of sunny tempera paints. She drew a sun rising over a body of water, the light shining as a cross in the sky, with the words "Sacred Lake Annual Meeting" below it.

"Works two ways," she said. "The church types won't be surprised, and the ones who don't want to be churched out in the middle of the woods won't come anywhere near us." She smiled, and the laugh lines over her cheeks stayed for a good, long while.

We were pounding in our signs for Quiet Camp, Family Camp, and the Late Owl's Camp when we heard Del's booming voice calling. "Jailbird's home!"

It was a long time before Hank let go of his mother.

His skinny legs draped over Sonya's lap, and the two of them pressed their faces together. The rest of us tried not to watch their tears or listen to Hank's whining and Sonya's soothing. All I could think of was Mara having to see young Sonya come and go, weekend by weekend.

Eventually, Sonya walked over to me, and I nodded toward the trees. We left Brett and Kate and Mark standing in the clearing, looking a bit wounded.

"So. You and my pseudo-dad." Her smirk was hard to read. She seemed tired.

"Yeah."

I took her to my spot by the river, around the bend from the swimming hole where the ferns grew hip high.

She gestured to my tent. "You're way out here?"

Only the top of my tent, an orange crescent, curved above the ferns.

"By the river," I said.

My first instinct had been to get some distance from David, from having to hide my feelings or lower my voice whenever Kate or Brett or Mark were near. But I also wanted to be near the sound of water. I found a small grove of pines and ashes, pleasantly noisy trees, and set my tent near the swimming hole, which wasn't a hole at all, but a deep, banked bend in the river where year after year winter melts carved into the land.

Talk started slowly. I made sure she was all right, that the police had treated her well, which they had, she assured me. We sat on the high bank, our legs dangling over water-carved earth. The local cops apologized over and over for holding her, she said, while NorA made a stink about survey flags in a kid's backpack.

"She did it herself," she said. "She knew what she was doing."

The jump surprised me.

She turned to me. "She told me. Exactly. She knew exactly what she was doing."

Out of every possibility I had considered, Mara calmly prepping bottles and walking along, lighting and tossing, is what I had always imagined. Mara was an incredibly calm and stubborn person.

"I know."

Mara had set fire to the canyon on her own.

She had burned down framed houses in a canyon where homes never should have been built, but the feds needed their new ecoterrorist campaign to win.

"I'm so sorry I couldn't do more for her, for your mom."

Sonya kept her eyes on the river and nodded. Her frizzy hair, tied back with a twisted handkerchief, had grown to her shoulders.

"I sent notes when I could. Drawings stuffed into books."

White pines Mara would know were from me. Raw organic cashews, too, and chocolate-covered peppermints, the good kind. I may have been the only person who knew that Mara, anti-consumerist that she was, would occasionally eat the cheap patties. Not that she ever received them. I don't know why I kept sending them.

"Yeah," Sonya sighed.

Yeah. Not exactly comforting.

"I'm so sorry, Sonya. It was awful, not being able to go to her."

She nodded and gestured back to camp. "You think they're okay?"

"We can talk as a group later." Kate would shake herself silly if we didn't. "You can decide how much you want to share."

"Yeah. You too, right?"

I couldn't tell if the shift was sarcastic or meant to sting, so I waited. "Can we walk?" I stretched my hand out to her. "You must have felt angry with us—"

"No." She hoisted herself up and stared at me, hard.

"I was forgetting," she said, and the rest poured out of her. "I could remember her face. Her smile. I have pictures, her growing-up pictures. But something about Hank's baby years, maybe because I was so busy and so stressed, I couldn't remember her voice.

"Her wavy hair. That stuck. Her hair was so big." She tried to smile. "But I was forgetting," she said, as if she was saying something inconceivable. Her eyes reflected deep hurt. "I was forgetting."

I knew that guilt. Having a life busy enough to allow you to forget. "I know," I said. "I know."

"You were close, right? Really close."

I did my best to hold her gaze. "We were so close," I said. "Your eyes are just like hers. They are." The red-brown curls and her smooth, beige skin, too, were Mara's. But Sonya's square cheekbones and the impossibly blonde frizz that lightened her hair, those were Gabe's.

"That's why I came. To stop forgetting."

I squeezed her hand. She let me, then she let go and turned to walk into the ferns.

We walked, silently, for a while. Sonya held her palms open, just above the ferns, and it occurred to me that Mara might be with us. I scanned the lacy green surface, everywhere between the trees, hoping Mara understood. With Sonya and Hank, I would do better.

"My mom always talked about you as a couple. Rebecca and David."

"We were, then," I said, not sure how much we needed to talk about David.

"I was kind of a shit to him." She smirked. "Definitely a problem for any relationship he tried to have. How do you explain a pseudo-kid to a girlfriend?"

"Marjorie liked the godfather idea," I said.

"There were some rough times."

"Sure there were."

"I showed up with a baby at nineteen, looking for a place to stay. He got kicked out of his girlfriend's place pretty quickly."

"I always wondered about Hank's father."

"That's when David told me about you."

"Yeah." Mara had aligned herself with one charismatic mess after another.

"He tried to hit me. Once. Hank's Dad." She looked up. "David doesn't know."

"He doesn't have to."

I wanted to tell her that her hard gazes from across the classroom, her real smiles, those were Mara's too. That whatever we talked about, only she and I would share, if that's what she wanted.

"We were such good friends," I said.

Mara and I, we wrote letters, we hugged and danced together at actions. I showed Mara the big lakes and northern rivers, and she showed me canyons and deserts.

"We met at a summer class in the mountains."

Sonya shook her head. "I don't think I knew that."

"That's how the Four Branches began," I said.

I thought of David meeting Sonya as an eight-year-old, taking her back and forth for weekends at the prison with Mara, becoming attached to a child who was about to be orphaned, and I understood the pull.

We followed the riverbank, Sonya feeling the ferns and me drawing deep breaths from the cedars that leaned over the water.

"I have her journals," she said.

"I always wished she would write more," I said. "She wrote the most earthy, mystic poetry."

"They read everything she wrote," Sonya said. "Everything. Her letters, her journals, my birthday cards. She couldn't tell me about you or the Four Branches. I had to get those stories from David."

Organizing was so much easier when we met as book clubs and passed notes from book to book. Now, anything said or written, every text and post was out there, forever, to be called up.

"Does anyone else know about your mom?"

Mara, a mother. It still made my chest ache.

"Brett," she said. "He's known for a while."

We stepped into the grassy ruts of the old logging road, circling back toward camp.

"She told me something else. 'Never let a man come between you and your sisters.'"

"She told you about that?"

Mara had stood there, telling me she wasn't herself, and I had stood, thinking of David and Mara, wronging me.

Sonya touched my arm. "Maybe David was her way of being close to you," she said.

I couldn't speak, so we walked. "Like me."

We could hear sounds of camp. Dull pounding. A shout for someone to hold a board.

"David didn't break you two up," she said. "It was the canyon and Fen's. She knew. It was your actions, yours and hers, that made it impossible for the two of you to see each other."

It was so good to hear her say so, that a nod and a squeeze of her hand was all I could manage. I wondered if Sonya knew about her father, about tall, square-faced Gabe who had stepped well out of his job role.

"Brett knows you and my mom were friends," she said, "but he doesn't know everything, what you started."

I smiled, hearing Brett's comic "Geez!" in my mind. Then I remembered Brett and Kate and Mark watching us walk off, without them. This was no way to start an action. Turned inside out.

I put my arm around Sonya's shoulder and squeezed her to me. "We have so much to talk about."

"A year's worth," she said.

She bent down to brush her fingers under the reach of a young white pine.

I did the same. We cooed to the tiny saplings with their long, silver-green needles.

Later, when it wasn't so painful to speak, I would tell Sonya how much her voice, on the page, sounded like Mara's.

Chapter 24

Report In

By the second full day, over a hundred people had come in. We hung Diane's Sacred Lake sign and added an arrow to the new Greeting Tent where we stationed Del and Zadie. Rue tended to run around camp, snipping at anyone who sat for too long or laughed too hard. Sometimes the energetic young husky accompanied Tammy and me on a scouting or supply run, her neck stretched between Tammy and the open window.

We put newcomers to work as soon as they pitched their tents and watered up: making maps, building privacy screens around toilets, readying workshop spaces. But as more and more people came in, most with only a day's worth of dried food, how to feed everyone became the focus.

"Who are these people?" Kate leaned into me as we walked camp, tallying supplies. "Even when we went to Randy and Diane's, we brought a cooler full of food."

When I defended them, some of them walking in with nothing but the backpacks strapped to their backs, Kate's real worry came clear.

"I'm sure the rigs are coming," she said. "My sweetie pie drill bit guy is on target. I know he is."

As any event planner knows, first you hope people show up. Then, you hope like hell that the event comes off as you envisioned it.

Eric and Mel and their Food for Peace truck came in just about the time we very much needed inspiration. Eric was honking, Melanie hanging out the side door of the refurbished postal truck, waving her arms and smiling as they drove into the center of camp and parked the bright yellow beast.

Melanie wrapped me and Kate and Del into a hug. She eyed each of us and said, "Thank you. Thank you. We came as quickly as we could."

I had met Eric and Mel years before at another action, and I knew the power their bright yellow truck would have on us, how much we would come to appreciate the bold blue earth painted across its back doors.

Eric had started Food for Peace when he was just out of school. His premise, he said, was simple. "People who are too busy surviving can't change the world."

Melanie was a bit more cynical. "That's how they want it. If feeding ourselves occupies our minds and what we do with our hands, people have no time to stand up and fight back, no matter how bad things get."

"Food is on!" Eric shouted an hour later. He and Del stood with their arms around each other, ready to serve our first hot meal. Melanie hugged me again. "Have to feed your kids. They're amazing!"

What was happening in camp, for the most part, was amazing.

Randy and Diane formed a transportation brigade and spent the day picking up travelers coming in by bus and train, a few from as far away as the East and West Coasts. David knew many of them, so he joined Del in the Greeting Tent.

He winked and told me he had dipped into petty cash, code for a generous donor who had paid for their travel.

The Marcies came in clumps as Kate had promised. "We'll know the Marcies right away. No worries."

Kate and Brett had been traveling to Ohio and Pennsylvania, learning from activists working against fracking in the Marcellus

Shale. In Pennsylvania, where the industry's private security forces tracked anyone who registered for a public meeting, security was a priority.

"People living on the Marcellus Shale," Brett told me, "they're a hardscrabble bunch with a good sense of humor, but they don't appreciate anyone messing with their privacy."

Every one of the Marcies, whether they came in alone or introduced themselves as a pack, gave the same introduction.

"Marcie Ann." A short, round-faced woman curtseyed. The older woman standing with her introduced herself as "Marcie Bea."

Later in the alphabet, when a newcomer introduced himself as Marcie Lee, the Marcies quickly hollered out, "Taken!" and the sandy-haired young man looked at his boots for a moment then smiled. "Well then, Marcie Mace."

Whenever someone walked into camp on their own, seeming a bit overwhelmed, we tried to find a common friend or organization they had come to support. There was always a place.

"My family's farm was almost bankrupted by the Great Springs fight. We're still struggling. We can't take another water grab," one middle-aged woman told us. "I know Pearl."

Pearl and the Water Coalition, the grassroots WC, was famous for taking on a bottled water conglomerate and winning. Pearl continually lifted our spirits as much as Food for Peace's bright yellow truck.

The WC had won their case with protests and blockades and continuous court battles, a group of teachers and nurses and farmers who were still together, selling music CDs and winter socks, organizing craft fairs and music festivals to pay off a decade of legal debts.

"It's ridiculous that it takes that much money to win," Pearl would say. "Hundreds of thousands. A million. But we won."

Late in the afternoon, Randy brought in a group of young people carrying serious backpacks. One of them, a tall, muscular young man whose forearm tattoos resembled the frond-covered ground and trees all around us, introduced himself as Sky. "Born and raised here," he said. Before the night was over, he and Brett were playing their guitars around the Late Owl's fire and planning a two-person lockdown at Randy and Diane's.

Who was climbing into the trees and who would lock clips inside metal-rodded PVC pipes was confirmed. Kate was going up, and Brett and Sky were locking down.

David introduced several new people as Green Watch types, acting on their own.

River was a tall young woman with auburn hair and amber eyes that were absolutely river-like. Her name would be hard to forget. She had been involved in seaport blockades and banner drops. "Quite the climber," David said. "You'll like her."

"Of course." Sonya plopped down next to me with her plate of food. "He keeps telling me that I'm grounded, but he's bringing in all of his old climbing buddies." I stared, too long, at her clay brown eyes. "What?" she said.

My biggest surprise was the door-sized man who came in at dusk, just as we were finishing off a delicious meal of lentils and tomato sauce over rice. Hot food in the middle of the forest.

"Levi?" I saw his tall shape bend and rise as he came through the trees. Sonya looked at me and then back at David. David and Levi shook hands, then pulled each other into a hug.

The last I knew, Levi had married and moved away from Fen's. He had taken a job at a migratory bird refuge in southern Indiana or Illinois. What I didn't know until after Levi and I had hugged several times and pulled our chairs close to talk, was that his wife, Carrie, had died a few years before. Another woman from the rust belt who developed ovarian cancer in her thirties.

Levi stood at the edge of the crowd we had become, lifting gear bags. Cheerfully, he called out, "Green sky at night, fractivist's delight."

"Our green sky guy!" Kate bounced over to him and gave him a big, noisy welcome.

"How long did it take you to come up with that one?" I teased him as we sat close.

"Practiced all the way up here."

Levi had always come up with the corniest sayings, like the Benten Bully Catcher at Fen's, a maze of cords and nets that hung up Benten's SUV when he came racing in to give orders and found himself wound up in the flimsy entrance gate his crews had erected.

"I can't believe you're here," I repeated as we moved about, cleaning up after dinner. Levi, with the same close-shaven hair and green eyes. Happy eyes. He picked me up in a bear hug, and I squeezed him back as heartily as I could.

"Levi's quite the supply guy," David said as we pulled chairs around the fire at dusk. "If anyone needs a special tool or some crazy new gadget, Levi's your man."

I watched everyone gather under the Big Tent, the one we had tack stitched together from several tarps. Some sat in groups, extending their hands to welcome others in. A few lingered near the edge, wondering where they belonged, and I wondered about their lives. Were Lakes and Leah, Kate's Marcie friends, sharing an apartment a mile from a Pennsylvania or an upstate New York college campus? River had to be a rafting guide, and what about Sky and all those forest fern tattoos?

The problem was, I knew Kate and Brett and Mark and Sonya. Goofy and grumpy Hank. I knew their lives beyond camp, which had me thinking I had one last chance to pack them into my hatchback and get them to safety. But what was safe in their world? The wind had stopped whispering. Winter was screaming in and melting back. The drought-baked West was either burning or flooding, and the Great Lakes were continually mentioned in water withdrawal schemes.

I watched Kate and Brett talk through last-minute plans. Mark set the Michigan map with the outlined Green Cross on the easel and adjusted it, just so, and I felt a deep sense of pride. They were doing what felt right.

I motioned to a woman about my age, with hair about as brown and shoulder length too, and invited her to sit with me. She smiled and unfolded her chair. Sonya and Brett leaned into each other. I squeezed Levi's hand, and with that, site reports began.

"Pep will be talking about the Straits," Mark motioned to the map, "where Lake Michigan and Lake Huron meet under the Mackinac Bridge. That's the location of the aging tar sands pipeline you've heard about. Line 5."

Mark let the groans pass, then he moved to the west and east points of the cross, framing the strip of land that ran across Michigan's north woods from lake to lake. "We'll hear from Pearl about the theatrics they're planning at new well sites in Manistee and Ogemaw counties. Down south, there's a frack well in the middle of a farmer's field, and all around it, a series of deep injection wells are going in."

Apparently, as fracking and pipelines and processing sites grew in the north, the southern section of the state was to become fracking's dumping grounds.

He stopped at the center of the cross, calling it the "Heartland," site of the Super Frac and in just a few days, a whole lot of action.

Kate and Brett passed out maps that named tribal lands and state forests. "All of the actions will take place within state forests, the commons," Brett said. "But even more important, we've got the tribes' backing. The northern treaty tribes."

The courts should go easier if we stayed on state land, land the public had an interest in protecting.

Brett promised more on treaty history later and introduced Pep, a young woman with noticeable freckles and wavy dark hair. She listened with an open smile and a great deal of energy.

Two teams, she explained, were assembling on each side of the Straits—one gathered on the northern shore, the Upper Peninsula, and the other to the south, in Mackinaw City. "We've got a confirmed count of over one hundred boats, and if the current is calm enough, we'll be up to twice that count if smaller boats join in." The Straits team would launch a fake oil spill under the bridge, rolling out strips of a dark, slimy mess.

"All natural, of course." Pep moved about as she spoke. "The idea is to keep the spill spreading. We'll start by placing floats under the bridge, then the boats will come out and expand the spill, like a real spill, but harmless. A very special eco slime."

A young man who introduced himself as Art talked about the Art-In they had planned, where they would paint signs and make the sticky-looking oil spill that would roll out from spools. The real "ooh" and "ahh" moment came when Art talked about the banner drops they hoped to complete from the huge cement rounds that supported the towers of the Mackinac Bridge. Amber-eyed River stood and waved as he explained.

"We're hoping to plant River and her team on one of the cement pads for a banner drop that will be really, really tough to remove."

I had gazed at those huge cement rounds myself, thinking about how wonderful it would be to descend from Big Mac's catwalk and sit, high above the Strait's gorgeously purple-blue water.

"Whoever takes on those banners has to be ready for arrest," Art said. "If we get River and her team up there, we'll have two mayors and the governor plenty pissed."

I asked about Werckz. "Is Werckz was still showing up at meetings and wooing the women of the north?"

Pep smiled. "Oh, we've got plans for him," she said. "The northern groups have recruited him to lead a puppet parade in Mackinaw City."

They had given him detailed instructions for starting the parade exactly where the tar sands bearing Line 5 rose from the sand and curved into a valve station before it sank under the water and extended across the floor of the Straits.

"We'll get coffee for Werckz and his gang, make sure they're all set, then we'll drive right back and put our boats in the water, just before sunrise."

David was baffled. "Who's Werckz?"

I explained Werckz's presence at meetings, the way he continually slipped up on his personal story, and the biggest indicator for me—his too-perfect pictures of frack well sites.

We allowed David to repeat some of our initial thoughts. "He could be shifting his story purposefully."

"He could be." Pep nodded and smiled.

"Could be an ex-insider."

Pep gave David one more nod. "The good thing is, there's so much support for shutting down Line 5, we're not even sure we can get all the boaters who have volunteered in the water."

A collective "Woo-hoo!" went up and Pearl stood next, laying out plans for the real parade. Zombies would take over two new well pads at the west and east ends of the cross.

I smiled Kate's way, and she wiggled. "Gotta be a Zombie Walk!"

We had dreamed of such a walk, a walk of the chemically dead.

"Protestors in hazmat suits will hold signs and hand out literature," Pearl said, "and we have news crews coming to each location.

"The idea is to keep our Zombies on the berms as long as possible, so when the police arrive, the Hazmats will form a blockade and keep them busy.

"Basically," Pearl summed up, "we'll accentuate the poisoning of the water, the excessive water withdrawals. The usual stuff, theatre style."

Brett stepped in to help as a geologist from one of the downstate colleges put up a large poster of Michigan's southern fault lines.

The geologist asked us, "How many of you felt last May's earthquake?"

Our first significant earthquake had come from the region at the bottom of the cross, where A-1 Carbonate wells had worried people from the beginning. Nearby fault lines were on a path with Palisades, a brown-listed nuclear plant that had been problematic since the day it went online.

I was home the day of the earthquake. I had just grabbed my first cup of coffee and sat outside on the patio, and I felt a wrinkle of pressure moving toward me. There were three distinct waves, stronger as they neared, then a buckle kicked up under me and shuddered on.

I had felt, immediately after, what Diane and Randy knew all too well, the sadness that settles in when home becomes unrecognizable. Water you're afraid to drink, air that makes you sick, land that sends up warning creaks and groans.

"Michigan has major fault lines in the south," the geology professor said. "So, at the southern point, we'll talk about the earthquakes that follow these deep injection wells, and how the nuclear plant sits right in this path."

Brett gestured to the center of the cross, explaining the absurdity of the Super Frac to come, destabilizing two shale layers simultaneously.

"That's insane!" someone hollered out.

"It is insane," Brett said. "What is sane is our reaction."

"We're going to come at this from the outside in," Kate said. "We've got some pretty special local plans at each site." She bobbed and smiled.

A rather short older woman with a skirt that fanned out like her graying hair, Mary Claire, gave a quick report.

"We'll have a circle of Dancing Grandmothers at each of the Super Frac sites."

Mary Claire was one of Kate's keep-in-touch-no-matter-what people. "She's a badass wise woman," Kate had told me. "And she's got a posse of pissed off grannies. Love, love, love to see the cops mess with them."

Mary Claire explained that they would be each site's first line of defense. "If any of you feel inclined to sing and sway with us," she said, "no dance skills required. You don't have to be over fifty, and you certainly don't have to identify as female. We've got scarves and skirts of all shapes and sizes."

A chuckle went up around the tent, then Mary Claire grew serious. "We'll learn some songs and chants, and eventually, we'll split up into arrest and non-arrest groups. With enough of us ready to be arrested, we can hunker down a bit more purposefully for Kate and Brett and Sky."

Frank extended an arm to Mary Claire as he stood. "It's shameful that a group of peace dancers, grandmothers, would get arrested, isn't it? Anishinaabek women, Water Protectors, are the backbone of the movement. They always have been."

He told us about the land we sat upon, where we were in terms of the lands seceded in the Treaty of 1836, and why what the DNR was doing—leasing to oil and gas without recognizing the tribes' rights to co-manage treaty lands and protect water—was not only wrong but also in violation of several agreements.

"Human and sacred," Frank said, "and protecting water is a long game, generations long. Of course, we don't expect NorA to listen, so we'll train observers." He held up a neon green National Lawyers Guild hat. "Free hats." He playfully demonstrated the hat's wide, bendable bill, then snugged the hat over his head and stood, arms crossed. "Tough look. Bright green hat. Official gear of Legal Watch."

He held the pose for a moment while we chuckled, then Mark introduced Diane as the spokesperson for State-Rudmond, Heartland North.

She stammered at first, apologizing for her lack of diagrams or a fancy plan.

"Our plan is simple," she said. "You might call it 'use what you got.' I don't know how many of you know the Twin Lakes area, but basically, we're a dried-up tourist town. Half the businesses around the lakes are closed."

She paused and smiled. "But we've got a lot of rusty old cars."

A hoot went up from the crowd, and her smile lines deepened.

"We've got a whole lot of rusty old cars, some just frames, half of them with engines, and we've got tow truck drivers ready to drag them out of the woods and pile them up on that long, banked curve that leads to the well site."

"Fucking poetry," Mark smiled. "Fucking poetry."

"Yup." Diane grinned. "We're going to show them some rural folk creativity."

Randy continued, "And when they call to get those cars towed out, none of the wreckers in town are going to respond. They're going to have to call wreckers from sixty miles away."

Randy reviewed the current state of the well site, passing some pictures around.

The last time I'd been at the lake house, I had sat up from sleep with the word "murder" pushing up through me. I had missed the fracking stages that came after. Now, the site looked like any other site in waiting. Three huge rust-colored condensate tanks and a series of coils sat off to the side. The wellhead had been restored to its regular height, with three red wheels locked loosely together with a chain. I always wondered how effective those chains were, with spray-painted directions running up the side of the well pipe: *23 turns, 1 ½ back, open.*

Brett announced that they had a name for their part of the action, but that name would remain secret until the centerpiece was revealed. "A really big fucking centerpiece," he chuckled to hoots and hollers. Across the tent, Sonya wasn't smiling.

Brett and Sky were going to lock down to a wellhead that NorA had plans for. Kate was going to be strung up in the trees to try to prevent them from drilling the new well behind Tammy and Del's, and Sonya knew exactly what such actions brought.

I tried not to look tired when Del stood to talk. "Let the legal efforts be successful," I told myself. Frank had a friend from the National Lawyers Guild coming in. But what good had that done for preventing other pipelines or frack well sites?

"At the south end of the Heartland," Del grinned, "me and this team of badass women are going to show the man what time it is. And it is ass-kickin' time."

Kate bobbed and shook, telling everyone that Del was their "kick-ass front man."

"My Marcie besties will hoist me up in a hammock," she said, introducing Lakes and Leah. The two young women were inseparable, one of those couples that made everyone smile, always intertwined and smiling as they walked. They opened their arms to Kate and took her in as their middle.

I turned to lock eyes with David, and he shrugged back. They were going to string Kate up, rather than put her on a platform? Effective, yes, but dangerous as hell. Smiling Leah and seemingly more serious Lakes better know what they were doing.

"We're going to need some stubborn unruly blockaders to help our dancing grannies slow NorA down for as long as we can."

"So there it is, people," Kate said, shaking her hands at the sides of her face. "We're younger and older, darker and lighter, we're from all over the gender map. As someone really smart says, 'We're coming together, not becoming each other.'"

The saying had been mine and Mara's, a wish for the future from a time not so long ago when men stepped out in front of women and the media reached right past us to designate a man—usually a white man—to speak for any action.

But here in camp, after morning and afternoon trainings, they would gather in circles to talk about racism and gender issues and creating a post-colonial world. They were doing better. I hoped Mara knew.

Kate threw one last nod to Levi. "Levi the light setter. What do you need?"

Levi stood, and in his low but gentle voice said with ease, "I could use three or four on my team. It would be best to have some experience on a motorcycle or an ATV. Tracking and GPS too, but I've got all the gear. I can train anyone to use it."

Randy called out, "We've got three bikes and two quads."

"Well," Kate bobbed, smiling, "you plan and you plan, and then the shit just happens."

We had always said if we could bring the people we'd met across the state together, we'd have everything and everyone needed to give NorA a good, hard time. Kate was right. The shit was happening.

"Welcome to the happens part, people." Brett smiled a full smile and stretched his long arms out to the signup sheets, inviting everyone to place themselves on a team. "And if you aren't sure where you want to end up, come ask us." He nodded, and Report In was adjourned.

After Levi met with the young men and women who would be his light setters, I grabbed him by the elbow. "Come on. Let's go get you set up by me."

"Not so fast, Teach." Kate clumped up behind us.

It was clear that she didn't know how to feel about Levi. She nodded and pursed out a "hey" his way, then turned to me. She was after the details she and Brett and Mark had been left out of.

"We're all here." She turned to gesture back to David. "Get this shit out of the way."

She agreed to give Levi and me an hour to set up his tent and get our asses back to the circle. Kate and Mark, Sonya and Brett and Hank, and David too, had set their tents close. I had wandered off into the ferns.

At least now, I'd have Levi. We locked arms and walked to his truck, Levi taking steps my size, and we traded "can't believe its" along the way.

Chapter 25
Elizabeth Stone

L evi and I walked hand in hand, promising ourselves that after the "Stone" talk, after my former students found out about Fen's and Caleb and the Four Branches, the two of us would go back to the high bank with a few cold beers.

Levi set his lawn chair across the fire from Brett and Sonya and Mark and Kate, leaving me to pull up between him and David. Hank draped himself over Mark, and Del and Tammy and Randy and Diane formed the rest of the circle.

I had planned to start with what we often called in literature, the "accidental activist" or the "unwilling hero," though I was, of course, no hero. Our initial group of four hadn't planned to become a center of impassioned action for Earth.

That was the start I had rehearsed. But when Brett swung his guitar into its case and he and Sonya both turned to me with their eyes full of support and connection, I said, "Yes, I was Elizabeth Stone."

It was surprising, still, how much people assumed that we, the original Four Branches, had done. We had done very little. We showed up where the action was and wrote about people like David and Mara.

"There were four of us, originally. We met at an environmental literature school in the east. Me and Mara, Sonya's mother, and Kyle and Ken.

"We came from schools across the country to work on writing projects. Like a naturalist's version of a study abroad program.

"The eighties were rolling into the nineties, and so many of the protections that had been put in place were in danger. The Clean Air and Clean Water Acts, wetland protections, the sanctity of public land. We were there to study environment and law and the growing attempts to alienate the public from regulatory agencies like the EPA.

"We bonded, especially me and Mara, and we talked, constantly, about how writing and music and art made the environmental movement what it was."

"Art sustains the revolution," Mark said, quoting a phrase Kate had written on our classroom whiteboard.

"Exactly."

"We talked about the need for journalists to dedicate themselves to environmental problems. That's how the Four Branches came in."

"Oh," Kate cooed. "Got it."

"Journalism as the unofficial fourth branch of government," Randy said. "The ultimate watchdog."

Diane smiled. "How old were you?"

"I was twenty, basically. We were all undergrads."

"Like us," Brett said.

I nodded. "Your history, the way you all met in class, is a lot like our start." Which was exactly why I worried about influence. I had to be sure I wasn't living vicariously through their camaraderie.

"The original idea was simple. We would write, monthly, sharing what was happening in our places. Ken had the East. I had the Great Lakes, everything in the middle and on down to the South. Mara covered the Southwest, and Kyle the Northwest. My job was to collect it all."

"You're running the Four Branches?" Mark shook his head like Kate did when she was having trouble grasping something she had heard.

I laughed. "I edited the website, once we had one. So did Ken."

"At first, we mailed paper copies. We put up notices in bookstores and took out ads in magazines. And it just grew.

"By the late nineties, we had a simple archive on the internet. Research links mainly.

"We created the Four Branches logo, got more serious about inviting other journalists and citizen researchers to send us their news, and by the late 2000s, we were well aware that we were being watched.

"The site got pinged and dumped every Thursday and Sunday, like clockwork."

Mark grinned. I had given him hints about website security, saying I had learned this or that from the techs at the college.

"At that original summer program, one of the visiting scholars was a futurist. He talked about the next wave being paid-for journalism. Advertisers were going to control content, and we couldn't believe it."

"Hah!" Diane scoffed. "Believe it!"

"Ken called the guy an extremist. Why would anyone let journalism get sold?

"But the more we studied with this guy, the more he made sense. Some heavy funding was pushing the anti-regulation movement and everything that followed. Anti-environment, anti-woman, anti-public workers.

"The goal was simple, really. Four Branches would be a clearinghouse for protecting the environment, to help people connect. The way it blossomed was way beyond anything we started."

"The site," Randy said. "That's why all the laying low. All they'd have to do is follow someone like Stone and they could take everybody down."

I checked on Sonya to see how she was doing. She was listening, intently it seemed, chin down and eyes up.

"What's with the name?" Brett said. "Why Stone?"

David leaned forward and smiled. "Our own bag of rocks," he

used to say, teasing me about my habit of picking up stones as I walked. When neither of us wanted to talk, we'd say, "My own bag of rocks."

"I pick up stones."

"Seriously." Mark's voice was flat.

Kate threw up her hands, cackling. "She does! I've seen it. I've totally fricking seen it!" She pranced, mocking me. "Every time we went out. Every fricking time! Stones all over the car."

Tammy patted Del's leg and sent me with a strong smile of support, her eyes and her heart-shaped face lit by the fire. "Tell us more about Elizabeth Stone. Explain to us what she does. What she's done."

I shrugged. "I watch and get the word out. I used to."

"Bullshit," Levi said. "You should see her climb."

"You can climb?" Kate blurted out. "Like, ropes and all, fricking climbing?" She slapped the arms of her chair. "You can climb and we spent two years bellying around in the dirt?"

David dipped his eyes toward me, uneasy.

"I can climb," I said. The memory of Caleb's body cooling between Steph and me, it could come back in an instant.

I sensed everyone go still. "I can climb. But a climber died."

For years Caleb came to me in dreams, and I would look to his forearms and know, again, seeing the dark purple undersides of his flesh. "Caleb. He loved beech trees."

I felt Levi lean into me.

"Rebecca?" Tammy spoke carefully. "We don't understand."

"I'm sorry. I'm doing this all out of order."

Other than Levi, I'd never told anyone about that morning when Steph and I brought Caleb down from the trees.

"Can I start over?"

"There's no order," Randy said, and around the circle everyone made some gesture of patience, so I started over, looking at Kate and Sonya and Brett and Mark.

"I can climb," I said.

"The Four Branches grew and we started to travel around to action camps and meetings. I met some really good climbers, and I trained with them."

Every summer for years, I trained in the forests of Minnesota, in the Adirondacks, and once in the scariest yet safest place of all, among the incredibly responsive redwoods of Northern California. Rescue climber. That was my role, whenever I showed up with my gear pack and a camera. Climbing went well with writing.

"Fen's was a significant wetland," I said. "The locals were proud of it and involved. Colleges from all over sent researchers."

"It still is," Levi said. "Thanks to what everyone did there."

"There was a tree sit and a blockade, a series of actions like you're planning, and a climber died under my care."

"What do you mean?" Kate leaned forward.

"I had trained him. Caleb. All the climbers. He was young, late twenties, and when he died, everything got more risky. The Four Branches was being watched at that point. We knew that, so we didn't try to hide. I showed up at Fen's as Elizabeth Stone. Stone, the Climbing School leader."

Levi gripped my knee and explained. "But when one of our climbers died, someone had to accompany him out of the action, take care of him."

"His heart stopped when he was up in the trees," I said. "I didn't want him to go to the hospital alone, so I went with him. I spoke to the police as myself, Rebecca Walton.

"Which meant, inside the action, there were a lot of people who were going to know that Elizabeth Stone and Rebecca Walton were one and the same."

I turned to Sonya, and she gave me a flattened smirk and a gentle nod.

"The best thing I could do for everyone was to leave and stay gone."

Across the fire, Tammy and Kate were holding hands. Brett's face was open and sad, and maybe a little gratified knowing that I had had good reason to hold this story back. Del seemed absolutely wounded.

"Rebecca?" Tammy's voice was gentle. "How did he die? Caleb, the climber?"

"He had a heart defect, which we didn't know about. An aneurism."

"An aortal aneurism," she said. "Then you couldn't have done anything. The climbing didn't cause it."

"No." I looked down and felt Levi's hand on my back. Unlike Mara, I wasn't built of so much mettle.

"But the article." Sonya sounded as if she just realized what I had done. "You put out a *Stone's Throw*."

"Yeah." Admittedly, that was a bit stupid, locating an old-school Fourth Brancher in the middle of Michigan. But honoring Hettie and Merle had seemed so right in the middle of the night.

"It's been years," David said. "No one thinks it's the same Stone."

"That was the feeling of the new editors," I said.

"We're safe," David said. "But some of you can't touch any action." He pointed, deliberately, to Sonya. "You." He leaned in to meet eyes with me. "You," and "You neither, Wizard," he said to Mark.

So Mark had been named. When it came to tech and communications, he was quite wizardly. Mark and Sonya and I would follow the story.

I could tell Brett was thinking. His eyes changed, and he and Sonya walked over to me and lifted me into a hug. Sonya's hug was so firm and lasted so long that it took all my determination to hold back tears. "It's okay," she said, and then Del's big arms wrapped us all up until Hank started to squirm and Mark gave us the out. "You know this shit kills me."

"Fricking A!" Kate shook, and I laughed. Sometimes Kate was so eighties.

Diane stepped back. "So what do we call you now?"

"I'm still me," I said. "Rebecca. Beck."

"Well that's good." Diane laughed. "Because I'd fail miserably if I had to learn a new name and keep my mouth shut."

Del shook my arm. "I always knew you were holding out on us." He looked from Levi to me. "So we're on the up-and-up here? Levi's just Levi?"

I smiled. "Levi is Levi."

Kate bobbed. "Well, you best haul out that harness and join my fricking team."

"You can run Climbing School, here at camp," David said, "but no action." He looked at Sonya. "You neither."

"Whoa, Daddio," Kate frowned.

Levi stepped in to mediate. "An original Fourth Brancher would be a crazy happy target for NorA."

Brett's gaze softened. "Everything that happened at Fen's, years before. That's why you didn't tell us."

Del threw an arm my way, teasing. "Looks like you'll be hanging with us in the Com Tent. Me, Zadie, Sonya, and the Wiz here."

I swore Mark blushed.

Brett picked up Hank as he whined and brought him toward Sonya, the kid tired and probably overloaded with our adult drama. "Come on, Hankster," Brett said. "Let's get you to the tent."

Brett leaned Hank toward me for a hug. "Night, Hector," I teased.

Del stretched toward him for a high five. "Give it up, little man."

Randy appeared at my side. "I remember Fen's," he said. "Damned DNR. The DEQ too. It's all rigged."

"Do you think I should leave?" I asked him.

I trusted his response. He knew how being outspoken could get you watched. "No," he said.

"Maybe I should offer?" I started, but he cut me off.

"Hell no."

Chapter 26
Doing Dishes

David came up next to me at the dishes station and put his hands into the cool, sudsy water. "Hiding out at dishes, huh?"

I felt comforted by his soft noise. So much of my personal life was missing noise. No pets, no partner, no housemates. Teaching had made me quite the solitude seeker. But in camp, I found myself, my body really, falling back into warm old habits the more David and I were near each other.

Thank god for Levi! I heard my own voice so loud in my head that I stared into the dirty suds (there was dirt everywhere!) fearing that I had said something out loud.

David's hand on my forearm brought my gaze up from the dish tub.

"You okay?" he said. "I thought the talk went fine."

His eyes were soft. Welcoming. What did I know about him anymore? How could I gauge any look? "The dirt," I said.

"The dirt?"

"It's everywhere."

He looked puzzled.

Sonya had told me about one serious relationship between David and a woman who lived on a houseboat. I tried to tell her that she hadn't caused the breakup, but she assured me that she had.

"I was thinking about the tenacity of the dirt." I swirled the suds aside, and David leaned in to look. "See what I mean? Even on the dishes."

Levi had broken every rule by coming to visit me the week after Caleb's death. I was still staring at walls, rehearsing, over and over, every climbing session. No shortness of breath. No dizziness. Caleb's complexion was so fair. Who would have known if he was unusually pale?

I had felt life leaving Caleb's body the way trees release their cool moisture, and his vapor had stuck with me. I felt it on my skin, in my lungs. I needed something to take its place.

Levi and I, we never talked about those three days we spent together. So much had gone wrong and we were such good, good friends.

"Beck?" David was close. He let his hand rest on my lower back. "They'll be okay. We'll all be okay."

I let the plastic plates in my hands drop under the suds, and I threaded my arm through his. We were standing there, head to head and rubbing each other's backs, when Sonya walked up.

She and I had been hiding out at the dish station a lot.

I released David, patting his back. "So. The Straits are coming along."

Sonya smirked, her head low and her eyes turned up as if to say, "I see what's going on."

"Oh, yeah," David nodded to Sonya. "River's going to be fine."

Sonya walked on with a flip of her hand, and David and I continued to talk strategy. River and the more experienced climbers were confident they could get to those huge cement bridge pads. They'd been scouting, David said, so he was leaving the banner drop to River.

Kate's team would require a lot of rope work. I was working with Kate and Lakes and Leah, practicing for things that go right and wrong, and David planned to settle in at Randy and Diane's with Brett and Sky.

David brought the best jail support, which I was sure Sonya

appreciated. He and Frank would do everything in their power to keep Brett and Sky safe. Still, stopping a drill rig from setting up, that was serious interference with oil and gas.

I had managed to slip in one quiet talk with Brett, when the two of us strolled in together, late for lunch.

"I know the risks," he had said. "We've got Frank, and the NLG, and the neighbors' support. We'll be looking at some jail time for sure."

Public support meant everything during the action. It could color media reports too. But when his case went to court, the law mattered, and so did the judge.

Brett and Sky would clip their wrist chains inside reinforced PVC pipe, and as Sky said in blockade training, "Once we clip, we're in your hands."

Locking down was a matter of complete trust. Trust in those who would make sure Sky and Brett got water and finger food. Trust in Legal Watch and the Dancing Grandmothers as a first line of defense. Trust in the blockaders who would chant and cheer as tow trucks painstakingly cleared up the pile of rusted old cars from that wide, banked turn that led to the State-Rudmond well site.

I had one, maybe two more days with Kate and Lakes and Leah, on Kate's ropes, so to speak. Lakes and Leah would be there, in part as a ruse to keep the police from cutting Kate down. They would claim that the lines they tended were the tree sitter's only support. Kate would be harnessed and clipped to the transverse above them all, but getting cut down was still a jolt. Mostly, Lakes and Leah were there to keep Kate motivated and to make tie-off runs with food and water. If she needed rest, they could take her place.

We moved the dishes to the rinsing tubs, watching Sonya stroll past the fire circle.

David said it first, throwing a shoulder in Sonya's direction. "She still doesn't like the idea of you and me, does she?"

I shrugged.

Over the breakfast dish tubs, Sonya had let her agitation fly. "Frankie and David. Where are they going to be a week from now? How are you hiding it? You know how this is going to end."

When I reminded her that Kate and Brett had sought out Frank's help, and David had come because she called him, she had walked away from me too.

But I understood.

David brought fresh pails of water, and I changed the tubs out. We rinsed in silence.

Kate wasn't without complaint either, watching David's effect on the guys in camp. "They're fricking smitten," she said when we caught sight of David and the boys, as Kate called them, in training. "Fricking bromance!"

We were throwing anchors and coiling rope, something Kate was surprisingly good at, and I could tell she was getting antsy. She had gotten embarrassed by how scared she was to slide that second foot out to cross the open space between the trees and her waiting hammock. So, I brought them all back down to the ground to throw anchors and pull rope, and we tallied new arrivals.

My *Stone's Throw* and David's network had brought in a dozen or so seasoned activists, but by and by, the people working in each action group had come because of Brett and Kate. Another handful of Marcies, more Dancing Grandmothers, and a lot of locals showed up with tents and signs, ready to protest.

Old locals too. To my and Levi's delight, the superintendent and her husband who had worked with us at Fen's strode in that morning.

The retired superintendent's hair was short and graying, and her husband seemed to have shrunken a bit toward her height, but they both grabbed Levi and me by the hands. "Kickin' 'em in the shins," she said, smiling. The saying had been a favorite at Fen's, our statement of perseverance. Both of them joined the Dancing Grandmothers.

"It's not just who you bump into," Kate said, inspecting her rope, and I finished the saying, "it's who you stay in contact with."

Kate gestured over her shoulder to David and Brett and Mark, role playing with the blockade line. David was giving them tips on how to stay calm and keep the line together when the police started to bark and reach in to pull people apart.

"I guess things got all turned around with you and him."

I nodded, seeing Brett's obvious attraction to David. Mark's too. David had a way of making people want to please him, and for the young guys, that usually meant trying to impress him. Thankfully, David knew enough now to push that prove-it shit out of the way and get them to focus.

Kate stepped close. "Sorry about me mouthing off when you first got here. They had my bestie in the county jail, you know? And Hank was a hot mess."

"It's okay." I gave her a shoulder bump.

She shook her hand toward David. "He does tend to take over, doesn't he?"

"He doesn't mean to." I sighed. Fresh into the knowledge that he had been there for Sonya, for Mara too, it felt right to give David a break. "He lights up, and that makes people want to find that switch, you know?"

"Oh, they're feeling around for it all right," Kate bobbed.

I laughed louder than I meant to and David looked toward us, nodding. Kate shuffled her bag. "Bromance is getting old," she scoffed. "Even Marko. Look at him!"

We had a good chuckle watching Mark's face as David looped his arms around both Mark and Brett, demonstrating the correct way to lock elbows. Mark, whose aloofness was easy to mistake as disinterest, was concentrating on David's every word and nodding expressively.

"Wonder how that's going to work with Sonya and Brett and all,"

Kate huffed as we picked up our bags and walked. "Sonya's not so keen on Daddio."

My chance to ask about Brett and Sonya had come up. "So they're a couple now, Sonya and Brett. Official?"

Kate shook and nodded.

"And you and Mark?"

"Not so clear on that one." She turned to the trail. "Kinda weird, isn't it?" She shook her head in David's direction. "With him on the scene, we're all shacking up."

I threw my arm around her shoulder. Kate, as much as David, had a way of drawing hugs. Shaky, little, strong-as-shit Kate.

"Just so you know," I said, "there's been no shacking up on my part."

I was feeling pretty good about being off and away, tent to tent with Levi.

Chapter 27

Bad Day in Camp

I was standing under the trees, following the tie offs from the oaks, visually checking each knot and rehearsing how Kate's entry into the hammock should have gone, when I heard Tammy's voice.

"How's climbing?" She smiled. She was carrying first aid bags and obviously didn't have time to stop, but all of the worry and nervousness I had felt as Leah and Kate swung on the ropes, all top heavy and refusing to listen to me as I told them, over and over, to loosen their knees and sit back—an entire day of worry came out at Tammy in a jumbled mess, and I could tell by the expression on her face that my rant didn't make her feel any better. There was so much work to do!

Lakes and Leah hadn't held the ropes with equal tension, and instead of communicating to fix it, they both overreacted and sent Kate over the edge of the nylon. Thankfully, Kate had grabbed the cloth and rode it down, squealing, until she hung there in her harness, and after a long minute, all three of them laughed so hard I had to walk off so they didn't see me laughing.

"They're giggling," I whispered to Tammy. "They're giggling, and NorA is coming."

"They know." I wanted to believe Tammy's calm, knowing eyes.

"No. They don't." I gestured to the path winding away from the trees, where Kate and Leah were still lying on the ground, laughing. "Listen."

At least Lakes had the sense to walk about, testing ropes, checking the transverse lines, trying to get it right. She looped her ropes and barely acknowledged me as she passed, heading for Kate and Leah.

"Damn it," I whispered to Tammy. I hadn't meant to make Lakes feel bad. Laughing it off was good, sure, but they needed to be steady.

In those few seconds as I watched Kate drop down off center and I knew the nylon was going to flip and throw her out, I was terrified, facing that feeling that I may have put someone else's well-being back in my hands when I swore never to do that again.

"Maybe River or one of David's crew should be doing this." I yanked on the rope hanging before me.

Tammy tucked her chin. "You don't mean that."

"I do." I yanked the rope again. "Maybe I do."

NorA was coming, and messing with the big guys' image wasn't well tolerated. Those golden sunbursts and green leafy shapes, the American flag waving with lasting power, so much depended on that image, and Kate and Leah were lying in the dirt, giggling about their mishap with the cross ropes while Lakes was pouting. And this was only an exercise. When Kate was truly hoisted up on those lines, Lakes and Leah had to know exactly how to handle those ropes.

"We need to go back to the house," I said. I needed to get back on site, under the actual trees.

"Come on," Tammy said, her voice low and soothing. "We'll go back. But right now, Del's cooking with Eric and Mel, and you and I need to grab a cold drink."

"I can't," I said, scanning the lines from the hammock, the grab line above. "I've got to run them through again, figure this out."

Tammy called to a young man heading to the first aid tent and handed off her supply bag, giving him her list of instructions. She held up a diagram labeled "Sprains and Strains." The paper caught the hot sun, and her permanent marker drawings gleamed. Eighty degrees and full sun, up north, in October. Every breeze that ruffled the oaks and pines and the younger maples and birches was welcomed. I watched the leaves behind Tammy and the young man flutter, the silver undersides of the maples flickering.

I took a deep breath, feeling as if I should say something reassuring to Lakes and Leah and Kate. Something like, "You'll get it, don't worry."

Tammy held me by the shoulders, like Del, her eyes serious and her tight grin purposeful. "They'll be focused when they need to be," she said. She eased the ropes from my hand and pulled me along the trail. "We'll be there for them. They know that."

I kicked my boots forward, enjoying the spew of dust. If I had to, I'd lift Kate up myself.

Tammy hugged me tightly. "They'll pull it off. We'll make sure of it."

Later, after receiving one of Del's long-armed hugs and sharing a beer with him, he made it clear that he knew exactly what I was feeling. Of course he did. He had witnessed the students and teachers of Detroit going up against a system rigged to make them look like the problem.

"I can't even go out there." He gestured toward Climbing School. "They're up in the trees, jackassing around, and my alarm starts beeping and Zadie starts whining. The minute I see those girls up on the ropes, I'm a goner.

"But they have to stand their ground, you know? Because this fucked-up ground we're handing them is going to be theirs a lot longer than it'll be ours."

He leaned close. "I know. The law and their favorite buddies are going to be here soon, and we're going to be watching from the Com Tent."

"Drink," Tammy said, and the three of us, with Eric and Mel pulling up to join us, clinked cups and did as we were told.

Del put on a big smile. "To the vital role of communications."

"Let's go back to the house," I told Tammy as we scraped lunch dishes. "I want to get another look at the distance between the trees."

My thoughts were, if we shortened up the ropes and were able to tie off two lines for each corner of the tripod, those lines could be a lot more stable and easier to traverse. Two ropes weren't always better than one, but in Kate and Leah's case, they would be. Lakes, clearly, was feeling my worry, and we needed our best climber to feel good.

We could lower the upper guideline so Kate could hold on just above her shoulders. We could create a latticed step rope. If we had to, we could run strips of wood so Kate could feel something solid.

Tammy sent me back to afternoon Climbing School with a reassuring push, and I walked, picturing a tiny fence that Leah and Lakes could roll across the tie offs. As soon as Kate was in, they could pull it back and hide it in the trees.

Chapter 28
Better Day in Camp

It worked. It was all working. Hank showed up for lunch splinted and wrapped for a broken forearm and a sprained ankle, injuries he had faked for First Aid trainees. And twice that morning, Leah and Lakes had rolled out the rope walk we created for Kate, and Kate had shakily but successfully made her way to the hammock without tipping. What had ever made me think shaky Kate would traverse a twenty-foot-high line without shaking?

"It's what I do!" Kate teased as I told her to keep her guide rope close to her chest.

When she went down to the nylon on one knee and then the other, she swung and whooped, but at that point I was ready to whoop with her. We all were. Lakes smiled and Leah let out a huge, "Katie-Did! Katie-Did!"

"That's exactly how it's going to go on site," I said, loosening the rope around my thigh to glide down.

Our second day was bringing good reports from everyone.

The Marcies brought in a nurse and a physical therapist from Youngstown, so Tammy was feeling prepared for both well sites.

Frank and the National Lawyers Guild attorney who came up from Detroit had their group well prepared. As we stood in line for lunch, we heard their recitations.

"This land is protected under the Treaty of 1836 and United Nations Article 32. You have no right to extract resources without tribal permission.

"The NLG strongly advises you to allow the tree sitter to come down of her own free will.

"We demand the right to observe!"

Hank came around at lunch, asking for signatures on his temporary cast.

"Aunty Becky?" he said, holding up a choice of permanent markers.

I pulled hot pink and drew a heart edged in red, with a bold blue vine trailing away. "To love and solidarity!" I wrote. Hank rolled his eyes.

Camp was feeling good. We had a system in place—morning circle followed by school and workgroups. After lunch, another round of trainings until dinner, when we reviewed progress and welcomed new people. At dusk, there was time for music and fun.

The main canopy was slowly being trimmed in braided twigs and lights. Everyone who came in added what they could: folding tables, chairs, a bottle of homemade peach wine. We had become a community.

David caught Hank and asked for the black marker. Next to my heart, he wrote "Ditto Schmitto," and Hank belly laughed.

"Hey." David plopped down in the chair next to me. Even the way we were talking sounded comfortable.

"Hey," I answered.

"A lot less tense today, isn't it?"

"So much better." I let out a long, slow breath. "Kate got into her hammock twice without incident. Not sure if I want to push for a third."

Blockade training was going well. "I'm hollering at them and yanking in for real today, but they're holding it together." David smiled. "They're starting to slip new bodies in."

The Dancing Grandmothers were moving through their songs, working with David on an outward-facing circle that would be able to flatten, switch directions, become a running ellipse or a figure eight. The line of mostly older women and a few men with scarves looped over their belts was working on some serious shape shifting.

"We're having fun, actually." David nodded and chewed. "Doing good."

All morning as we ran through Kate's set, we could hear the chanting and the singing, and occasionally, David's fake harassment.

"We could hear you." I smiled, thinking of the squealing we had heard following David's barking. When the police lost their patience and started prying people apart, it never hurt to cry out in pain while your partner screamed, "You're hurting her!"

"It's a time warp, isn't it?" His eyes lit up with a look of pride and amusement that wasn't yet tainted with worry. Sonya wasn't going up in the trees or locking down.

"Frank and the NLG. You think they'll be able to keep the charges down?"

"Sky and Brett?" he said, and I nodded.

"Kate too," though it would be tough for them to make a resisting arrest charge stick once they cut her down with everyone watching.

Across the clearing, under the shade of some scraggly jack pines and the flicker of young birch leaves, Sonya and Brett were leaning against each other. Brett smiled and told some story with his hands as Mark walked up to add to it.

Smart, sensitive Brett. Why was it that the kindest ones ended up in the toughest spots? I'd seen it happen so many times.

"We had a good ear, all the way to the top," David said. "But now? The forces of dismantling are building. I know Frank will fight like hell."

When I asked Frank if he would stay in camp, he had chuckled, "Hell, no. None of that sleeping on the ground for me." We had walked to his truck and patted each other's arms a quick goodbye. "I'll come and go from Del and Tammy's," he said.

David switched gears, calling out to Mark, "Come out and tape us this afternoon!"

Mark turned to give David an exaggerated thumbs up.

"Will you cover them?"I asked David. Meaning, would he put his legal team on Brett and Sky and Kate if they needed help. Rally his donors?

"Of course," he said, looking as if I had insulted him, but then he smiled and waved Mark's way.

After dinner, good news continued to blossom. Tammy had two first aid stations and a pair of medics for each site. Mary Claire and the Dancing Grandmothers demonstrated their moving dance line, and we were all impressed. Any one of them could call for a change in shape and direction, and somehow, they all shifted. The blockade teams marched in for dinner trying out chants. We were getting comfortable with the routine and our roles. I was even getting comfortable falling asleep to Levi's snoring, though a couple of times each night I had to call out, "Levi, turn over!" and he'd grumble and quiet down.

When Kate left the evening fire abruptly and came back jumping and whooping, it took a while to calm her down.

"It's official," she yelled up to the sky. "It's fricking official!

"My sweetie pie drill bit guy!" She held up her phone in a crazy dance of fire-lit energy. "He just called. He just called!"

She took a deep breath and bobbed. "Two Redding 120's packing up early tomorrow morning, and he just got word to put his drill bits on a trailer and head up tomorrow.

"Fricking hell!" She stilled with the realization. "They'll be here in two days."

We would have to be in place, ready for action, the night before they arrived.

"This is it, Teach." Kate and I walked arm in arm, talking quietly after camp had erupted into a good, solid cheer. She jiggled her phone. "Time to make shit happen."

She and Lakes and Leah and I gathered for a quick hug and pep talk. "Oh, I'm going to make your shit happen tomorrow, all right," I said. "You all better get some sleep."

"Tonight?" Leah whined. "Everyone's celebrating."

Lakes looked at me with raised eyebrows.

"In your tents by midnight," I called after them, as if I had anything to say about it.

Diane huffed up, making a good show. "Well, that wasn't mother hennish at all!"

Once they were out of sight, she bent down as if in pain. "How are you doing this? They're killing me! Come on. Tammy and Del and Randy and you and me, we're going to worry this out together."

She threw her arm around me in a gruff hug. "And yes, your boys can come. Already invited."

Chapter 29

Report Out

After lunch, Tammy and Diane and I set out to scout both well sites. David and Frank and Mary Claire were going to gather everyone together for a serious talk about lining up on arrest and non-arrest sides of each action. No sense doing something in a moment of passion that you hadn't fully considered.

We had had another successful morning of Climbing School. With action day looming, Kate and Lakes and Leah had been quite serious. Lakes told Leah and Kate as she rolled out Kate's rope ladder, "We have to be able to do this when things go right or wrong. Stay focused."

Tammy was quiet as we walked from the back of her and Del's property onto the smooth, dry well site behind them. She'd seen the array of vats and tanks and metal coils, the diesel motors and light racks at Randy and Diane's, but for over a year the well pad behind them had remained empty, waiting for the rig that never came.

"Until now." Tammy sighed. "I'm sorry." She reached out to Diane and they hugged, a wrap of summer-rich taupe and pink freckled arms, Tammy's smoothed dark hair and Diane's blonde fray. "I know I shouldn't be so selfish," Tammy said. "We've seen it all at your place."

Anywhere a frack well pad went felt wrong, but for Kate and Brett and me, Tammy and Del's felt especially wrong. Del was already suffering.

The limestone had been freshened and groomed, and in the afternoon heat, white dust rose as we walked. Bright red and blue battery cars sat in one corner, and there were stakes and conduit pipes sticking up everywhere, prepped for the compressors to come.

Sometime in the next twenty-four hours, a stream of trucks would bring scaffolding and the drill housing and the sharpened bit that would transform the land forever.

The trees around State-Miralette were mostly pine—fields of tall, rather branchless red pines that had been planted by the CCC after logging. But forest succession had also brought birches, maples, and those scruffy jack pines. Along the access drive, where we needed stable branches, we'd found a beautifully healthy white pine and two thick, strong oaks. I stood under them, thinking they must have been saplings, adolescents at most, to have survived the last logging. They'd grown up together.

"Come on," Tammy said as I stood under those trees, listening, looking, checking the ground again. A tree sit made sense here. Kate would hang over the access drive where we stood, preventing any trucks from getting to that flat, groomed square now covered with limestone.

The State-Rudmond site at Diane and Randy's was bustling. NorA was returning here, replacing equipment that had been loaded in before, so they worked fast.

From the sandy two-track that led to the house, I photographed truck after truck bringing in all sorts of tanks and vats. They lined huge plastic chemical vats along the periphery, and parked the tall blue glycol tanks and orange drilling fluid trailers near the wellhead. We were standing on the berm when a semi hauling the natural gas tank that would power the drill drove a broad circle around the limestone, then backed the tank along the wooded side of the berm.

Between arrivals and drop-offs, Tammy and I paced out measurements between equipment, and Diane recorded our counts. We wanted to bring back accurate information about our entry points and the working space we would have between fixtures.

Already, the grime and scents of oil and gas had returned. The air felt heavy with diesel and sharp with vinegar.

"All quiet so far," Diane reported, bringing Tammy and me some iced tea.

For all her nervous jitters the night before, Diane was all business now. She and Randy had people watching the truck route.

"We'll know the minute they turn off the expressway," she said. The rigs were due to arrive the following morning.

The three of us stood gazing at the red wheels on the wellhead.

Before the light of morning, Sky and Brett would thread their pipe through the chain and those wheels, making it impossible for NorA to get started.

Report Out went well, once Kate and Brett got everyone hushed.

"Places, people. Places," Brett said with the biggest grin on his face. "I've always wanted to say that." That got us smiling.

Levi and his crew were heading out to check the lights and test the timers.

David and Brett and Sky were heading to Randy and Diane's to spend the night at the lake house, and Lakes and Leah and Kate were packing up for Tammy and Del's. Sonya and Mark and I would set up the Communications Tent at the edge of Tammy and Del's property. Excavators had taken down the pines beyond their property line, leaving an abrupt edge where the oaks and maples and youthful white pines of their backyard met scraped, leveled land, so we would have clean sight lines.

Pep sent a trusted friend from the Straits to let us know that River and her team were set to go, and Art's creative crew had the oil slick spooled and ready. Over a hundred boats were ready and waiting. That brought up a cheer.

Werckz was safely stationed at the pipeline on the Mackinaw City side, where there would be no parade. They had given him a false launch site and time, just in case he called in the troops before they got the boats in place.

Frank had eyes that were dark and serious one moment, and bright with a grin the next. He looked up, serious now. "When we speak of a spiritual relationship to land and water, to the need to heal our relationship, our voices are sidelined. Ignored." He shook his head. "So we speak in legal terms. About the lack of consulting with the tribes. About treaty rights and consent decrees. About the public trust, and how we have a duty to protect water and Earth, but still, the well sites and the pipelines come. So we act."

He squeezed Brett's arm and nodded to Kate and Sky.

"We're ready. Ready to support Brett and Sky and Kate and her team." He held up a lime green hat. "Remember, you'll have a legal team on each site. Have to say it here, for jail support."

Kate raised her chin, smiling. "This is how people power comes back, people. Place by place.

"To the heartland!" she called out, and the call went up from the crowd.

After making cleanup rounds with Sonya and Mark, making sure we left no trace among the maples and birches and the high tufted pines, I went to my river spot, gazing upriver where the shade of brush and trees gave the river bottom a coppery green tone. Such a beautiful, typical, northern Michigan forest floor. I held my palms over the ferns as I walked the old logging road toward Del. Time to take down the Greeting Tent.

We were moving from the can-do comfort of camp to the

adrenaline-fueled power of standing together in action, with just one more night to go.

David and I packed the makeshift canopy that had shaded our meetings and sprinkled the night with a hodgepodge of lights. We were standing close, bringing the folds together, when Sonya and Brett came to tell us that Randy had arrived, ready to take Sky and David to the lake house.

They ducked back through the cedars, giving us a private moment.

"If I end up getting arrested," David said, "Cal will be able to get me out quickly. Brett and Sky too. Don't worry."

Frank's mention of jail support had sobered us.

I frowned and he added, "If NorA pulls any serious shit, I'll jump in."

"I'll worry about Kate then," I said.

"Me too," he nodded.

He opened his arms for a hug, and I let my face rest on his shoulder. "When this is over," he said.

"We'll figure it out," I answered.

"We have an it, then? To figure out?" He looked at me and smirked.

I was about to tell him that he had smirked like Sonya, when Sonya's voice wafted through the cedars. "They're ready for you, Pops."

David's face changed. He wanted Sonya's approval, her belief in him, so badly. He pulled Sonya into a hug, and I could see in her tight smile that she cared.

"Hank's at the truck," she said.

"Let's go say goodbye together," David said.

The two of them moved through the cedar boughs. David turned to smile and wave before they disappeared behind a wall of deep purple-browns.

Chapter 30

Green Cross

The radios were silent. Cell phones nearby. True darkness had fallen.

Del and I were sitting under the Com Tent, staring at the dark well site, and I was thinking, best-case scenario, Kate would come down on her own and get off with trespassing, and Brett wouldn't get more than thirty days in jail. The spectacle of the oil slick in the Straits and the Zombie Walks on the big lakes would do the job of drawing in public support. But these were bests.

The solar lights that Levi had set up for Lakes and Leah and Kate began to glow, sending subtle blues and greens, and where they blended, the softest purples into the trees. A cool pine breeze rippled the canopy above Del and me, and we watched bands of blue and purple move like waves of water through the trees.

I was tempted to radio Kate, to get her out here to see the lights, but she and Lakes and Leah were inside where they needed to be. I set the radio back on the table and caught Del's attempt at a smile.

"You're used to this feeling." Del gestured to the site. "The night before."

"I don't think the feeling ever goes away."

His eyes were shining in the lantern light. Del was such a crier. "Feels like we should be yanking all the young folks out of the trees and climbing up there ourselves."

"Hear, hear," I said, raising the cup of caffeinated tea Sonya brought before she and Tammy and Mark went back to the house.

Zadie whined, and we both reached down to give her attention. She still got all out of sorts when Del didn't go to bed at sundown. I cupped her chin and said into her pale blue eyes, "What do you know?"

"I'm proud. Proud as I've ever been," Del said, "But every damn ounce of me wants to get them the hell out of here before dawn."

Randy and I had discussed doing exactly that. He had come to me, asking, why not have us older folks go up in the trees and lock down? Let Tammy and Diane and the kids provide support.

I had talked with Brett and Kate, with all the climbers, and David had prepped the blockade teams.

"If you're doing this for any reasons other than your own, you have time, right now, to decide if those reasons still make sense. Each of you. Think about the risks. Are the worst of the risks worth it to you? Only to you.

"If, at any time, you decide that you can't be the one, no one will think less of you. Walk away or stay. Every single one of us will be here for you."

Zadie whined and pushed her snout under my hand.

"I had a talk with everyone," I said to Del.

I made sure to address their decisions in groups and with each of them, separately, though Kate's talk had not gone so well.

"You giving me the walk-away speech, Teach?" she had snickered. "I know this one, you know."

"It doesn't matter how much you know it." I tried to be calm, but she was making it difficult. "You have to live it."

"Oooh. That's deep."

"Damn it, Kate. You want me to send Del to you instead?"

She'd gotten serious then. Downright pouty.

"No." She looked at the ground, then back up at me. "Fricking hell, no."

"So," I said as we both held the harness she was about to clip into for run-through number three on our last afternoon of training, "think about it, tonight. Look around and ask yourself if you're caught up in the fun, if you're doing this for Del and Tammy or Randy and Diane.

"Because you know how this ends. You're going to come down alone."

Finishing alone was the only truth. Hundreds of people can cheer you on, send money for supplies, risk a slap on the wrist for running over a berm and squirting water into your mouth, but no one can get sent to jail or stand trial for you.

"They'll cut every last person away from you," I said, looking straight into her eyes. "And even though we'll be there, hollering and chanting and throwing obstacles their way, you'll be on your own for a while."

Kate had looked at me, her chin forward and bobbing until her bangs shook. "I know the bastards' game plan. I've seen it a few times."

Del shook his head. "Damned Kate."

"She knows what she's up against," I said to Zadie and to Del.

Del and I watched the breeze send waves of color through the trees. "Damned fireball Kate," he said.

He stood, telling Zadie to stay as he put one of his long arms around my shoulder. "Zadie's good company. Keep her close tonight."

Zadie stayed, but her eyes were on Del. His tall form wavered toward the house, and she half sat, squirming.

I whispered to her, "You can go after him if you want, girl."

She tipped her nose up to me, demanding a hug. Together we watched Del step into the house. Tammy reached out to guide him over the lip of the slider.

Zadie let out one sharp, instructive "Yip!" and Del disappeared inside.

"That's a good girl," I said, ruffling her neck. "He's off to bed."

—

My phone vibrated, and Zadie growled.

It was David. "Your girls in bed?" We'd been joking about our girls' and boys' sites, though gender orientation had nothing to do with the planning. Literally, the ease of peeing into a urinal and the weight of the tree sitter were paramount.

"Everyone's been put to bed here. How about the boys?"

"Randy and Brett are still playing."

I had a vision of Diane's off-tempo table slapping. "Oh, boy."

"Yeah," he sighed. "Is Sonya okay?"

Mark and Sonya and Hank were in the house, sleeping, hopefully. They'd end up on watch if we made it to a second night, and we wanted to keep Hank away from Randy and Diane's. Tree sitting was intense in its own way, but a lockdown was visually grueling.

From the house, I caught a whiff of laughter and heard Rue's yip. Tammy was coming out to join me.

"Hey," David said, and I turned back to the trees around the site, smiling at the metallic appearance of the leaves. "I meant what I said, when this is over."

"Yeah." I tried to keep my phone close, but I had the feeling Tammy understood the nature of the call. "When this is over."

We hung up when I heard Diane call out, "Bedtime, lover boys! We gotta be sharp come four a.m.!"

A surprised "Oh!' came out of me when I looked up to see Tammy's face framed with dangling braids.

"Don't say a word," Tammy said, sitting in the chair beside me and passing me a cup of coffee. Her usually pulled-back hair had been decorated with ribbon and yarn. A thin braid hung down from each side of her part, braided with delicate cloth ribbons, and her bun had been replaced with a gathering of twists and braids and beads that caught the light.

"Leah and Kate." She tried to frown.

"It looks great," I said, smiling with her.

They had been trying to convince me to let them braid ribbons into my hair, but I had the excuse that I needed to keep my hair safely tucked away, for climbing.

"They promised me they would go to bed. I tried." Tammy nodded toward the house. "Kate's in there dying her bangs."

We laughed and drank strong coffee.

"You were right," she said, squeezing my arm. "Watching is the hardest part."

We didn't wake Del when we saw the Green Cross. There wasn't time, with all of us transfixed on Mark's screen as he brought up satellite imagery of our earth, turning slowly.

I whispered to Tammy, "The lights of the Bakken." A diffuse golden ellipse rolled past, then the glare of Chicago, then fainter but seeming to brighten in contrast to the huge black lung of Lake Michigan, was our own beautifully huge and subtle Green Cross.

Levi had done it. He'd done it! Again.

We cheered quietly, squealing into our hands so we didn't wake Kate and Leah and Lakes. They'd be in the trees in just a few hours.

Mark and Sonya saved the image and posted it on the website. I sent it to Ken, to everyone. We were silent as Sonya typed the caption.

From the ground, to the trees, to the stars
For the water, for the animals, for the bedrock below
We shine in solidarity
Green Cross

Mark leaned back. "Let's hope the stars are listening."

"Time to call Thompson." He nodded to Sonya. "Let the media coverage begin."

Chapter 31
Day of Action

Kate was lying in her hammock, breathing deeply with her eyes closed, when I noticed two young deer below us.

I had made the journey with her, gliding along a transverse line tied to the white pine that hung over the access drive, following as Kate laddered down from Lakes's oak. It was intense, sliding toward a hammock hanging in midair as you wobbled down ropes that held the cloth taut, but she made it.

I had looped the temporary rope and was about to take it to Leah when I saw the young female deer looking up from below, standing where the blue-white glow of limestone fell off into the red of pines.

"Don't roll." I grabbed the edge of the hammock as gently as I could.

Kate opened her eyes and scoffed. "I'm not moving a muscle."

"If you can, take a peek. Company," I smiled.

Lakes noticed and cooed silently.

Kate clamped her hand firmly over mine.

"I'll keep you steady," I assured her.

The young deer stretched their necks to gaze back at Kate and we all forgot, for a moment, that we were doing anything but cooing at two young does whose haunches were just beginning to fill out.

"All good up there?"

Del's voice boomed from my radio, and Kate slapped down into the fabric. We swung, together, as the deer kicked up their front legs in unison and curved their long necks back into the trees.

"We're good," I radioed Del. "Update in ten."

"You'll get used to the swing." I gave Kate's arm a squeeze. "You did in camp."

"I'm good," Kate said without opening her eyes. "Good-good-good."

She was higher here, suspended on longer ropes, so I had run an extra hold line above her. I placed her food and water pack alongside and slightly above her, where she could easily drag it across her chest to peer inside. Her waste bag, complete with the bedpan Diane had decorated for her, I set on her other side.

"You want to use it before I head down?"

Part of the reason we'd put Brett and Sky on that awful grating at Randy and Diane's was that it would be much easier for them to use a urinal out there, in plain sight, and still find some privacy. That, and Kate was just under one hundred twenty pounds, the lightest candidate for a suspended tripod.

"Hard part's over," I said, looping the extra rope and nodding for Leah to take it up.

Kate released her breath in a calming stream. "Yup. Hard part's over." Her bangs looked lavender in the early morning light.

Sometimes, having someone watch a brave act was more nerve racking than the act itself. I prepared to let go, telling Leah and Lakes to hold the ropes. Del and Tammy and Sonya let out a cheer that got picked up by the protestors and blockaders gathering at the end of the access drive. Mark stayed on the ground for a while, talking to Kate, and I went to work anchoring fake supports.

When NorA and the police came in, it would appear that Kate had been raised up and was supported by the poles that I brought up under each edge of her hammock. For effect, Mark and I ran ropes from the poles and staked them into the ground, good and deep, creating a web of supposed support across the access drive.

Lakes and Leah would convince NorA that to cut any of those lines or to pull out those poles meant Kate would free-fall. The ropes that actually held her were tied off and knotted under Lakes and Leah.

The Dancing Grandmothers hugged and patted me as I called up a temporary farewell to Kate. "Going to check on the boys for a bit," I said. "Del and Sonya are in the Com Tent. Mark and Tammy and Frank are on Meet and Greet, out front with the blockade."

"Tell Marko to keep the video coming." Kate's voice boomed from my radio, and I turned down the volume, handing it to Mark. "Tell him yourself."

I left ropes looped for both Lakes and Leah to send down to me so I could get up fast if I needed to. Lakes and Leah would lift food and water and haul down waste. When NorA stopped us on the ground, as they eventually would, the support team would run supplies in, clipping bags to the supply ropes so Lakes and Leah could haul them up.

I stood where the two young deer had been moments before, coiling my rope into my bag. A climber's ropes were sacred. These would stay with me.

The bustle and noise of a lockdown was so different from a tree sit. Standing at the edge of the sandy two-track across from the State-Rudmond well site, it took me a moment to step into all that color and noise.

David handed me a megaphone and had me announce that everything was a go at Heartland South. "Tree sit accomplished!" People held up their hands for high fives and patted David and me on the back as we passed through their cheers and chants.

For the most part, the only sounds in the south were the voices of Mark and Sonya and Leah keeping Kate company, as well as the nervous radio checks from Del. State-Miralette, for now, was cool with pine scent and a breeze that crackled last year's oak leaves.

At Heartland North the well pad was bright with voices and

shaking signs, and the sun reaching over the trees made the chunky white rocks around Brett and Sky sparkle. We were due for another eighty-degree day.

Brett and Sky demonstrated the spin of the PVC pipe, showing me how they could knee-up from their cushions and walk on their knee pads over the covered grating. They were equally tall, so their knee walk around the grating was smooth. They walked a 180 and back, grinning. The thick plastic and moving blankets, I thought, might get awfully hot over that metal, but it was better than breathing in whatever poisons wafted up from the greasy swill that filled the silo beneath them.

"Check it out." Brett pointed to the symbol painted on either side of the pipe, where metal rods were held tight with layers and layers of duct tape, widening the pipe so it couldn't be pulled through from either side of the wellhead's red wheels.

"Au Sable Sacred" was painted in a peachy red, rimmed in bright yellow, over a map-like blue vein of the river forking north and south.

"Diane's idea." Brett smiled. His hazel eyes were bright under the bill of his hat. "I figured she needed one." Diane and Kate had painted the decal together. "Show it to Del. And these too." He had me take a picture of his "up north" camouflage shorts.

He and Del had become close. "Man close," Kate said.

Sky and Brett posed over a "Ban Fracking" banner, holding up peace signs with their free hands. Brett's short, dark hair poked out from his hat. His thin face looked to be all chin beard and smile. Sky's smile was wide across his tanned face. Both of them were energized with adrenaline. Morning sun colored the limestone around them a faint blue, and I got candids of David and Randy bringing plates of hot eggs and bacon.

I stood on the back wall of the berm, capturing the action in clumps. The support team bustled around Brett and Sky, adjusting their cushions and strapping water camels on their backs. The blockade line was several people deep across the span of the triangular metal gates. Beyond the gate, the Grandmothers were weaving and practicing shapes, a few stepping out to drink coffee or walk over to Brett and Sky to give them long, thankful hugs.

I picked up a stone, a round of peach granite, its red and cream pattern gleaming as the sun rose over the trees.

"Take care of Brett and Sky," I said, my thumb gliding over its hollow.

I didn't ask for care from the pines that were dry and festering with bark sores, or the youngest trees that were leafless and brittle, trees too close to last summer's drilling and fracking. I spoke to the trees that still felt alive and able, older oaks and maples and birches that stood sentinel over the grassy clearing between the woods and the berm, where this year's big-leafed youngsters were bound for trouble.

Just when I thought I was going to have time to get sappy about how good and close and "we got your back" this action had become, my whole body startled and turned to a scream, the recorded scream of Roger Daltry's long falling bridge in The Who's "Won't Get Fooled Again." Diane came revving up the access drive, driving a golf cart with a boom box strapped to the dash. For an outdoorswoman, she sure was loud.

Cheers went up as she circled Brett and Sky in the cart she had labeled "Official Site Spokesperson" on the front bumper and "Vote for Diane—Township Board" on the back.

This was the fun site all right.

At some point, NorA and the state troopers and the sheriff's office would arrive, and these theatrics would happen only in brief stunts. In the meantime, Diane and Randy were making good on their promise: "In solidarity and fun."

I had to cover my ears as Diane stopped to pick me up. "Hop in!"

We puttered down the access drive, high-fiving blockaders and waving with the Dancing Grandmothers as we headed into the banked turn of Woods Road. Diane bopped to the music and smiled.

An impossibly high mound of cars sat stacked across the road and strewn into the sharp gullies. Some of the biggest cars and pickups were tipped over with their hoods pointed skyward.

"Oh my god!" I called out. "I had no idea!" It would take hours, maybe even days for tow trucks to pull apart the mess of car bodies.

"How?" I laughed. "How?" I knew it was going to be big, but the sight of it seemed impossible, still.

"Lot of backhoes and winches around here."

I leaned into her arm and hugged it. "It's amazing!" That crazy pile of cars might keep NorA away!

Diane turned her body to the two-track where the cars had sat ready for days. A single dozer sat parked in one of those dozer push-outs the industry was famous for—push-off points during excavating, when they were hurrying to get all the downed trees and brush out of the way.

She turned down the music. "Well, lookie there. Someone left us a dozer."

I was a few miles down the road from the fun at State-Rudmond when two semis passed by, hauling trailers with bright orange vats. Drilling fluid. I was tempted to turn around and catch the action when they rounded the long, banked curve and saw that pile of rusted metal, but I settled for a call to David, who hung up quickly to get everyone in place.

The noise at the fun site was just beginning.

NorA would know within minutes.

We got word from the Straits that Werckz was traveling around with his buddies, trying to drum up help for the parade that would never start.

River ended up alone on one of the cement pads that supported the base of the Mackinac Bridge's huge blue pillars. I watched Pep's brief video, thinking, I hope River has food and water. Supplies would have been spread between climbers. She could be on that cement pad for a long time.

In the stills, River was beaming, waving in front of the banner she had dropped on the way down. "Now is the time! Decommission Line 5!"

At the Straits, at the future Super Frac sites in the west and the east, especially at the heart of the cross, the anglers, clean energy groups, people from the breweries, and the ban groups continued to arrive, and as the day wore on, a thousand people lined each shore under the bridge. The now notorious Line 5 had drawn a lot of attention after the pipeline rupture that dumped over a million gallons of sticky tar sands bitumen into the Kalamazoo River.

Someone at the Straits organized a traffic stop, and the story was posted on all the online news sites. Hundreds of protestors stood in the traffic lanes at the peak of the bridge span, their signs and their chants vibrating into the air. They lined up along the catwalks between the roadway and the rising suspension cables, dropping banners from the railings. And coloring the water below, a sea of boats rolled out the oil slick that continued to spread with the currents.

"That's right!" their signs read, "Oil Out of Water!"

Back at State-Miralette, we heard the trucks before we saw them, engines gearing down as they turned off the county road and onto the access drive to the well pad. The first few semis rolled to a stop, and the roar of the protestors swelled.

I had my camera on a tripod, and from the Com Tent I watched Frank and Tammy through my zoom. Del narrated what he saw through his binoculars.

"The first guy's getting out of his truck," he said. "Frank's standing out front and Tammy's got the video camera rolling."

Frank and the driver exchanged a few quick words, which we couldn't hear, but again, we heard the protestors roar. The driver shook his head and walked back to talk to the drivers of four other trucks that had pulled up behind him.

"Looks like the dog house," I said, inviting Sonya to take a look. The first truck carried metal framing and sheeting, the platform and siding that would enclose the first two stories of the drill rig once it was up.

"What are they saying?" Mark asked Del.

"Frank's giving them the treaty lands talk."

Several drivers approached Frank and Tammy. The protestors grew quiet, then they burst out with chants as the drivers went back to the first truck and appeared to make some calls.

Del radioed Kate. "Looks like go time, kiddo. You okay?"

Kate bounced back. "Hell yes. Who's visiting?"

"We definitely surprised them," Del said. "A whole damn line of trucks. We'll let you know when our good friends arrive."

Tammy's video confirmed what we figured had been said. Frank told the driver that NorA had no right to set up the drill rig or extract resources on treaty lands.

The trucker in the video slumped. "Man, I'm just a subcontractor. All I know is I've got an order to park this equipment before sundown."   •

Frank responded with his sarcastic grin. "Looks like you're parked right there."

I was hanging in my harness twenty feet up when two DEQ officers and two sheriff's cars arrived. I'd left a climbing rope in a sturdy oak near the access drive, where I could see and hear most of the movement. People rarely looked up into the trees.

The deputies inspected Kate's ropes and took a few pictures. Tammy and Frank stayed with them, and Lakes and Leah called out warnings.

"If you move those ropes, you will endanger the tree sitter."

"You will cause a dangerous free fall."

Legal Watch added, "The Lawyers Guild strongly advises you to let the tree sitter come down of her own free will."

The older of the DEQ officers made several calls while the younger man, "fresh out of college," Del radioed as he watched him get out of his truck, walk along the row of protestors, and scan the blockade.

The older DEQ officer put away his phone. "Frank." He nodded.

"Mitch." Frank nodded back. "I believe you know Tammy."

"NorA has a security team on the way," the DEQ officer said. "They hold a valid lease."

Frank countered, "There isn't a tribe in Michigan that recognizes the validity of their leases."

When several men arrived wearing NorA's red logo on their hats and their royal blue polos, the protestors whooped and chanted. "Hey, hey, hell no, oil and gas has got to go!" Their voices were so loud that Del radioed in from the Com Tent. "Hearing it all now!"

Frank motioned for the chanting to stop, and he delivered his statement to the men in blue and red, NorA's security uniform.

"NorA and its foreign investors have not consulted the tribes on access to treaty lands. There is a higher law, and these nonviolent protestors are exercising the right to protect land, air, and water."

He held up a treaty map. "Every tribe in the state recognizes the sacredness of this land."

"We have a paid lease here," the NorA supervisor began. "Both the DNR and the DEQ have approved work on this site."

"Yes, they have." Frank nodded. "And we have a legal case, all the way up to Washington, that disputes the DNR's leasing of treaty lands.

"We support these protestors." Frank gestured to the crowd behind him, bringing his hands back to the circle of NorA men before him. "NorA is the only trespasser here."

In the roar that followed, I missed what NorA's security supervisor said in response, but his body language, as he stepped toward Frank and put a hand over Tammy's camera lens, was clear.

Del and Mark came rumbling up on an ATV. Mark looked up and threw me a quick shrug. They were supposed to remain at the Com Tent.

The NorA supervisor's voice was loud and firm. "Legal action or not, we have twenty trucks on the way to park equipment, and they're going to park it, today."

"Well, isn't that handy." Del stepped out from the ATV, smiling. "You need a place to park?"

Both Tammy and Frank threw tight grins at Del.

"Got the perfect place. Big parking lot, all vacant and waiting, and NorA pretty much owns it already.

"You know the place," Del teased, and the NorA supervisor glared. "Strip club up at the county road. Big, empty parking lot."

An hour or so later, just before I retreated to the Com Tent, I caught a conversation between NorA and the sheriff on video.

"Now Jerry," the NorA supervisor said to the sheriff, "you know we can't let this turn into one of those damned pipeline standoffs. You need to get some men out here. Now."

By lunchtime, we were watching helicopter video of the bridge teeming with protestors. Police cars blocked both sides and started moving in. The Straits had made national news before; now Randy and Diane's car pile was making the rounds too. As Mark had said when we first heard the plan, those rusty old cars were poetry. Tow truck drivers and mudders alike, using what they had to make a very local statement.

A shot of a single tow truck driver hooking the bumper of an upside-down old Pontiac made Thompson's first report, with clips of the blockade.

"No more boom and bust!"

"Industry out of our woods!"

David told us that Brett had cringed at the possessive implications of "our" woods, but Frank assured Brett that the people meant no harm. It wasn't a claim. It was a statement of obligation, of the duty to protect and preserve a forest that was two generations into its ecological succession.

Diane, on the other hand, fully claimed her right to be the police liaison, insisting on having direct access to Brett and Sky, which the police and even NorA's site supervisor were tolerating, for now.

"What they're doing here," she said as Thompson interviewed her, "purposefully destabilizing the ground, taking advantage of all the riskiest processes to free up oil and gas for what, for an instant? It's insane. NorA won't live with the consequences. The locals will, for generations, and we're united in our response to that."

She eyed the camera and let loose a grin. "And what we're saying, what everyone is out here saying together is hell no!"

The segment ended on Brett and Sky, both looking a bit red and hot in the full sun, but also determined.

With a continuous news presence, NorA was standing around doing a lot of griping, but they weren't hauling people off, yet.

Midafternoon, Sonya and I posted an article with photos of the huge car pile at State-Rudmond, noting that only one tow service, a driver from over sixty miles away, had responded to NorA's and the sheriff's calls, and his progress was slow. The Zombie Walks were a favorite on social media. Zombies walked the west and east site berms and moaned, at times falling into each other and snarling as they stumbled. They created quite the backdrop as Pearl and other spokespeople read lists and side effects of the hundreds of toxic chemicals in a typical fracking cocktail.

The Zombie Walks were so much fun, so impressive in their mood and tone, that I loaded Mark's laptop into a supply bag and had Tammy hoist it up to Kate so she could watch. NorA's blue and red squad had set up a table on the well pad, but so far, they weren't trying to stop Tammy or Frank or the Legal Watch team in lime green hats from interacting with Kate.

Frank came over to the Com Tent to tell me he had a surprise coming, a visit from friends, but he made me promise to keep it quiet when he drove off in his bright blue truck. Sonya and I walked toward the access drive when we saw Frank and three women in long skirts piling out of a van. An older woman with short dark hair swung out of the front seat, then leaned back in to grab a copper pail. The other two carried pails of water as well.

They were Water Walkers, Indigenous women who walked the waterways of the Great Lakes region, stopping to speak with township boards and city councils along the way, reminding the public that we all needed to care for the water.

"Three generations," Frank said.

They had paused their walk when they heard about Brett and Kate and Sky.

"It was a good time to take a break." The older woman, Jan, smiled. She had high cheekbones and smile lines that could rival Diane's. "Good to support these young Water Protectors."

Frank introduced Sonya as Brett's girlfriend, and Jan held up her hand. "Wait here," she said, handing her pail to Frank. "I'll be right back."

Ellen, Jan's daughter, was much taller but had the same wide smile. "We're from the Grand Traverse band," she said, "same as Brett."

The granddaughter, Annie, was tall and narrow, like her mother. Something about the way her long brown hair framed her face felt familiar.

"Ban fracking now," she said, and I smiled.

"The auction protest," I said to both of them. "You hushed the room."

She shook her head. "I was so nervous."

Jan returned, smiling. She must have been seventy or so, yet she was walking waterways, carrying a pail of water. "For your son." She handed Sonya an olive green day pack with a beaded zipper pull. "We heard he could use a new backpack."

Sonya accompanied the Water Walkers onto the well site, where they stood under the trees in their long skirts and tennis shoes, each holding a copper pail, and visited with Kate and Lakes and Leah.

"NorA could get pretty nasty," I said to Frank.

He nodded toward the Dancing Grandmothers and the Water Walkers gathering under Kate's hammock. "We'll just have to keep NorA away.

"Some of our own folks aren't sure about the old ways, the old dances," he said as we watched the women lift their pails to show Kate. "But I know Brett will be glad to see them."

He looked at Sonya and me. "They want to go and see Brett. Then they'll come back here and stay for the duration."

Frank had suggested, early on, that legal action had the best chance of winning at State-Miralette, where NorA had not yet drilled and fracked the land.

"You go," Sonya said to me. "I'll stay here with Mark and Del."

I asked Jan and the others for a few minutes to get in costume, and they laughed, gesturing to the beadwork necklaces that hung over their matching summer T-shirts and loose skirts.

I came back in sparkly jeans, a straw hat, and aviator glasses. Jan smiled. "You've had troubles with the law."

Frank grinned. "Nice hat, Stone."

On the way to State-Rudmond, Jan told me they kept watch on the Four Branches, on all the groups around the Great Lakes.

"We're on Facebook too," she said. "We keep up."

At the well site, Jan walked up the access drive, leading with the eagle staff she carried on their walks. Ellen and Annie walked alongside her, and Frank and I followed. Michiganders had witnessed, with fracking, new and tragic levels of mistreatment of water, and the arrival of these original Water Protectors felt immediately ceremonial, a gesture of unity.

The protestors parted, with smiles of respect and relief. Even NorA seemed to understand. They stood aside as Jan and Ellen and Annie passed the gates and made their way toward Brett and Sky. Their message of responsibility was clear. Water was so heavy to carry.

It was hot, with the Rudmond well pad left scraped and dry for the summer, and NorA had light racks on Brett and Sky nonstop now, even in daylight. Diesel grime hung in the air, the noise peaking as the engines chugged up in cycles.

Frank asked NorA's security team to turn the generators off, but the supervisor, dressed in NorA's blue and red security garb and a radio belt, refused. Without a suit there to make the call, he explained, he couldn't turn anything off.

Jan thanked Brett and Sky for the land and waters they protected. In her pail, she told them, she carried water from the Au Sable, water she had scooped from the river today. The others carried water from the nearby Manistee River and Lake Michigan—waters that were connected, waters that connected us all.

The NorA team looked a bit nervous when the Water Walkers curled around Brett and Sky and Frank and I drew back, keeping them from looking on.

Jan told the story of the Nibi Song. One of the Water Walkers had written a song for the water, and it had become the song of their movement, a song about speaking to the water. She translated some of the lyrics: "Water, we love you. We thank you."

They sang, and the initial call to "Nibi" hung on the air so powerfully that it was the only word I retained. A beautiful, haunting "Neh-eh-beh" drifted over us, and I hoped the others near the gate could hear it.

I was sure the NorA guards couldn't hear anything but the chug of their diesel generators.

The last lines, Jan said, honored the water and expressed respect.

Limestone dust tamped up in puffs around their feet. They asked that no one film them, but Jan requested that I take a few photos when they were ready to pose. Brett smiled as Annie fist-bumped him and Sky. Jan leaned close to say something to Brett and Sky, and they listened, their faces full of concentration.

Heat radiated around them. I hoped Jan was giving Brett and Sky strength, a centering chant or some mantra to ward off the pain and fatigue. Certainly, these women who had carried pails of water along hundreds of miles of shoreline knew how to persist.

The borders of all my photos were filled with scraped, dry land, accentuating Brett and Sky's vulnerability. The strength of the sun felt like an interrogation of everything that was wrong about a frack well site.

"That plastic," I said to David, showing him the steam wavering in my images. "It's getting too hot in the sun."

Before they left, Jan drew close to Brett, and as she spoke, he bowed his head. She rested her hand on Brett's shoulder, and they traded words again, Jan pronouncing and Brett carefully repeating with her help.

"You've been holding out on us," I said to Brett, patting his skinny shoulder. His loose T-shirt was soaked with sweat. He and Sky both looked so hot. "I saw you trading lines. I didn't know you could speak Ojibwe."

He smiled, taking the bowl of grapes (water fruit) and the smooth granite rubbing stones I gave both him and Sky. "Looks like you have too," he laughed. "Great shades."

I wanted to ask Brett what Jan had said, but Brett wasn't a person who needed to be drawn out. He was quiet because that was his way.

I started to turn, to tell David to get wool blankets over that hot plastic or Brett and Sky would be steamed, literally, but I waited because Brett's face was full of thought.

"A prayer for healing," he said. "With the original name for the river."

He smiled. "It was a really long name."

"Wool," I said to David, a few minutes later. Why hadn't any of us thought of that? "Wool blankets over the plastic."

"On it." He got on the phone, calling for wool.

In the wake of all the reverent listening, several people decided to take advantage of the slow moments that followed.

Brett and Sky had been shaded by a canopy all morning, until NorA pulled it up and dragged it away, claiming they needed clear sight lines to the wellhead.

One of the neighbors climbed over the berm and across the limestone, dragging another canopy as the NorA security team watched. Brett smiled and thanked the middle-aged man and the protestors who came to help him hoist the canopy over them. Sky raised his water bottle in thanks.

The stocky, bearded man gestured toward the NorA team. "They're the ones who took out all the trees. This is just too damned inhumane. Arrest me if you want, but these boys need some shade."

Thompson got it all, and so did I, including the NorA security supervisor being interrupted by a call, then quickly turning away from the cameras, refusing to comment.

Diane walked up next, bringing finger food to Brett and Sky. They both seemed to be concentrating, or trying to, on her every word. They looked tired, but then they all laughed and fist-bumped, and Diane called to Randy and David. "Potty break!"

David and Randy came in carrying the "Ban Fracking" banner that served as a privacy curtain so they could pee in Diane's aptly painted "pot to piss in."

The NorA team, seeing Randy and David wrapping the banner around Brett and Sky, ran over, pointing and yelling, and I could hear David state in response. "What more can they do that they aren't doing in front of you right now?"

Randy took off his NLG hat, pointing to the logo and saying something that made David bend back in laughter.

When they came back, I asked what had happened, and Randy said, "I offered to let him hold the urinal."

David laughed. "But then he said, the big guy tends to miss. Watch out."

David walked me to my car, and I chuckled. "What would we do without Randy?" Without Diane and her golf cart and her music? Without Del and Tammy, and now, Frank's Elders and the tribal members who had joined both blockades. The answer was simple. This was a local response to threats to water and home. We could only do this together.

By early evening, stations across the state were airing the snarling Zombies, the oil slick under the bridge, and the fake gas cloud the geology professor and his team had released from the injection well sites at the south end of the cross. People marched through the streets of town wearing gas masks and painter's masks, carrying signs and flags that mimicked the green-yellow-red gas hazard signs posted on well sites.

National outlets aired Diane's "Hell, No!" speech and Frank's call for the US to officially recognize Indigenous rights laid out in the United Nations Article 32. David fielded calls asking for interviews with Brett and Sky and whoever was responsible for the Green Cross. The image of the lower peninsula, crossed by a subtle green glow, had been posted by organizations around the world. The world!

"For some dumb reason," Mark smiled, "we never thought of that."

Thompson's interview with the Water Walkers was being aired alongside the fake oil spill under the bridge, which, with the Coast Guard and the police in boats, wouldn't last beyond the evening.

We expected them to clean up the action at the Straits quickly. What we didn't expect was NorA's departure, just before dark, from both well pads.

Diane and Del and I figured the split up of the convoy had worked to our advantage. NorA had taken Del's advice and sent the trucks bound for State-Rudmond to the strip club's empty parking lot. With a third of their trucks stranded on the access drive at State-Miralette, with several more trailers stuck on Woods Road, and the remainder of their fleet parked several miles away, they needed security in all three places.

At State-Miralette, a typical wellsite security trailer was sitting on a flatbed, trapped between the trucks carrying the scaffolding and the heavy haulers carrying loads of long steel pipes. NorA's security team decided to use the guard shack as it was, loaded on the semitrailer. They powered up the diesel generator and set their chairs on the road below.

Randy and a team left the lockdown at State-Rudmond to make some noise and flash an occasional light from the woods bordering the strip club lot.

"All those eighteen-wheelers and all those tires." Randy grinned. "They better keep watch."

At Del and Tammy's, NorA left only two men at the security trailer. The young DEQ geologist pulled up and stood talking to them for a while, then he walked out on the well pad.

Mark and I both leaned forward.

He stopped under Kate's hammock, tipping his head up toward her.

"Can't hear you," I whispered so Kate would remember to press her speaker button.

"What's the word?" she was saying.

We saw the young geologist turn to look behind him, his tall form narrowing in the shadows spreading across the well pad. Everything was bluing.

His voice came across rather weakly. "No plans tonight."

"You trying to sweet talk me down?" Kate giggled.

"Nope," he said. "Just giving you a heads-up." He stood for a moment, then waved with both hands toward the trees. "Night, ladies."

"Hey." I thought Kate was going to peek over the edge, but she didn't, thankfully. "Thanks," she said. "You've got a tough job."

He turned rather abruptly and jogged back under the hammock. Mark sat forward, listening to the radio in my hand.

"How old are you?"

Mark turned his hands up, mouthing, "What?"

"Hmmm," Kate was stalling. "You first," she said.

"Twenty-six," his voice came back.

Del had been saying, all day, that the young geologist was sweet on Kate. "Sight unseen and she's got that one charmed."

"First DEQ job?" Kate asked.

Mark continued to gesture his annoyance.

"Yup," the young geologist answered. "Two years now." He put his hand on his hip, relaxed, it seemed. He stopped watching behind him.

"You from around here?" she asked.

"The UP," he said.

"Fighting the mines up there," she said. "Sorry if we're making you look bad."

He looked at the ground for a moment. "You didn't tell me your age."

"What the fuck?" Mark said out loud. I had to work not to laugh.

"Probably more than you need to know," she said, her voice kind.

"All right," he said. "All right." He looked up at Lakes and Leah. "See you tomorrow, ladies," and they called back a "Good night."

Mark popped up out of his chair. "I'm going to go see if I can catch him."

"Mark, he might make a good ally." When he kept walking, I called after him. "Kate wouldn't appreciate you going all man-to-man with him."

He waved me off at first, but eventually he turned around.

—

Levi and his crew kept watch from all sides of the berm. The NorA guards had climbed inside the security trailer that sat sandwiched by the long row of trucks. Mark and I walked up and down the access drive taking photos. It was quite the visual: crawler cranes and forklifts, winch trucks and heavy haulers, load after load of those long, rusty pipes. Over a dozen trucks were stranded, unable to turn around. But eventually, no matter how hard we fought, all that steel was destined to be driven thousands of feet into the ground.

In a rare span of solitude, I sat under the tarp of the Com Tent and watched night settle in. The wall of pines around the well pad turned flat and black, their prickly tops resembling fence posts against a beautifully clear aquamarine sky, and I looked toward Kate, hanging over the access drive, no doubt soaking up the moonlight reflected off those white, white stones.

Levi's lights came up, and I remembered that Kate and Leah and Lakes hadn't seen them.

I grabbed the radio. "Kate. Are you moving?"

"Yeah. You see that too?" Kate radioed back.

"Levi rigged some lights for you. I forgot to tell you."

Lakes was on too. "The leaves are shimmering. It's beautiful!"

Kate giggled, then hollered out, well beyond needing the radio. "Levi the Light Setter is fricking amazing!"

"So noted!" Levi called from the far side of the well pad.

Kate and Lakes and Leah played with the lights for a bit, moving the ropes and oohing and ahhing at waves of soft blues and greens. The oaks that were holding them appeared to sway as bands of green and purple traveled through their leaves, and the white pine, with its long branches arching over Kate, appeared frozen at the tips, tufts of needles gleaming like blue ice.

Tammy and I delivered hand warmers and blankets, loading them into supply buckets. "It could get down into the fifties," Tammy said. "Bundle up before you get cold."

Del radioed from the tent. "Zadie wants to stay with you all tonight. She's a hell of a lot faster than I am these days."

"Night, Del!" they called back.

"Where's that Zadie badass?" Kate laughed, and Zadie ran up and over the berm, her back haunches working with amazing speed for an old dog.

Sonya and I settled into watch duty, and Del and Tammy made their way to the house.

"I've got plans," Del said. "Going to sneak in a big girl's breakfast tomorrow."

Sonya and I sat, sipping Tammy's strong coffee. Every now and then, Levi's lights sent ripples of color into the trees, but we had become good at distinguishing between the bounces of small, repositioning moves and the more wave-like sweeps of light.

"Repositioning," we said in unison.

My phone vibrated. "David," I said.

"They're out." David sounded out of breath. Chilled, most likely. "Both of them," meaning Brett and Sky.

"They're out?" I repeated, and Sonya raised her eyebrows. They had faked a potty break, which NorA didn't seem too concerned about, so they snuck in Brett and Sky's doubles.

"We took them up to the lake house for some rest."

I put the phone on speaker so Sonya could hear.

"We're watching Woods Road, the access drive, all around the berm, and there's not a sign of NorA. All but two of them got sent to the strip club."

"Same here," I said.

Sonya seemed wary.

"Randy will keep them busy."

I was about to hand my phone to Sonya when she held hers up to me, Brett's name on the display. She stepped away with a gentle, "Hey," and I heard Brett's low voice vibrate, "Hey."

"She doing okay?" David asked. "Hank too?"

I had given Hank a ride up to see Kate after dinner, once we were sure NorA wasn't going to return. He paid close attention to every detail, to the eight, to the way we had to wrap and unwrap the rope around my thigh as we transferred our weight for our slow glide down.

"Top-notch student there, Teach," Kate had bobbed.

Hank had fist-bumped with her before we descended. "Kick some ass," he had said, and Kate had promised. "Giving it my best, buddy."

David hung up and Sonya came back, quiet. I put my hand on her arm. "Go up to the lake house," I told her. "My keys are in the car. I'm not going anywhere."

She stared at me, debating.

"Go. I'll let Hank know."

"I'll be back before breakfast." Her hug was firm. Happy.

I called to tell David she was on her way, and he laughed at me. "Where the hell is Stone the hardass?"

Levi and I fell asleep together on the cot, hours later. We were exhausted. Neither of us had slept during setup night.

I woke to the sound of Brett's voice, hollering out in pain as NorA thugs dragged him away from the wellhead, his arms bent behind him at an impossible angle, and I sat up to find Tammy above me.

"Morning," she apologized, holding a carafe of coffee for me to see. Her tiny, ribboned braids hung down toward me.

I was dreaming. "Levi." I flipped over. He was gone.

I heard Del's voice and realized he was sitting in one of the chairs, his back to me. "Long gone," he said. "Checking lights. You sacked out hard, Teach."

"Sorry." Tammy handed me a cup of coffee, and I went to take a sip but stopped. "Kate?"

Del jiggled the walkie-talkie in his hand. "Girls already had breakfast. Mr. Sweet-On's the only one back so far."

Tammy frowned. "Del, give it up."

"Oh, oh, oh!" He sat up. "Look out. He's coming for morning coffee."

Tammy and I turned to watch as the young geologist strode up the access drive, headed toward Kate's hammock.

"Watch this." Del grinned. As thin as he had become, at six-foot-five with broad shoulders, he was still imposing when he stood up with purpose.

The young geologist had almost reached the hammock when Del told Kate to key in and he spoke into the radio. "Anyone touches a hair on that sassy little blonde's head and they're going to have me and my vicious dogs to deal with!"

Zadie and Rue, hearing Del's booming voice, stood shoulder to shoulder out in front of Kate's hammock, growling and yipping. The young geologist froze, looking over at Del who waved as if nothing had happened.

My head was pounding. Too much caffeine and not enough water. And with the stress, stress the size of Montana, Levi and I had joked, I had to remind myself that only when you knew someone well enough did their antics start to wear on you.

Tammy swatted Del's shoulder. "Actually, you oaf, she dyed her hair blue."

Del whistled, and Zadie and Rue backed down.

"He's all yours," Del whispered into the radio, and we heard Kate giggle. "But you key me in if there's anything more than courtin' going on."

Lakes or Leah must have said something, because the young geologist tipped his hat back and seemed to relax, though Zadie yipped each time he tried to take a step.

"For the water." Tammy frowned, explaining Kate's blue bangs.

I stood between the two of them, trying to move the kinks out of my back.

"You and Mr. Levi sure were looking snug," Del said.

"Barking up the wrong tree," Tammy warned.

She knew I was tired and not exactly pleased that our whole small world seemed to have come upon Levi and me before dawn.

"Sonya's not back yet?" I asked.

Tammy answered. "Just called. She's on her way."

I set my coffee on the folding table and put a hand on each of their shoulders. Our community had become close and strong. Yes, it was a bit too local right now, but this was the way we would win, by standing together in the tightest little knots.

"I'm sure glad you're both here," I said, hugging them to me. "So glad we're all right here. So, so close."

Tammy patted my hand and laughed.

Levi and I had talked, briefly, sitting in those same two chairs in the middle of the night.

"Get some sleep," he'd said, brushing my arm as I nodded off.

"You too," I said, pulling him out of his chair.

He had held up the walkie-talkie, and I nodded at him to bring it with us.

"Not like before," I said, trying to let him know that I wasn't inviting anything but warm, comfortable sleep.

"Jesus, Stone," he put his arm around me, "that doesn't even count."

We had fallen asleep as friends. Me, thinking about how much beefier Levi was than David. So much shoulder to lie on! And Levi was probably missing tall, thin Carrie.

Del turned toward me. "I guess we're family now, because I believe I have just been told off, good and proper."

Tammy swatted him. "You think?"

"Wow. A second day." My voice shuttered with nervousness and a zap of joy. "Can you believe it?"

Del gestured to Zadie and Rue, still standing under Kate's hammock, keeping the young geologist at bay. "Maybe we should keep the dogs on site today."

Mary Claire and her Dancing Grandmothers gathered in a circle under Kate, singing something we couldn't distinguish, though it sounded low and peaceful, like a hymn that makes you want to close your eyes and breathe it in.

The blockade team was assembling at the gate, and thanks to Pearl sending her zombie teams to us for the second day, there must have been two hundred people lining the access drive, carrying signs. NorA was going to get a proper greeting this morning.

Del smiled his wide, real smile, gesturing to all that movement and color and tufts of laughter and noise. "Makes you feel young again, doesn't it?" His legs fidgeted with energy.

Tammy leaned back in her chair and hollered into the radio. "Fricking holy hell damned well yes it does!"

Kate radioed in, "Say it, sister! What's up?"

Chapter 32

Second Day Pileup

Mark came running from the house with his laptop in one hand and his other hand waving. "You've got to see this. Holy fricking shit, you've got to see this!"

Sonya and I leaned over the screen, hearing David's voice on the video as he brought into focus the pile of rusty old cars, this time topped with a school bus.

"There was a bus?" I asked, and all Mark could do was nod furiously as we watched.

David walked along the well side of the pile with the chants of protestors accompanying him, then we watched the camera jiggle as he dipped down into the bank and came up panning what he called the "keep out" side.

"This is what they'll see today," he said, "when the rigs come in."

"They did it again?" I grabbed Mark. "That's a whole new pile?"

Mark nodded, and I grabbed both him and Sonya. "NorA is going to be pissed!"

"Keep watching." He smiled.

David zoomed to Randy and Diane, the two of them standing off to the side of the road, chatting and drinking coffee as if they hadn't just pulled off a miracle.

Sonya pegged it. "That's got to be Randy's idea."

Randy was clowning all right.

"You get ahold of that last driver?" Diane asked as she sipped from her "Ban Fracking" coffee cup.

Randy held up his "Oil Out of Water" mug, looking at the camera with a wry smile. "I don't think he's coming back today."

Diane and Randy clinked their mugs together and the video cut out.

Mark connected us all on screen. I leaned forward, peering at Randy and Diane standing in front of the blockade. The faded yellow of the old school bus looked buttery atop the dark blues and burgundies below it. A school bus!

"You guys are incredible! Incredible!"

"More than anyone needed to know, right?" Diane winked.

"Damn, Diane!" was all I could say.

Randy leaned in. "And don't worry. The members of the Spring Lake Protection Society are taking full credit for today's pileup."

There was no Spring Lake Protection Society, of course, but Randy's quote would make it into our writeup. Sonya was taking notes and asking Mark questions.

"It's brilliant!" I hollered. Randy turned the screen to face the new pile and the protestors gathering around it, signs dancing as they cheered.

There would be no turning around for the tens of trucks and trailers coming in, hauling drill housing and fluids and power shovels. The road into State-Rudmond had been raised and widened, but it was still too narrow for turns. Nothing but two miles of one-way possibility for trucks that big—in or out.

"We'll keep NorA away from the kids as long as we can," Diane said, turning the screen back so we could see half of her face, on a tilt.

Sonya and I smirked at each other.

"You get back to Kate and your crew now," Diane added. "When they can't get through here again today, they'll be coming your way for sure."

She was right. If NorA couldn't score a quick win there, they would come at us hard and fast. Whatever was quickest and easiest, that was the NorA way. Cutting Kate down was going to be a hell of a lot easier than getting a second pile of cars and that buttery yellow bus hauled away.

NorA got an unexpected greeting on our site too, but not from us, from two young sheriff's deputies. They came to tell NorA that they couldn't park any more trucks on the access drive. The trucks were stopping at the county road and blocking traffic.

Four of NorA's red and blues were on the well pad, sitting at a camping table with fold-out chairs. Kate had been having fun all morning, singing her water songs, telling them stories of dead frogs and the "Five Minute Escape Pack" that motivated her writing.

When the NorA suit approached the deputies, it was obvious that he had already heard the no-parking news. From the Com Tent, we watched his arms gesture to Kate's hammock, back to the blockade at the gate, down the line of backed-up semis and trailers, all to the audio of protestors' chants.

We heard snippets of conversation from Kate's radio.

The young female deputy spoke first. "It's a safety concern, sir. The trucks are backed up on the county road, and Miralette is a residential area."

"Just whose side are you people on?" He had a deep southern accent.

That got the protestors hollering, and we couldn't hear the rest, but we could sure see it.

"Whoa. He's a bit heated," I said as we watched from the berm.

The NorA suit, wearing jeans and the NorA blue polo under a dark jacket, was giving the deputy an earful, his boots right up to hers and his face growling down at her. Her male partner didn't step in.

"Not sure I want to hear that conversation," Mark said.

"Pig," Sonya said, and I had to agree.

After another terribly uncomfortable moment—the guy must have been spitting in the deputy's face—she motioned for the NorA suit to walk with her, away from the protestors.

The suit gestured and hollered all the way, his arms up toward Kate, then punching the air toward the blockaders. They chanted louder, which really got him going. He made a big sweep of his arm, a brigade charge, and the entire security team hopped in his white SUV.

Sonya and I stood listening to Tammy and Frank chuckle about the number of expletives coming out of the guy's mouth as we watched his final exit on video. He rolled down his window while shimmying the SUV back and forth into a turn. With the trucks blocking the drive, even the SUV was a tight fit.

"We'll be back with the real sheriff." The suit pointed at the deputy. "You!" he shouted. "You pack it up and go on home."

"She radioed in and they left." Tammy shrugged. "After all that commotion, they left."

"They'll be back," I said, noting the line of trucks parked and waiting. "They probably got word of the car pile at Randy and Diane's."

We got a call from Pep that another hundred protestors from the Straits were coming in. Where did we want them?

"Send them to Brett and Sky," I said, thinking about NorA driving off to the sheriff's office to raise hell.

David sent a text that didn't make sense—"Brett and Sky are okay!"—until we received his next video. David's face poked into the shot. His eyes were wide and his face red with heat. "Big wig. All the way from Denver."

The man, wearing jeans and NorA's dark jacket, kept his head down as he and the State-Rudmond security supervisor strode past the Dancing Grandmothers and the protestors and their chants. David followed them as they ducked into the trees to get around the wall of people on the blockade. Like the police, this new NorA suit had to walk into the site. With the car pile blocking Woods Road, there was nowhere to park except for the sandy two-track that bordered Randy and Diane's property, and Randy made sure the road was crowded with cars.

The suits weren't used to having to face the people, and when Thompson stepped in front of this particular NorA executive with a microphone extended toward the man, I knew the new suit from Denver was going to lose it.

"Is this typical, for NorA to withstand two days of delay due to protestors?"

The NorA exec turned toward Thompson. There were words between him and the security supervisor, and then suddenly, instead of going for Thompson, the man broke past his own team and strode toward Brett and Sky, ripping up the stakes of their protective canopy, arms flailing, pole to pole as he yanked away. We couldn't understand what he was saying, but we could hear his growl. He looked like an angry animal making a display of territory.

In the background, we saw Brett say something to Sky, and the man charged. He knelt in front of Brett, pushing close with his chest, and he screamed in Brett's face.

Diane's voice bellowed off camera. "Get away from him, now!" The local police who had been relaxing in the shade ran out and tried to talk the man back. His security team stood off to the side, holding the mangled canopy.

"Hotheads are losing it," David said. He taped the suit being pulled back by his own men.

"Last chance, shitheads!" the NorA suit hollered back at Brett and Sky.

Randy appeared, speaking to Thompson. "Did you see that? He just charged us and went nuts. He threatened to have us all put in a dark hole."

Brett's face was calm, so was Sky's, but I could see their fatigue.

When Brett was tired or deep in thought, though his face was more chiseled now and his chin was covered in a neatly trimmed beard, he still reminded me of that quiet young man who used to listen to Kate and Sonya and only once in a while speak up. He was so thoughtful, so agile in his mind. But his body, tall and thin, and the way his eyes could look so emotive sometimes gave me twinges of concern.

At the close of the video, Brett turned his head toward the camera. He must have been seeing David, but it seemed as if he were looking directly at Sonya and me. He held up a peace sign, and I felt my hand wanting to return the gesture.

David glanced over his shoulder for a second, and that was it.

Sonya replayed the video, and we watched again as the NorA suit screamed in Brett's face. When Brett lifted his head to look our way, she asked me, "Is he okay?"

We walked to the house to get a few quiet minutes, and Del, who must have sensed the worry passing between us, met us at the slider.

"I'll go back out on watch." He nodded, giving Sonya's arm a quick squeeze. "It'll be okay, kiddo."

Sonya and I weren't inside the house for more than ten minutes, but that was long enough for Del to find trouble.

"A-okay," Tammy said as she and Del hurried toward us in the yard. Her grip on his arm and her head-down focus weren't convincing. Del threw us a grimace. "Go ask Frank," Tammy said without looking up.

They brushed past, and we heard Tammy say, "Just what do you think would happen to Kate if you got yourself arrested?"

That got us moving.

Apparently, Kate had received a visit from a hothead of her own.

The man had parked a diesel truck with a tool trailer and walked up to the blockade, asking for Sally. Tammy had politely told him there was no Sally on site, and he'd gotten angry.

"We escorted him back to his truck." Frank motioned to the house. "That's when Del decided to get on the cart and help."

Del waved at us from the deck. Zadie yipped but stayed put. *Oh, Del.*

"If we're not careful," Frank said, "Del's going to be our first casualty."

"The guy did get pretty nasty," Mark said. "He ran around Del, hollering, 'Where's the little whore who set me up?'"

"I thought Del was going to deck the guy."

"He was." Frank's eyes widened. "I had to grab him around his waist and hold him, but all that did was slow him down." Frank turned back to the well pad, watching NorA's movement. "Uh-oh. With half my team gone, I better get back on Meet and Greet."

Tammy appeared next to Del on the deck, and Del promptly sat down. She brought out a pitcher and a glass, said some words to Zadie and Rue, who stood at attention, listening to her, then she stood behind Del, her hands on his shoulders.

"Who is he? The hothead?"

"The drill bit guy," Mark answered.

"Oh."

"Hey. The younger DEQ guy said NorA called a meeting in town," Mark said.

"You and the DEQ are talking now?"

Mark answered, a bit sheepish, "He's not a bad guy."

Mark had, once again, accompanied Del out to the well pad. The two of them weren't exactly following protocol.

NorA's blue and reds watched me walk across the well pad while Frank kept them busy. I stopped under Kate's hammock. "So. Sal?"

The fabric jiggled and Kate's eyes and pursed lips bounced over the edge. "Guess he was right pissed," she said. "I felt kind of bad, really."

"You stayed put?" My warning tone was clear.

"I stayed put, Teach."

Her drill bit guy would tell NorA about Sally soon enough. Kate didn't need to be connected to months of scouting and planning.

"I thought Del was going to have a fricking heart attack." Her face and hands appeared over the edge again. She was getting much more comfortable. "But it was kind of funny." She bobbed and the hammock rippled with her. "I hope Del's okay."

The humor had stopped when NorA called the sheriff, threatening to have Del charged with trespassing. In Mark's retelling, Del had walked toward the officers, yelling, "What happened to protecting the land and people who live here?"

He had gotten wound up and hollered at the NorA bunch too, something about the county not being theirs to run.

"He'll be all right," I said. "Tammy's got him grounded."

Tammy must have ordered Zadie and Rue to stay on him. Del often teased, "Zadie and Rue know who's boss."

To the north, on State-Rudmond, police officers started to walk in to arrest protestors. In response, the protestors spread out across Woods Road, away from the blockade at the gate, making the officers' trip back and forth between the protestors and the cars all the longer. A good two hundred people from the Straits were on site. People from the east and west well pads had also come in, many of the Zombies still in costume. As soon as four or five officers each grabbed a person and walked them toward the cars, another eight or ten protestors would step in. After an hour or so, the police gave up, and the pile of rusted cars, yellow bus included, wasn't getting much smaller.

Sonya called me to check out her latest post on the *Four Branches:* video of the second day's car pile and the neighbor putting a canopy over Brett and Sky. We also watched Thompson deliver the barb that sent the NorA suit into his canopy-ripping charge. Thompson stuck a microphone in front of him. "Is this typical, for NorA to withstand two days of delays due to protestors?" When the suit walked on, refusing to acknowledge the question, Thompson called out, "Has NorA ever been bested by activists for two straight days?"

That was when the suit pushed past his own team and went for Brett.

"I cut the video there," Sonya said. The closeup of Brett locked down and defenseless as the hothead screamed in his face—no one needed to see that.

"Is anyone watching NorA?"

Mark turned to me, understanding, I thought. He frowned. "We don't have anyone following them."

NorA wasn't going to wait for another day. They could be assembling a private army somewhere off site. I picked up the binoculars and panned Miralette Road as far as I could see. No white or black SUVs. No sheriff cars either.

"They're up to something," I said. "Why meet off site?"

The meeting must have been a round-'em-up session, because NorA came back to us with a Humvee full of armed conservation officers, both DEQ reps, and three sheriff's cars, one of them driven by Sheriff Jerry himself.

I was wrong about their army. It wasn't privately funded. They were going to use the people's forces to take the people down, just like Del said.

David and I were on the phone when twice as many troops arrived at State-Rudmond.

"Three state cars, two county sheriffs, and the Imperial Storm Troopers," Randy reported. "Two Humvees full of them."

Worse yet, the new suit, who we identified as the head of American operations out of Denver, had county commissioners and the director of the DNR on site, demanding action.

For an observer, the last few hours of an action are nothing but phone calls and speed posts, verifying as quickly as you can what you are seeing and hearing, often from a distance, so you can accurately report. I could feel us moving into that mode.

David sent video of NorA's official statement. With a circle of conservation officers and state troopers around the wellhead, NorA and the DEQ gave Brett and Sky their final warning. Give up or get cut out. The saws were on their way.

We witnessed a close conversation between Diane and Brett on a video that Randy sent. Diane held the back of Brett's neck. His eyes were fixed on hers as they talked, and then Diane hugged both Sky and Brett, clinging to Brett as he used his free hand to hug back.

"Sky and Brett both," David said, "They want to make it through day two."

It was doubtful with the new car pile that NorA would gain access before dark. They would move trucks all night if they had to, to be in position the next morning. The Green Cross would burn on, night after night. Levi said it would take a week or more for the batteries to run out. *EcoNotes* and *Fracking Times* and the *Four Branches* would continue to cover everything that happened hereafter. Had we given Brett and Sky an out? An easy, supportive out?

"Of course we did," David said. "But they're firm on staying."

In the video that Randy sent, Diane stood up from her crouch in front of Brett, pointing to him and hollering out to the officers that rimmed the metal grating. "He's Ottawa, did you know that? He's a member of the tribe. He has every right to be here. He's obligated to protect this land."

"Go, Diane," Mark said.

Sonya bumped my shoulder. "You were right."

Sonya had questioned, in camp, whether Diane was the right spokesperson. She was tough. Fearless, really, but she wasn't necessarily eloquent, and she was prone to awkward outbursts.

"Let her go off on them," I had said. "Let them feel the anger and distrust."

Hour by hour, Diane became our voice. She was angry, yes, but full of honesty and compassion. Full of grace.

The protestors filling Woods Road and the people clamped together on the blockade were being pulled away and arrested, sort of. Their hands were zip-tied behind them and they were told to stand where they were positioned, near the car pile, but with Woods Road still blocked and the sandy two-track around Randy and Diane's filled with cars, the police couldn't transport them out. So protestors simply walked back to the tent to get their ties cut.

"Another day, your rigs away!" they hollered. The next chant made us smile. "Day two, fuck you! Day two, fuck you!"

David and Diane and Randy were pushed back to the two-track across from the well site. "David and Diane are trying to talk themselves back on site," Randy explained, "but I don't think so. The Empire's got a wall of troopers on us."

At State-Miralette, we heard the same warnings. Protestors on the access drive were warned by the sheriff, with our NorA suit standing by, that they were trespassing.

"We're on state land!" they hollered back. "The people's land!"

When conservation officers and sheriff's deputies started to remove protestors who refused to leave on their own, chants changed from "Show me what democracy looks like!" to "This is what the Empire looks like!"

So many boaters and Zombies had shown up on both sites that it took the police hours to clear the access roads and get to the people on the blockades, but they did, eventually. All we could do was keep an accurate list of who retreated before being arrested, and who got hauled away. Even the Dancing Grandmothers, winding in and out of the woods to dance across the well pad, were captured, sometimes with a lot of effort.

Tammy and Frank took video of the dancers lying on the ground below Kate's hammock, singing. The COs dragged them across the limestone while dust plumed up around them, and Lakes and Leah screamed from the trees that they were hurting our Elders.

"They are peace dancers!" they called as conservation officers dragged the women away.

"Rebecca, it's shameful," Tammy said. "Their skirts are ripped, and some of them have awful scratches on their backs and legs."

Tammy showed a DNR spokesperson the images we were posting, and he convinced the sheriff to get stretchers or emergency blankets on site before they dragged any more Grandmothers across the limestone.

The Water Walkers and the remaining dancers gathered in a circle below Kate. Jan and Ellen and Annie's copper pails had been decorated by another granddaughter for this second day.

Jan had invited the Dancing Grandmothers to join them, to hum along. Together, their voices filled the well site with the Nibi song, and I stopped to listen to the opening line, which had been sounding in my mind since I had first heard it the day before.

"Ne-he-beh" drifted on the air once again, bolstered by a firm, choral hum.

Frank videotaped an announcement, setting up the tripod and taping the circle under Kate's hammock. Lakes and Leah descended partway to appear in the shot.

"The tree sitter will come down of her own free will, tomorrow, at sunrise," Frank stated. "Until then, we will remain to see all three of these brave water protectors down to the ground safely, in the morning."

Tammy brought us video of the NorA suit addressing the DEQ

and DNR staff on site. We couldn't hear what he was saying, but his face and their submissive, uncomfortable postures told us everything. The cut down was coming.

Sonya radioed Kate. "You want company, or would you rather be alone?"

"Company sounds fine," Kate said, her voice soft.

Mark took the radio. "You okay?"

"I'm not moving after what those grannies did. Did you see that? Fricking badass."

"We could try to sneak you out." Mark looked at Sonya and me. "I'm sure the grannies would help us with a good distraction. We've got a lot of protestors standing by, too."

"I'm good, Marko," Kate said. "Me and Brett and Sky, we're going for two here."

Mark looked down. "I know."

I heard, again, the sound of the water song.

I tried to hold on to the long-voweled rise of "Ne-he-beh," to a sense of peace that could get us through whatever came next. Jan had told us the song was meant to inspire us to speak to the water, to make peace with the land.

"Sonya?" Kate sounded calm. "You should come hear. It's beautiful."

I agreed to let Sonya go out on the well pad until NorA made their move. Mark walked with her, standing under Kate's hammock briefly, then he shuffled back from the berm.

"Mark. When we leave"—I nodded to the Water Walkers and the Dancing Grandmothers swaying under Kate—"tell everyone to walk with them. Walk the rivers and the lakes." Not to absolve ourselves as humans for our mistreatment of the natural world and each other, not to shed a history of domination and destruction, but because we had been invited into a simple, temporary partnership, invited to walk along, to support each other's efforts.

Some days, Jan told me, she walked alone.

Mark nodded, then looked up at me as if he had considered, for the first time, that we would leave.

"Kate speaks to water," Jan had said. "She knows to do so, every day."

Video of Brett and Sky being hooded came to us, and I was thankful that Sonya wasn't watching. A stiff, dark hood went over Brett's head, heat and dust rising around him. No call, just a video that must have been taken from across the street.

There were two firefighters and a police officer partially blocking our view, but when the dark hood, supposedly for protection, went over Brett's head, I saw his eyes tilt up into it before the hood covered his face and shoulders. The video jiggled from the severe zoom or the heat, we couldn't tell which. The hoods, shuddering and black, made Brett and Sky look like flat, dark caricatures.

Mark and I were both on the phone, calling for an update, when Levi called.

"They're going to cut Brett and Sky out," I said before Levi spoke.

"Shit," I heard him say.

Mark waved me over to see another video. "Hang on." We got a snippet of David and Diane, wearing lime green NLG hats, striding toward Brett and Sky. Conservation officers approached them and the video cut out.

Levi sounded hurried, out of breath.

"Is there any way they can get to Randy and Diane's from the road that heads south of State-Kitfield?"

"What road? There's a road beyond the well pad?"

A summer ago, when Sonya and Kate and I had scratched paces into our boots, the earthy-smelling road they had compacted around the wetland ended at the State-Kitfield wellsite.

"It ends at the county line," Levi said. "And by GPS it lines up with Woods Road."

"But there's no connection to Woods Road."

"Not yet," Levi sighed, "but I believe there will be soon."

We had seen how fast they could turn a trail into a compacted thoroughfare for heavy equipment. Who could forget the steel-toothed machine that had shaken the ground so badly that we had heard the groan of its engine and felt the tremors it stamped into the ground from the other side of the wetland?

"They've got dozers and earthmovers and they're coming behind them with a wide track. This is a one-time road, Beck. It has to be."

Had anyone scouted the land north of Woods Road? Everything was planned to strand the rigs on the long drive in from the south.

I looked at Kate's hammock, hanging over scraped earth. Mark's head was in his hands.

I saw, in my mind, the oily heat and dust rising around Brett and Sky.

"They try to break the human spirit," Frank had said. "But it's coming back stronger, generation by generation. These young people are done with this bullshit."

Now, the Water Walkers were about to have their hands zip-tied behind them.

The night before, talk in camp had turned to NorA's Great Lakes tunnel—a ludicrous and as yet unverified NorA scheme to replace the aging pipeline under the Straits with a ninety-nine-year tunnel that would take ten years to build, a tunnel dug deep into the lake bed, a tunnel that would carry sticky tar sands bitumen and the chemicals needed to make it flow. The same types of neurotoxins and carcinogens used in fracking, the same chemicals that had caused the formation of Koosh-ball-like clumps of organics and synthetics that the locals along Talmadge Creek and the Kalamazoo River had fished out of the water and stored in canning jars, showing anyone who would listen. The cleanup was not working.

The same administration that we just learned had poisoned Flint's water was making secret ninety-nine-year deals with NorA for a project that would split the Great Lakes in two.

Here and now, the idea of a Super Frac seemed as threatening and as ludicrous as any. Tomorrow, it would be a tunnel. Not because any of it made sense. No. Because they could.

We could never let our guard down.

We might win, place by place, but beaten, their plans would fester.

They will drill into the bedrock for whatever mineral or gas or liquid they want. They will burrow into the big lakes, disrupt the ancient glacial basin forever, all with some flimsy conduit or a concrete barrier between violence and water.

Why? Because they can.

To feel a part of land and water and sky, to love rocks and rivers and the life that knows them, brought so much joy and so much grief.

"Levi? I'm so tired of watching."

It was my grief that turned Sonya's head. She watched me, listening.

Levi sighed. "Then let's get them their second day."

I turned away. "What are you thinking?"

"How'd you like to stretch a few wires across the north end of Woods Road and hold on with me?"

"But where?" Sonya said. "Shouldn't we call David?"

I grabbed everything I could find. Bungees, coiled fencing, a bucket of hammers, stakes, rods, nails, and threw it into the back of Levi's truck.

"I'm going to meet Levi. Check it out."

She smirked.

"We'll be fine."

She put her hands on her hips. "With his truck?"

"Everyone needs to stay focused on Brett and Sky and Kate. Agreed?"

She stood firm. "Would you let me leave if I refused to tell you?"

Her frizzy hair was held back by a headband, making it clear

that she was eyeing me, hard. I wanted to tell her that Mara would
be proud of her, that Mara *was* proud of her, but Sonya had been left
for the greater good before. I couldn't say anything so final. I gestured
north. "Just south of the county line, where Woods Road ends. NorA's
got a crew out there."

"You can't do anything stupid. Promise me you won't do anything
stupid."

"Easy," I said. "I won't do anything stupid."

I opened the truck door and gave her a long, strong hug.

"You know David's going to kill me," she said.

"Tell him you didn't know where I was going."

She smirked and did not wave as I drove away.

Chapter 33

What Zadie Knows

Sonya waits as Mark opens and closes windows in a flurry. "Teach and your dad," he says. "That's still a trip."

Yes and no, she thinks. She and Brett have talked about Rebecca several times. The power of secrets.

"Marko. Where's Thompson?"

"Well. Out there," he says, gesturing to the screenshots open in front of him.

"Where? Exactly. Can we get him out to County Line and Woods Road?"

Mark turns, looking behind her. "Why?"

"I need you to trust me."

"Jesus." Mark's whole body dips. "What the hell are they doing?"

The wind makes Diane's phone voice falter. "We're taking care of Brett, hon," she says.

Sonya feels a pang and closes her eyes. "I know."

Diane walks as she talks, asking for Thompson. "They're bringing in a medical guy. Did you hear that? Your dad got rid of the firefighters. He'll have someone who does casting."

She lets Diane go, because listening to her run about, hollering here and there, is more nerve racking than lying to David. She's decided to honor Rebecca's request, mostly.

"Diane. Tell Thompson to call me right away. And tell David to keep the video coming."

Conservation officers and NorA's team walk under and around Kate's hammock.

"Shit, it was nice to have Rebecca here." Sonya tries to smile for Mark. Another woman, another mentor and mother figure has left to face off with the man. She lets out a growl, feeling trapped for a moment, and Mark half-turns to her but his eyes stay with Kate, who is counting on the two of them to stay focused.

But then the mad rush of Zadie and Rue, yipping and tearing past them, up and over the berm, distracts them. The dogs jump and yip under Kate's hammock to let Kate know, "We're with you!" and then they tear back to Del.

Del approaches, holding up the radio. "Time to kick in with jail support. We ready?" But before either of them can answer, Del says, "We got this. We got this."

Zadie and Rue sit on either side of Del, squirming. Their panting is hot and interrupted with whines.

"Frank and the NLG are going to kick their legal asses," Sonya says. "Kate and Brett will be all right."

Of course she knows the lack of precedence in her statement. Rebellious women and Indigenous communities have not won many battles.

Del puts his long arms around both her and Mark, tears filling his eyes. "You sure I can't let the girls go?"

Zadie and Rue look up at Sonya with their wolf-like eyes, waiting for any motion that will send them back to the well pad. When Sonya lifts her head but does not lift a hand, not even a finger, Zadie turns her snout to the sky and lets out a mournful howl.

Rebecca jumps down from Levi's covered pickup, wondering what the hell he has been doing. There's an arsenal of equipment in the back: steel, poles, mesh, even a generator or some kind of compressor.

Levi's motorcycle sits parked in the trees, and she can hear him talking to the oaks and pines, explaining his plan.

"Where's NorA?" she says, looking toward the snaps and rumbles.

"Less than half a mile away."

"How fast did they chew through the first half?"

"Hour. Maybe more."

She admires this friend, her best friend after Mara, who is clearly in make-it-happen mode. All she can do is take instruction and not interrupt him with a lot of questions, but she has questions.

"Levi." She motions to the truck. "What have you been doing?"

"Construction fencing," he says. "They put up a hell of a lot of security."

He opens the tailgate and they empty out the truck. Rolls of heavy-gauge fencing, short and long poles, something she questions with her eyes and Levi says, taking the heavy tube with a giant ball on top, "This is one handy fricking pole jammer."

She holds up each pail and roll and gadget and he points to where, on the road, she should place it. Standing above it all, Levi lays out his plan. "Tree gate," he says.

"That's it? Tree gate?"

"Angle the truck across the road, engine forward." Then he huffs out, "Later."

Later, when the two of them are strapped in and have nothing better to do than trade ideas, they will come up with a name.

From her hammock, Kate listens as NorA and the troopers discuss how they're going to cut her down.

Tammy and Frank are wearing neon green NLG hats, repeating into their cell phones everything the police and NorA say. Tammy hollers out, "You will endanger her life if you cut any of those lines.

The National Lawyers Guild strongly advises you to allow the tree sitter to come down on her own."

Kate practices. "Scissor, scissor, hold on tight." She readies her fingers. "Topmost edge and hold on tight."

She hears Zadie's long, rising howl and pauses to listen.

"I'm okay, girl," she whispers, squeezing the hand-sewn leather anchor that Teach gave her to commemorate her first successful climb. Kate raises the okay signal to Lakes and Leah.

"We got this," Lakes says.

Leah's voice shakes. "We go down together."

Kate rehearses.

If they cut one rope, she'll know which way to roll. If they cut them all, she'll scissor and squeeze and slow the fall.

She's still shaking over the Grandmothers being dragged away. Mary Claire clung to every root and stone along the way, waving as Kate curled up over the edge of the fabric to watch.

Badass grannies! Tammy too.

Leah and Lakes are hollering up a storm. "You are endangering the sitter!" Kicking back as the officers try to hook their ropes and pull them down.

Maybe the good DEQ guy is still down there. Lakes calms and says, "The smartest thing you can do, please, let us make sure she doesn't fall."

Brett tries to ignore the sweat. The desire to wipe it away from his eyes, off the back of his neck, is overpowering.

They took his water and the towel-off crew long ago.

People from the trees swung down to slug him some water before they were chased away, but they don't seem to be making it through anymore. He's heard a scuffle or two and the shouts of NLG observers. "You can't leave him without water in this heat. You're endangering his health. We demand that you let us give him water!"

David had knelt in front of him and Sky. "They're going to hood you. Supposedly to protect you from sparks and fragments, but more to get you to give up sooner."

"Listen," David had patted the center of the pipe, "if it gets too hard, unclip. But you agree and unclip together, got it? Don't make a move without each other."

The saw pings and thunks, and a bolt of heat races over him. It feels like a bottle rocket shoots off the blade and the sound stops.

"Gonna be a pause here," the tech tells him. Brian.

He can release his back for a moment!

Brian's voice comes close and quiet. "Jesus, you guys wrap enough land mines in here or what?"

Brett tries to laugh, but his mouth is so dry that the skin on his lips catches and tears. "Yeah," is all that comes out. He listens as Brian explains to the NorA supervisor that he has to change another blade.

After they cut Sky out and realized, with David screaming at them to get a smaller medical saw, that both he and Sky were clipped independently, and thanks to the metal rods and mesh built up around the PVC pipe, that they were going to have to cut Brett out separately, things had gotten hotter all around.

The guy from NorA was in and out of his face. One of the more decent conservation officers warned him that he could be crossing over into felony territory if the rigs arrived and he wasn't sawed out yet. The heat of the sun had become unbearable under the hood.

But then he heard Diane's golf cart revving up over the berm, heard The Who's "The Kids Are Alright" blaring around the well pad, and he grabbed on to her support.

Randy's voice, now, comes in on the breeze, leading a local version of "This Land Is Your Land."

"Going back at it," Brian says, and Brett hears Brian's helmet click shut.

He feels the hot wind that shoots sparks up toward him, and he sets his position against the grinding vibration. His head wants to fall back, even in the grimy, scratchy hood, so he concentrates on David. He can hear David screaming.

He likes the guy. He likes him a lot. Sonya loves him, but she doesn't dare to show that love because, as she has said, love hasn't stuck around.

And Hank. Brett loves that little guy. His goofy name games, his rolling laughter that bursts out more like Kate's than Sonya's.

For a moment, he thinks he can hear the Water Walkers singing.

His back is in crisis. His legs are going numb. "You're costing me $300,000 a day!" That's what the NorA guy had spat at them. Little did the guy know that his screaming was exactly what made the two of them decide to hang on.

"You want to come off with me?" Sky had said before he was pulled away.

He didn't know if Sky heard him answer. "Nope. Going to stay."

Rebecca makes sure that the nail strips are covered, barely, but once again, placement is everything. They want the trucks to make it to the north end of Woods Road and then get stopped where the lane of dirt is tightest to the trees.

Levi has talked her through the looped cords hanging from her body, how they relate to the tie-down strips stretching into the trees, to the metal poles that will form the fence between them. Now, he is carefully weaving the two of them together.

She lifts her arm when he taps it. "I was thinking about something David said."

Levi tightens a cord over her shoulder. He holds another in his mouth, nodding for her to tell him.

"He was lecturing me about why I shouldn't jump into the action. Because . . ." She starts to all-out giggle and Levi stands back, pondering. "Because I need to be the one to pull it all together."

Levi pulls the cords down to the clip at the back of her harness, and she widens her stance to avoid being yanked about.

"You and David. Think you'll get back together?"

"I don't know." Timing had always been so incredibly important in her life. "Maybe our time has come and gone."

Levi snaps a cord, testing. "There's not enough of the real stuff to waste, Beck."

She can hear the equipment getting close, the snap and groan of the trees. The smell of soil is in the air.

"They're going to come after me first," she says. "Try to get you to do something stupid." Especially out here, away from any cameras, without any observers.

"I love you," she says.

"Love you more," he winks.

"I'm serious. Don't help them out."

Levi holds her shoulders. "Squat down and hold against the pull. It won't last, but until these rods snap up and we lock in to the pipes, you're going to get pulled right past me."

"I'm heavier," he says, as if she doesn't understand.

"Levi, don't let them egg you on." She grabs his shoulders. "Stick together. Stick to the plan."

He leans close. "Beck. We don't have a plan."

"Sure we do. Hang on. Don't let go."

He weaves cords, in figure-eight fashion, around them. "Ready?"

It takes all of her strength to plant her feet and refuse to be yanked into him as he ties them to the buried pipes and uses his pole jammer to seal the deal.

She hollers against his effort. "What would Carrie think?"

"About this?"

"Yeah."

"She'd approve. She might not be happy, but she'd know why."

Many times, she has worried about influence. That her history and her cynicism have driven Kate and Mark and especially Brett and Sonya toward a more absolute vision. Yet here she is, feeling more inspired by them rather than the other way around.

What the theoretical environmentalist often fails to understand is the power of place. Pure, sacred place. And we can only care about each other's places by becoming part of our own. Mara didn't know about the cancer. She had one last chance, that was all. One last chance.

Levi grabs the sides of her face, forcing her focus. "You good?"

She loves the fierceness in his green-brown eyes. "Good!" Levi has always been part tree and part ground.

"Last big pull," he says. "These cords are going to yank you up until I get us clipped. Go with it."

He secures the poles between them and reaches across her.

"When the fencing starts to snap, shuffle." He demonstrates. "Shuffle out with it."

"Click and shuffle," she says, and she's moving before her words float with her on the air. She is lifted by the trees and she laughs out loud, looking into the oaks and maples and the pines. She can feel their fibrous connection, her body a trunk, airborne with them.

Climbing, she has always been a rider of sorts. She has wrapped her arms and legs around trees and felt their trunks swaying to their roots, but this, this is wildly different. For a moment she is taken up by the trees, and though they may be testing and protesting, she can feel in their lean down toward her, as they set her down and she hears the clicks and snaps that plunk her down hard, their decision to support.

She and Levi have become part of the forest.

David stares at the peach-colored dust, leaning into the metal bars that cross just below his hips. The hot sting causes him to step back from the gate, and he reaches down to touch it, to lean against something, anything, as he watches Brett's head hang heavy in the dark hood.

How the kid is hanging on in this heat, without water, without an unobstructed breath, is beyond David. He's worried that Brett has passed out. He's been screaming at them to make sure Brett is still conscious, but the police chief and sheriff hauled him back because the med tech trying to saw through the PVC pipe started hollering to get him out of the way. David wipes sweat from his forehead and squints, trying to figure out if Brett is moving at all anymore.

But then Brett seems to feel David's worry, his desperate stare into that dark hood, because Brett straightens his back, opening out with his one free arm toward David as if to say, "I'm good, man. I'm good."

The guy cutting into the pipe rises from a kneel to load another blade, and Brett holds up three fingers, which David echoes into the air, pumping his hand and hollering out, "Three blades!" All sorts of supportive noise erupts from the road.

The Au Sable Sacred has wrecked three blades, and Brett is okay! The kid is okay!

If they grind into his hand or saw off a finger, they'll have no problem justifying it as the risk Brett knowingly took when he refused to unlock and withdraw his arm. Yet somehow, the kid continues to refuse.

Kid's got guts. David smiles, holding up three fingers to the crowd. *Fuck, he's got guts.*

The med tech on the saw is talking to Brett, and David considers whether he should tape what will probably be the end of the action. It would be awful for Sonya to see Brett hooded and alone, but negligent if he didn't send it. People had to know.

David showed the tech exactly where to cut, right down the middle of that bright red Au Sable Sacred. "Don't cut anywhere else," he told the young guy on the saw. "He can't move if you make a mistake here."

David steadies the camera and presses record.

The tech says something to Brett and Brett straightens, then the tech lowers his face shield and buries the blade in what is left of the Au Sable Sacred.

Del flinches as Mark opens the video, but it's too late. Del's hurt startles Sonya.

There, in the closeup, the dark hood over Brett wavers as the sound cycles up to a high pitch that throws sparks and then stutters. There's a growl that seems to throw the man operating the saw.

They can hear David's voice hollering in the distance.

The saw whines to a high pitch again, the tech testing it as he talks to Brett. There's a pause, and she watches Brett slowly, purposefully straighten his back and set his shoulders.

"He's okay." Sonya puts her hands to her face, nods to Mark to let the video roll.

The large dark hood rises and settles and she knows, Brett is okay.

"He's okay, Little Man," Del says, and Sonya looks down to see Hank.

Del presses Hank to him as they watch the sparks drown out Brett's form until he's nothing but slices of dark paper, the dark hood wavering beyond the heat of the saw.

Mark squeezes her hand, she squeezes Hank's, Del pulls them all in, and they concentrate on Brett's image.

"He's okay."

Brett feels a cold, wet bottle pressed to his hand, and Brian says, "Quick. Here."

He finds his mouth, but with the hood covering his shoulders, he gives his face and his chest a dousing. Sweat has pooled between his collar bones.

He concentrates on the heavy heart stone that hangs over his sternum. With the cold water sliding under it, the stone feels cool again. It's the only thing that feels cool.

Brian takes the water bottle and his tone changes.

"NorA's talking to the sheriff. Something's going on up near the county road." He quiets and says, "I think this one's going to do it."

Brett nods and breathes, gets ready to know. This is it.

"It'll get really hot. You might even feel like the blade is touching you, the wind from it feels like a line of pressure. But I'll be inches away. Ready?

"Keep still," Brian says.

"I don't care if you take his fucking hand off," the NorA guy says. "Get on with it."

The heart stone's coolness sticks to Brett, the necklace Hank made for him. His heart beats against the stone and he draws that beat forward, away from the high-pitched whir and the hot electrical smells.

He centers on the Water Walker's words, timing the rhythm of her voice with his heartbeat, his breath, the stone.

The whir of the saw becomes a hot line of pressure, and he recalls the old woman's deep-set eyes. He sees deep into the forest, the water, the movement of the river.

He takes slow, shallow breaths, and beyond the incredible heat that radiates in and out under the weight and the scratch of the hood, he feels Hank and Sonya with him, smiling.

Kate gazes into the canopy of maples and pines above her. The blue jay returns and cocks its head as if wondering why she is such a different human, sharing this place, the cardinals' and the chickadees' place in the maples under the oaks and pines.

"Thanks for the space," she says to the jay, and it tucks its beak toward its chest in a nod.

"It's a great place." She smiles. "I can see why you've stayed."

It is a privilege to be up in these trees. To see the way the breeze moves the leaves, or as Brett would say, the leaves create the breeze.

She is filled with understanding. The network of veins and roots, the feel of birds lifting off and landing, the trees and the birds working together. She has even come to terms with the spiders that have used her ropes to extend their webs above and below her, the dew on the webs catching Levi's lights and the sun's rise too.

She thinks she should spend more time up here, but then a light, inquisitive pull snaps under her feet. She hears Zadie and Rue yip and one of those piggish NorA voices says, "Git her down."

Her radio slides out of her grasp and she scissors, gathering the cloth so it won't slide too fast through her jeans. She grabs high. *Topmost edge and hold on tight.*

Rebecca remembers the video camera strapped to her chest.

"Kickin 'em in the shins, Levi."

"Yup." He straightens and pulls the huge zip ties between them tighter. He grips her hand and feels her sweat, the bones of her knuckles.

"Kickin 'em in the shins, Beck. Real hard."

They set their feet and breathe, deeply, keeping time with each other.

No more rationalizing.

No more wrangling with words.

The gleam of a truck grill, they see it flash in the trees.

"Hey!" she hollers. Diesel engines growl into successive downshifts, moving into the curve that straightens before them. "We didn't come up with a name."

Levi nods to the flash of chrome. "Stop the Fuckers for a Few More Hours Tree Gate," he says, and she smiles. She wants to add, "Let's hope like hell we're on state land!" Because if they're not, if they're on private land leased to NorA, they'll face felony charges for sure. One more time, that bag of essays comes to her, and she quiets, thinking, some of them will understand, most of them will not, her students and her supervisors.

She feels the vibration of the trucks approaching, feels the promise of Levi's hand around hers, and she closes her eyes to invite her favorite places in.

She breathes in the violet mist and the wetland rainbows at Fen's. Caleb's ivory skin, the wide smile on his upturned lips, even as she puts her forehead to his to say goodbye.

She sees Mara, tall and lean like Sonya, with her long red-black hair unwavering as she calmly walks and tosses fire.

She sees the reed-lined shores of Spring Lake behind them, feels the music of precious nights at the lake house, mornings of acorns raining down as the woodpeckers laugh.

And then, Del is healthy and strong, and they are canoeing the Au Sable. All of them. Randy and Diane, Tammy and Del and Frank, Brett and Sonya and Hank, she and Mark and Kate, paddling along its bronzy purple surface, oohing and ahhing when patches of sand light up to gold.

"Fucking poetry," as Mark would say.

The first truck slows to a stop. She is strapped as tightly as she can be to Levi and the trees, yet she is free.

Overwhelmingly, what she feels is freedom.

No more waiting. No more rationalizing. No more of the pain of observing—of knowing and photographing and writing but stopping short of doing.

They will get Kate and Brett their second day.

She squeezes Levi's hand and whispers, "No more."

Acknowledgments

First, I thank the editors, writers, and musicians whose work appears in this novel, with permission.

An excerpt, "The Ultimate Out of Balance," first appeared in the anthology *Fracture: Essays, Poems, and Stories on Fracking in America*, edited by Taylor Brorby and Stefanie Brook Trout (Ice Cube Press, 2016).

Erin Lesert, my spirited and humorous sister, is the poet behind "Bitches Combat Training."

I thank Sarah Barker, songwriter and performer of "Silent Spring," for her passion and her Rachel Carson–inspired song.

This novel was inspired by people I met across the state of Michigan and beyond when I embarked on a multi-year mission to learn as much as I could about fracking: the process, the science behind the risks, and the sensory story of living with fracking. The characters and well sites in *Land Marks* are fictitious, but the dedication and commitment of people and groups working to protect the Great Lakes is real.

When fracking came to Michigan's forests, concerned citizens showed up (and continue to show up). They organized educational events, shared the science, their stories, and their songs. They stood up in protest at Michigan Department of Natural Resources Oil and Gas Mineral Rights Leasing Auctions and delivered comments to our state's Natural Resource Commission.

Circle Pines, a peace, social justice, and environmental steward-
ship center in southwest Michigan served as a gathering place for indi-
viduals and groups across the state of Michigan working to protect
state forests, recreation areas, and tribal lands from oil and gas devel-
opment. College students formed groups such as Citizens Against
Drilling on Public Lands and Kent County Water Conservation.
Ban petitioners and local grassroots organizations such as Michigan
Land, Air, Water Defense helped to educate the people of Michigan
on the dangers posed by horizontal hydraulic fracturing. Deep Water
Earth First! (and many others) made some noise at leasing auctions.
Members of Clean Water Action, Food and Water Watch, the Sierra
Club, West Michigan Environmental Action Council, Northern
Michigan Environmental Action Council, and For Love of Water
(FLOW), were (and are) active in these efforts. Phil Bellfy, professor
emeritus of American Indian Studies at Michigan State University and
a member of the White Earth Band of Minnesota Chippewa presented
the argument that the 1836 Treaty of Washington and a 2007 Inland
Consent Decree established treaty tribes as co-managers of treaty
lands and waterways, and therefore oil and gas development under-
taken without consulting involved tribes was a violation of treaty laws.
I thank family friend and Michigan attorney Zeke Fletcher (Grand
Traverse Band of Ottawa & Chippewa Indians) for more recent legal
talks about fracking and related efforts to put an end to tar sands pipelines. A special nod goes to Earthwork Music Collective, whose name
says it all.

Indigenous women are at the forefront of the movement to protect water. Special thanks to Holly T. Bird (Pueblo/Apache/Yaqui/
Perepucha/European), Michigan attorney and Co-Executive Director
of the Water Protectors Legal Collective for her energy, her work, and
her time. I thank Pat Lynn, a friend and Water Walker, for her friend-
ship and guidance in my attempt to honor the powerful presence of
the Water Walkers who walk from the headwaters to the mouths of

rivers and lakes, raising awareness along the way. The story of the "Nibi Song" (written by Doreen Day) appears on the Mother Earth Water Walkers website. I remember, often, talks with the late Larry "Pun" Plamondon, activist, author, and Native American Storyteller (Grand River Bands of Ottawa Indians, Turtle Clan), especially our talks about writing and listening to the land.

At the time of this writing, Michigan is actively fighting a proposed Great Lakes Tunnel Project that Enbridge, an international company headquartered in Canada, wants to build to replace Line 5, its 70-year-old tar sands bearing dual pipeline that spans the bedlands of the Straits of Mackinac, where Lake Huron and Lake Michigan meet. This is the dangerous and ludicrously short-sighted plan feared by this novel's narrator as a plan to "split the Great Lakes in two." To learn more, visit the websites of FLOW (For Love of Water) and Oil and Water Don't Mix, two Michigan-based organizations doing incredible legal, awareness, and policy work to protect the largest body of fresh surface water on our planet.

You know activists, citizen researchers, and experts close to you. I hope you thank them often for showing up.

I am grateful for visiting writers Peter Annin, Megan Quinn Bachman, Kathleen Dean Moore, Michael Nelson, Mary Pipher, and Stephanie Mills, who listened to and inspired my students, students who continue to inspire me, sometimes when I least expect it.

Several writing and arts organizations provided support when I needed it most: Pierce Cedar Creek Institute, GilChrist Retreat Center, Crosshatch Center for Art and Ecology, and The Writer's Colony, with special thanks for the Moondancer Environmental Writing Fellowship. A sabbatical awarded by Grand Rapids Community College and a snowy winter residency at Hill House offered me time to begin this novel. Storyknife Writers Retreat in Alaska was pure comfort and magic when I was missing both.

I deeply appreciate the insights of readers Deanna Harbolt Hayes,

Taylor Mallay, Jennifer Furner, Stacey Danevicz, Barbara Saunier, Steve Losher, Scott Kruis, and Katy Yocom. Thanks, too, to Gail Collins-Ranadive for sponsoring Homebound Publications' Prism Prize for Climate Literature.

She Writes Press has shepherded this story into the world with professionalism and enthusiasm. I thank Brooke Warner, Addison Gallegos, Kimberly Glyder, and Kiran Spees for their patience and support. Theirs is a job that marks an end and a beginning, and She Writes has managed the transition well.

Always, I am grateful for the love and support of my best friend and partner Greg, our son Max, and our daughter Aurora. I wish every writer a family that sends them off with love and encouragement each time they are inspired to begin another writing journey.

About the Author

photo credit: Barbara Lesert

Maryann Lesert writes about people and place in equal measure. Her first novel, *Base Ten* (Feminist Press, 2009) featured an astrophysicist's quest for self among Lake Michigan's forested dunes and the stars. *Land Marks* grew from two years of boots-on-well-sites research on fracking. Before novels, Maryann wrote plays, including three full-lengths, five one-acts, and collaborations with a memoirist and a local symphony. Maryann lives in west Michigan, where she teaches writing, enjoys time in the natural world (shared with family and friends), and writes by the big lake.

SELECTED TITLES FROM SHE WRITES PRESS

She Writes Press is an independent publishing company founded to serve women writers everywhere. Visit us at www.shewritespress.com.

Gravity is Heartless: The Heartless Series, Book One by Sarah Lahey
$16.95, 978-1-63152-872-9
Earth, 2050. Quinn Buyers is a climate scientist who'd rather be studying the clouds than getting ready for her wedding day. But when an unexpected tragedy causes her to lose everything, including her famous scientist mother, she embarks upon a quest for answers that takes her across the globe—and uncovers friends, loss, and love in the most unexpected of places along the way.

Provectus by M. L. Stover. $16.95, 978-1-63152-115-7
A science-based thriller that explores the potential effects of climate change on human evolution, *Provectus* asks a compelling question: What if human beings were on the endangered species list—were, in fact, living right alongside our replacements—but didn't know it yet?

The Alchemy of Noise by Lorraine Devon Wilke. $16.95, 978-1-63152-559-9
In this timely and provocative drama, an interracial couple's new and evolving relationship transcends culture clashes, police encounters, and resistance from select family and friends, only to have a violent arrest leave them questioning everything—including each other.

Ferry to Cooperation Island by Carol Newman Cronin
$16.95, 978-1-63152-864-4
Former ferry captain James Malloy is a loner—but in order to save his New England island home from developers, he'll have to join forces with the woman who stole his job.

The Same River by Lisa Reddick. $16.95, 978-1-63152-483-7
Two women living on the Nesika River in central Oregon—Jess, a feisty, sexy, biologist who fights fiercely to save the river she loves, and Piah, a young Native American woman battling the invisible intrusion of disease and invasive danger in the same place 200 years earlier—learn that wisdom comes from the recovery of wildness.